THE HOLLYWOOD  MURDER MYSTERIES

BOOK FOURTEEN 1960

DEAD MEN PAY NO DEBTS

PETER S. FISCHER

www.petersfischer.com

To my beautiful daughter Meg
always cheerful, always there
to brighten my day and always there
when I need her most.

CHAPTER ONE

I am 40 years old. I suppose I should be depressed but I am not. What I am is mostly confused, uncomfortable, unsure of myself and wondering what is in store for me as I enter the fifth decade of my life.

My name is Joe Bernardi and I am a film publicist who gets second billing in the firm of Bowles & Bernardi, Artists Management, an outrageously successful agency in the Hollywood firmament. I am a millionaire several times over and even I have to admit I have come an awfully long way since 1947 when I went to work for a poverty row studio named Continental Studios for a weekly salary equal to what I now spend on a business lunch with a valued client. I have rubbed elbows with them all, the giants and the minnows, the good and the bad, the kind and the crude, a host of delightful ladies and gentlemen as well as so many others who are not and never will be. I have flacked for some of the finest pictures of the last decade and also for some better left in a dark room to grow mold and disintegrate. I have many friends in the business but those closest to me have nothing to do with the film community and I treasure their friendship deeply. They keep me grounded and constantly remind me that the glitter of Tinseltown has little to do with real life.

For the past year I have been married to a lovely woman whom I had pursued for thirteen years before she finally stopped running long enough for me to hog tie her and drag her to the altar. Bunny is part of my core. Without her I am nothing. Also part of my core is a seven year old little girl named Yvette who is my daughter. Like Bunny she brings me nothing but joy. My health is good so why, you may ask, is this wealthy successful man with a loving wife and a cherished daughter so at odds with himself? The answer may bewilder you. I have become a successful first time author with a best selling book to my credit and suddenly something of a celebrity on the literary circuit. And because of this I now have no idea who I am.

I wrote "A Family of Strangers" in 1948 and after a lot of pitfalls and detours it was finally published. Because the publishing house had little faith in this maiden effort it snuck into the world unheralded. A few critics noticed and wrote some wonderful things about the book and about me but within months "A Family of Strangers" had disappeared from bookshelves the country over and the many unsold copies found their way into remainder bins and outlets like St. Vincent de Paul and the Salvation Army. So much for Joseph F.X. Bernardi, popular and revered American author. Joe Bernardi, Hollywood movie flak, went back to work in earnest while dreams of a Pulitzer wafted into the air and disappeared like the vapor that once belched from long forgotten Stanley Steamers.

And then a strange thing happened. A man who was a total stranger read my book and found it worthy and on the afternoon before the day of his death, he wrote a long and persuasive letter of praise to a publisher of his acquaintance recommending that he rescue my novel from obscurity. Howard Lowell, a respected professor of literature, gave me, in the last tortured hours of his life, the gift of a second chance to pursue my dream. He thought he had done me a favor. So did I, at the time. But we were both wrong.

My new publisher, Poseidon Literary House, did everything right. They garnered rave reviews from highly thought of authors and critics, shipped a dozen copies to every major bookstore in the country and set up a grueling schedule of interviews and media appearances in nineteen major cities over the first three weeks post publication. On the day the book first went on sale I appeared on the Jack Paar Show with my good friend Tennessee Williams at my side. Paar brought out the best in both of us and the next day, the book started disappearing from bookshelves everywhere. A dozen copies per store were not enough. Poseidon's presses went into overdrive. Within two weeks we were number 39 on the *New York Times* Best Seller List. A month later we had climbed to number 16. A month after that we had edged up to number 12 and I was exhausted. So was Bunny. She'd join me on the road for a few days, then fly back home to resume her duties at *The Valley News* where she was the associate editor, taking on more and more responsibility as the paper grew in circulation.

My partner, Bertha Bowles, had let me embark on this odyssey without a murmur, knowing that I was living out a lifelong dream. By now we had grown out of our 10th floor offices in the Brickhouse Building and taken additional space on the floor below. Our staff had grown to ten junior managers, five male, five female, as well as six full time publicists. None of our clients was being shortchanged and when occasionally they would ask for me personally for what they called 'the Bernardi touch', Bertha would smile politely and say, "Be patient. He'll be back soon."

And I was. Three weeks ago the rat race came to an end. Christmas and New Year's have come and gone and I have returned to my desk with hopes of settling down to work. But now a new type of obligation has encroached into my life: the guest appearance. Invitations have been coming in from everywhere for the past four months and in the beginning I was delighted. Anything to promote the book. But now the book has been adequately promoted, sales have been monstrous, Poseidon is happy, I am happy and still the invitations continue to pour in. I can't respond affirmatively to all of them and now I have no wish to appear at any of them. The East San Antonio Ladies Literary Society and its ilk will have to carry on without me. I am exhausted. I have been away from Bunny and Yvette far too long.

I am standing at my office window and looking out over the city that has been my home for the past thirteen years. Much has changed. Oh, the old studios are still integral to the business. Paramount is mere blocks away and in the distance I can make out the 20th Century Fox lot. They continue to thrive but they are no longer the dream factories that once dominated the industry, headed by giants like Zukor and Mayer and Warner and Goldwyn, men whose approval could make a career and whose displeasure could permanently dash the hopes of a struggling actor or director. Today these men and their successors are often supplicants, vying for the distribution rights to new and innovative films developed and produced by small independent companies headed by big stars or by hungry newcomers with a lot to prove and the talent to succeed, firms like The Mirisch Company, John Wayne's Batjac Company, Kirk Douglas' Bryna Productions, Hecht-Lancaster, already winners of a Best Picture Oscar. There are dozens of others, assuredly more, and all of them totally obscure. Some will succeed, most won't. Movie making is still one of the toughest rackets in the world and it shows no mercy to the incompetent or the ill-prepared.

"Boss?"

I turn to find Glenda Mae staring at me from the open doorway.

"Sightseeing or planning to jump?" she asks in her own irreverent way. She has been a part of me for the past dozen years and I couldn't cope without her. She is still as beautiful as the day she finished second in the Miss Mississippi beauty contest an indeterminate number of years ago, a date known only to her and possibly to God.

"Enjoying the view," I tell her.

"Of what? The smog?"

"It's early yet," I tell her.

"Well, if you're through surveying your domain, Bertha's off the phone and wants to know if you have a moment."

"Always," I say as I move past her to the doorway. "Phineas is after me for a lunch date. If he calls, ask him where and when and tell him he's buying." Phineas Ogilvy is the film columnist for the *L.A. Times* and one of my closest friends. Lunch with the man is always a delightful and often unpredictable experience.

"Will do," Glenda Mae says.

Bertha smiles when I walk in the door. Bertha smiles a lot even when she doesn't feel like it. It comes with the job. No problem is too tough it can't be overcome, no client too troublesome that he can't be shown the door. She's also a realist and when she has to, she speaks her mind bluntly.

"You look like hell," she says, looking up at me appraisingly.

"Thanks," I say. "You don't."

"Thanks, yourself. Have you been getting enough sleep?"

"Not that I've noticed."

"You need a vacation."

"I thought I just had one."

"I would hardly call what you've been doing rest and relaxation."

"No argument here," I say.

"Pull up a chair before you fall over," she replies.

I do as I'm told. She eyes me thoughtfully.

"David Niven's overseas fumbling around the Greek islands in that war movie with Greg Peck and before he left he gave me a key to his place in Montecito. He said if anybody needed somewhere to kick back they were welcome. I think you qualify. I'm sure Bunny's got vacation time coming—"

"I don't need to kick back, Bert, I need to get to work. What's going on?"

"Nothing you need be concerned with."

"Elmer Gantry?"

"Jerry's handling it and doing a first rate job, according to Brooks who isn't the easiest man to please."

I nod. Jerry Marcus is a special protege of mine. He's sharp and he's pleasant. People take to him instinctively and he knows his job. If Richard Brooks, the director, is happy, Jerry doesn't need any help from me.

"Speaking of Gantry," Bertha says, "I got a call from Burt last night. He's crazy about Shirley. She's lighting up the dailies."

I smile. I am really delighted. Six months ago Shirley Jones approached us, looking for help. For years she'd been playing a dozen varieties of Miss Goody Two Shoes, and she longed for something more substantial. Honestly I didn't see it but Bert did and she dug in her heels to get Shirley the part of LuLu Baines, the vengeful prostitute opposite Burt Lancaster's Elmer Gantry.

"You never miss, Bert," I tell her.

"Oh, I miss a lot, Joe. I just try not to let you find out about it. Now what do you say? Montecito for at least a week?"

I shake my head.

"I don't know, Bert. I appreciate the offer—"

"Joe, there's nothing here for you right now. Every film and every client is being covered. A week from now something may pop up. If it happens earlier I'll call you. Promise. Besides it'll give you a few days to think about the next book."

I don't respond because I have no response. A lot of people have been asking me that. How's the new book coming along, Joe? What's it about? Can't wait to read it.

I get up from my chair.

"I'll talk to Bunny," I say.

"Good," she says. "And maybe Jill will let you have Yvette for a few days."

"Could be," I say.

"By the way, how's Jill doing?"

"Better, I hear, but I haven't seen her in weeks," Bertha nods.

"Well, you get back to me on this."

"I'll talk to Bunny tonight."

By the time I get back to my office, Phineas has called. Luncheon at one at Musso's and reluctantly he has agreed to pay. I find I also have a visitor waiting in my office.

Barry Loeb has been my literary agent for the past ten years and for the most part it's been a thankless job. Aside from the flurry of activity when my book was first published in 1950, I have done nothing since. Then when Poseidon expressed interest, I called him and put him back to work. He accepted with delight, as if the intervening nine years of non-activity had never happened.

"If you tell me I look like crap, you're going out the window," I tell him.

He grins.

"Never entered my mind. You look like the same handsome debonair snake oil salesman you've always been," he says.

"At last. An honest man. Pull up a chair. How about a cup of coffee, soda?"

Barry sits as I plop myself down behind my desk.

"Can't really stay, Joe. Got an appointment at Universal at eleven but I had to swing by." He smiles. There's something about that smile, something that he knows and he can't wait tell me.

"Let me guess. You've just won the Irish Sweepstakes," I say.

"Better than that," Barry says. "Got a call early this morning from Poseidon."

"Don't tell me. We've shot back up to number 12 on the *Times*

Best Seller list."

"Even better. You've been optioned, pal," Barry says.

"What?"

"The book's been optioned for a motion picture. Five thousand up front against a hundred thou when the picture gets made."

I shake my head with a smile.

"And what studio has lost its collective senses to make such a rash and risky offer?"

"No studio. A guy in New York. A television director, actually. Fella named Stuart Rosenberg. Great reputation."

"Never heard of him."

"You ever watch 'Naked City'?"

"Sure. Good show."

"Rosenberg's directed at least a dozen of them and he's in New York now directing his first motion picture."

"What picture is that?"

"A low budget programmer for Fox featuring a lot of nobodies. It's called 'Murder Inc.', about the mob in the '30s that was for hire to kill people."

"Murder Incorporated? Naked City? Does this guy know my book's not about cops and robbers?"

"He knows it."

I shake my head dubiously.

"I don't know, Barry. I like the idea of 'Strangers' getting turned into a movie but shouldn't we wait and maybe get an offer from one of the studios."

"The studios aren't making many of those deals these days, Joe, unless you hit number one with a runaway best seller which, I remind you, you did not do. Most of the option deals are coming from the indies. Look, for all we know, in a few years this guy Rosenberg could own Hollywood."

"Yeah, but—"

"Joe, there is no 'yeah, but'. Poseidon controls the movie rights. You get a nice piece of the action but it's their call. You have nothing to say about it."

I slump back in my chair. The idea of a movie version of "A Family of Strangers" had been kicking around in my brain for months, ever since the book first got noticed. But I had visions of a call from Walter Mirisch or Sol Seigel at MGM or maybe even my old boss Jack Warner. This guy Rosenberg is probably a damned good director. He may also have delusions of grandeur. The movie business is not for the faint of heart and the back alleys of Hollywood are littered with the bodies of ambitious wannabes.

I muster up enough enthusiasm to thank Barry for coming by with the news. After he's left I return to my desk and stare up at my ceiling, trying to figure out what I can do, if anything, to wriggle out of this arrangement.

CHAPTER TWO

"Naked City?"

"Naked City."

"I remember Naked City," Phineas says. "A fine movie. My dear friend Mark Hellinger produced it. Barry Fitzgerald. Don Taylor."

"Not that Naked City. This is a television program", I say.

"Television? I never watch it," Phineas says dismissively slicing into his juicy rack of lamb.

"It's a pretty good show," I reply.

"I seriously doubt that," Phineas says, slathering some mint jelly on his lamb. "That accursed little box has reduced story telling to paint by the numbers and made midgets of beloved icons who once were giants. Loretta Young, Barbara Stanwyck, Walter Brennan, Robert Taylor, all reduced to six inch miniatures mouthing obvious inanities to an audience with the taste level of an amoeba." He shoves the forkful into his mouth, adding yet another few ounces to his corpulent frame which threatens to top three hundred pounds. In response I take a dainty bite of my Cobb salad.

"Times change, Phineas," I say.

"Yes, yes," he says impatiently, "but I needn't change with them. Our marvelous world of shadows and dreams on a twenty foot screen in a darkened theater is being replaced by Alka-Seltzer commercials and laugh tracks from long dead audiences of the Jack Benny radio program. Not for me, old top. Not now! Not ever!"

For one of the few times since I have known him he has raised his voice in frustration and suddenly the diners nearby are staring at us. He becomes aware of it, casts his gaze belligerently at our neighbors who quickly look away as he returns his attention to his plate.

"Then you don't approve," I say.

"Of what? This man Rosenberg? I don't know him. He could be a genius awaiting his first big opportunity. Maybe your book is it, old top. I sincerely hope so."

I nod and take another bite of my salad which, of course, is delicious. Musso & Frank is a Hollywood institution. The stars have been coming here for decades, as far back as the silents and a couple of the waiters have been here since the place opened. Invariably the place is crowded, not only with a few real stars as well as producers and writers but also armies of tourists from Nebraska and points east looking for a glimpse of Natalie Wood or Troy Donahue.

Suddenly I am aware that silence has descended on the table, odd when Phineas is present. I look up and he is staring at me curiously.

"There's something else troubling you," he says.

"Not really," I reply, avoiding his look.

"And what sort of a dolt do you take me for, Joseph? We've known each other far too long."

I raise my eyes. He's right.

"Do you remember Joan Weber?" I ask.

"Who?"

"Joan Weber. Six years ago she came out with a song called 'Let Me Go, Lover'. It was a sensation. Climbed to number one on the charts. And she never made another record. A one-hit wonder."

Phineas nods sagely,

"Yes, I see. Margaret Mitchell. Emily Bronte. One brilliant book and then nothing more. Is that what you fear, Joe?"

"Not fear, Phineas, but concern. I think maybe I poured it all into one pretty good novel and now I have nothing left to say."

He shakes his head.

"You've been in the midst of a whirlwind for months, old top. No time to think or to ponder. Don't let it bother you."

"I've had twelve years to think and to ponder, Phineas. I've started and stopped a dozen times. I'm telling you, there's nothing there."

"I don't believe that."

I smile.

"Spoken like a good friend but I know better. I've tried to dig down deep and I keep coming up empty."

Phineas shakes his head.

"I remember well the first few chapters of your book, life in the oil fields, the wildcatters who would hit dry holes time after time and then when things looked darkest, suddenly they'd hit upon a gusher. Your gusher is waiting to happen, Joe. I believe that. You're too good for it not to happen."

I smile as I look into his eyes, He's a marvelous friend but he's wrong. I nod appreciatively but nothing has changed and I want to get off this subject. I ask him about this morning's column which chronicled Frank Sinatra's world-wide pursuit of Ava Gardner. Instantly he is into an unflattering dissection of Sinatra's adolescent behavior, he in Spain and she in Rome, fending off photographers with their 35mm's poised and reporters from every part of the globe hovering with pencils at the ready to capture the greatest love story since Wallis Simpson and the King of England. Or so they would lead us to believe. We finish lunch with Phineas regaling me with the latest gossip around town and I relax enough to shunt my misgivings to the sidelines.

After lunch I return to the office where I chat up a couple of our newer people. They couldn't be more delightful but I can read the body language. They have things to do and people to call and I am wasting their time. I slink back to my office and scan the trades and finally give up in frustration. I touch base with Bunny who tells me she'll be tied up until seven or so. I tell her I'll handle dinner. On the way home I stop by Bernie's Deli and pick up a broiled chicken, cole slaw, macaroni salad, a pint of vanilla fudge and a six pack of ginger ale. In the old days it would have been Coors but Bunny's been sober for nearly four years and my gift to her is abstention in her presence. I'm delighted to do it.

Food in the fridge, ice cream in the freezer, I pop open a Canada Dry, grab my copy of Allen Drury's "Advise and Consent" and go out to the back patio where I flop down on the chaise lounge. I'm either going to read or fall asleep, don't know which though the odds favor reading, I like this book a lot.

Ever since I became one of the so-called literati. I've been taking my reading much more seriously and I've developed a critical eye I never really had before. Drury is good. He's very good and there's talk of a Pulitzer. He handles dialogue with wit and passion and he knows his stuff. A former UPI reporter assigned to the Senate, he has painted a picture of that august body which is not always flattering and is certainly never dull. He wrote a couple of novels after graduation from Stanford but this is his breakthrough. He has dissected a subject he knows well and I wonder if he has any misgivings about where his next inspiration will come from. Annoyed with myself I sip my ginger ale and try to concentrate on Chapter Ten. My fear of failure is becoming an obsession.

I don't know when or how it happened but suddenly I am on the Senate chamber floor in a heated argument with Senator Seeb Cooley, an opinionated old curmudgeon, while majority leader Bob Munson is trying to pull me away before I throw a punch. Furious I stride to the Senate cloakroom and open the door and there's Kirk Douglas in his Spartacus outfit, delighted to see me. He opens his arms wide and gives me a huge embrace and then plants a wet kiss on my lips. I'm aghast. What's the matter with the man? Has he lost his mind? In a panic I open my eyes and suddenly Kirk has disappeared and beautiful Bunny is coaxing me to consciousness the best way she knows how. I respond in kind and when I come up for air I check my watch. 7:06 and it's getting chilly.

"Must be a helluva book, sleepy Joe." she says.

"Actually it is but at times a nap's more fun."

"Hungry?"

"Starved."

We grab the chicken and give it a minute or two in the oven as we set the kitchen table and lay out the slaw and the macaroni. For a while we'd been eating on trays in front of the television but after a week or so, instituted a new house rule, a quiet supper in the kitchen where we get a chance to share our day's activities. I tell her about lunch with Phineas, she tells me about a couple of Valley politicians who are about to be collared on charges of corruption. The story will be big when it happens and all hell is going to break loose. I don't ask which party's involved because I'm pretty much non-political. I vote for the man and hope for the best. This election year I kind of like John Kennedy but most of the so-called experts don't think he can beat Hubert Humphrey for the nomination. It's not just his Catholicism, it's the shadow of his old man who spent too many years in the company of too many unsavory characters. Doesn't seem fair but there it is.

Bunny's in the midst of spooning out the ice cream when the phone rings. I reach for the receiver hoping it's Yvette. Sometimes Jill lets her call right after supper before it gets late.

"Is this who I think it is?" I ask.

"I doubt it," comes an unfamiliar male voice. "Sorry."

"Who's this?"

"Stu Rosenberg. We just wrapped and I wanted to get through to you before it got too late."

"Oh, sure," I say, momentarily blank.

"I guess your agent must have told you, Mr. Bernardi. About the option, I mean."

And then it hits me.

"Mr. Rosenberg. Right. Nice to hear your voice," I say.

"Likewise," he says, "and please, it's Stu."

"Okay, Stu. I'm Joe."

Bunny looks over at me with a curious look. I raise my eyebrows and shrug.

"Good. That'll make it easier working together," Rosenberg says.

"Working together? I thought you optioned my book."

"I did. Say, didn't they tell you?"

"Tell me what?"

I think I hear an audible sigh.

"Those guys. I made a big point of it, even tried to get it in the deal memo. They said they couldn't speak for you, it'd have to be your decision. They really didn't say anything?"

"I have no idea what you're talking about."

Bunny's scooped my ice cream into a bowl and I can see it's already starting to melt. I stretch the cord over to the table and grab a spoonful before it starts to get soupy.

"The screenplay, Joe. I want you to write the screenplay."

That stops me cold.

"Oh, no. Sorry, Stu, I've never written a screenplay in my life."

"So what? It's not that hard, Joe, and the book is so visual it'll probably write itself.

"I really don't think—"

"Joe, I swear to you it'll be a cinch. And who knows the material better than you and more importantly, who cares about the material more than you do? Oh, sure, if I could get Budd Schulberg or Paddy Chayefsky or Ernie Lehman, that's different but guys like that are way out of my price range and neither one of us wants to see 'Family of Strangers' butchered by some low-rent hack. Do we?"

"No, but—"

"No buts, Joe. Look, why don't you hop a plane to New York. I've got two weeks left on this feature and you and I can spend a couple of hours a day talking about what needs to be done."

Hop a plane to New York City in the middle of February? I'm officially a Californian now. I have little use for snow and 20 degree temperatures.

"Look, Stu, I appreciate your faith in me but honestly—"

"But honestly, Joe, I need you. And stop worrying. Ray Chandler wrote the screenplay for 'The Blue Dahlia' and got an Oscar nomination. And maybe you don't remember who wrote the screenplay for 'Viva Zapata'. A guy named John Steinbeck. Maybe you've heard of him. Want more? How about Scott Fitzgerald, William Faulkner—"

I break in, surrendering.

"Okay, okay, you're a hard man to dissuade, Stu."

"I've heard that about myself," Stu says. "Tell you what, Joe. Sleep on it. Talk to your wife or Bertha or anybody else whose opinion you respect and then call me sometime after lunch. Can you do that?"

"Sure. I suppose."

"Great! Here's where you can reach me."

He gives me a phone number and we chat for a minute or two more and then I hang up. I turn to Bunny who still has that curious look on her face.

"Well?" she asks.

"I just got offered a job," I say.

CHAPTER THREE

I've just snapped shut my seat belt and put my seat in the upright position, awaiting further instructions from the guy in the cockpit. We are starting a slow descent above the sea of lights that the natives call New York and the out-of-towners call everything from "awesome" to "god-awful". Most of the latter are first-time tourists who have just had their first run-in with a downtown hotel bill or a restaurant check, both of which they equate with armed robbery. Me, I love the place. Always have, even when I couldn't afford it. It's a fantasyland without peer.

Dead ahead is La Guardia Airport and I can hear the pilot lowering the landing gears in preparation of arrival. I have spent the past seven hours alternately reading, dozing and staring out my window at the country below, pondering what lies ahead. I know I have reached a crossroads and I am just as uneasy as I was a couple of months ago. Stu Rosenberg has merely exacerbated the situation.

Bertha has let me come East with her blessing. She reads me well and she knows I'm wrestling with some crisis though she doesn't know exactly what it is. Take your time, she'd said. Work it out. Write the screenplay, stay with the company or do both. Whatever you decide to do will be fine with me. Of course, there was a price to pay. With Bertha it's always some little thing. Nothing time consuming. A small favor, Joe, that's all. When she said that I checked to see if my wallet was still in my inside jacket pocket.

"I guess you'll be hanging around Rosenberg's set while you're there," she'd said.

"Not if I can help it," I'd told her.

"Oh, too bad."

"What's too bad?"

"Oh, nothing."

"What do you mean, oh, nothing?"

"I mean, oh, nothing."

"Come in, Bert. Spit it out."

"Well, there is this actor."

So then I knew. She wanted me to do scout work on some up and coming talent. She's always on the lookout for tomorrow's big star, either sex will do, hoping to corral him or her before the competition catches on.

"What's his name?"

"Peter Falk."

"What's he done?"

"Television."

Television? Phineas will be delighted.

"He also does stage work, Joe, off Broadway. Did some guest shots on the New York live TV circuit and a couple of walk-ons in features but people I respect tell me he's a comer."

I frown, digging into the recesses of my memory.

"Falk. Falk. I know that name," I'd said.

"No, you don't," she'd responded quickly. Too quickly.

"Yes, I do. Isn't he the guy with the glass eye, the one who recently screen tested for Columbia ?"

"The eye is not a problem," she'd said.

"It was for Harry Cohn," I'd replied.

"Harry Cohn was a boor."

"I think he said—"

Bertha had glared at me.

"I know what he said, Joe. It doesn't bear repeating. Now will you check out Mr. Falk or won't you?"

And, of course, I'd said I would, so now as I sit back, the wheels hitting the runway, I prepare to do double duty. Check out Peter Falk, he of the glass eye, and also sit at the feet of Stuart Rosenberg as he tries to turn me into a screenwriter.

It's a few minutes past ten when I shuffle into the lobby of the Hotel Astor. I'm a semi-regular hereabouts so my tenth floor room with a great view of the city is ready for me. As soon as I close the door behind the bellman, I flip on WRCA for the late news and then head for the bathroom to start a hot bath. I grab a cold Piel's beer from the mini-bar and drink most of it while I'm undressing, After a fifteen minute hot soak, I towel off, catching glimpses on the tube of a near riot going on in Brooklyn. In less than a week they're going to demolish Ebbets Field and even though the Dodgers have been gone for years, hundreds of protesters on Bedford Avenue can't come to grips with reality. Dozens of police are holding back the crowd while Gabe Pressman interviews a guy in blue and white makeup carrying a sign that reads 'Bring Back the Bums'. Brooklyn, you gotta love it. The closest thing we have to our own private foreign country.

I turn off the television, slip into some fresh skivvies and climb beneath the covers. Even though I am a Cardinals fan, I remember the old Dodgers with affection. Guys like Reese and Hodges and Snider and of course, Jackie and the way he'd stretch a single to a double and then end up stealing home. Somewhere in the midst of all this nostalgia, sleep claims me.

The next morning I'm up and about by eight o'clock. I've already arranged with Stu Rosenberg to meet with him at the studio at nine and after grabbing a quick breakfast I hail a cab and make my way to 126th Street in Harlem. The place doesn't look like much on the outside and I suspect the inside isn't much better. Bertha had told me that 20th was making this one on the cheap and she wasn't kidding. No-name actors, black and white photography and a short production schedule and yet, for some odd reason, it's being filmed in Cinemascope. Why? I haven't a clue.

I jog up a short flight of stairs and start to turn the corner when a shadowy figure coming the other way slams into me and knocks me against the wall. I yell something at him as I grasp at the bannister to keep from tumbling down the staircase. The guy hesitates for a second looking back at me. He's a ferrety little man with bad teeth and worse hair. His wide eyes reflect anxiety and if he has any thought of apologizing, he dismisses it and continues to dash down the stairs two steps at a time as if a blood thirsty vampire was hot on his tail. I reach the landing and look back. Whoever he was, he has fled the premises.

I start down the corridor in search of Stu Rosenberg. One of the office doors is slightly open and I look in. It seems to be a very small production office with a couple of desks and a mimeo machine and a cork message board. There are no messages tacked to it. A grey-haired rent-a-cop is sitting on a folding chair chomping on an apple while an elderly secretary with blue framed glasses and a frizzy perm is busy typing. She looks up when I ask where I can find Mr. Rosenberg. Try one of the sound stages, she tells me. End of the hall, turn right. I thank her and step back into the corridor which is when I notice the man standing at the top of the stairs, hands on hips, looking around in puzzlement.

"He went out the door less than a minute ago," I say loudly.

The man turns and as soon as he faces me, I think I recognize him. I know for sure that he recognizes me.

"Joe?" he asks tentatively.

"Right."

He forces a smile as he approaches me, hand extended.

"Harv Jessup, Joe. My God, man, it's been a while."

As we shake, I, too, force a smile because it has, indeed, been quite a while, at least a dozen years. I'd just started at Warner Brothers and Jessup was a young up-and-coming press agent with a high-powered public relations firm. In those days he'd been trim and handsome, a suave ladies man, nothing like this pudgy figure with watery eyes and thinning hair now standing before me.

"Good to see you, Harv," I say to him.

"Same here, Joe."

He's nervous and ill at ease and having trouble making eye contact. He reaches in his pocket for a pack of Camels and lights one up.

"Are you working the picture?" I ask.

"Just temporary," he says taking out a handkerchief and wiping the sweat from his face. Outside the temperature is in the mid-40's. Here, inside, it's maybe mid-60's, not even warm, but Jessup is sweating like it's August at Pismo Beach. "20th asked me if I'd fill in just for the shoot."

"Who are you with these days?" I ask.

"Myself. One man office. Lean and mean, nobody to answer to. I like it this way."

He dabs again at the sweat beads forming at what's left of his hairline. He reminds me of Eddie O'Brien, the toady press agent, in 'The Barefoot Contessa'. It's clear the intervening years have not been kind to him.

"So what are you doing here, Joe?" he asks hesitantly. I know what's bothering him. He wants to know if Bert and I have been hired by 20th to handle the picture and ace him out of his job.

"I've got an appointment with Rosenberg. Personal, Harv. Has nothing to do with this picture," I tell him.

Relief floods his face.

"Sure. I get it," he says. "Stu's on Stage One talking to Rescher.

End of the hall. Turn right."

"Thanks, Harv. Nice seeing you again."

"Likewise, Joe," he replies.

I start up the corridor, then stop and turn back.

"By the way, Harv, who was that guy who went out the door? He nearly knocked me down the stairs."

Jessup hesitates for a split second.

"Some reporter looking for an interview. I told him it was a bad time. He got a little pissy and I told him to fuck off."

I nod, then turn and continue on toward Stage One, more than a little puzzled. The little weasel on the stairs was no more a reporter than I'm a tenor at the Met. And if he was, this is a quiet time before filming, perfect for a star interview and beyond that, no press agent ever tells a member of the press to fuck off. I'm still wondering why he lied when I walk onto Stage One and spot two men off in a corner. As I approach one of them looks in my direction and then smiles as he points in my direction, pistol-style.

"Joe Bernardi," he says.

I return the pistol point.

"Stu Rosenberg," I say.

We shake hands warmly and he introduces me to Gayne Rescher, his Director of Photography. I've never met Rescher but I know his work. He shot 'A Face in the Crowd' for Elia Kazan. This picture's in good hands. After a minute or two of chit chat Stu and I head off to his office. It's cramped and windowless but it does have a desk and two chairs and so we make do.

For the next fifteen or twenty minutes over lukewarm coffee and day-old donuts we discuss the book and I immediately realize he knows the novel inside out, not only the incidents, but also my intent. The more we talk the more relaxed I become. This pipe dream may actually turn into something.

He leans back in his chair.

"Okay, Joe. Let's imagine you're at your desk. You've just typed 'Fade In' and you're getting set to write the opening scene. Where do you start?"

"At the beginning, " I say.

"Really?"

"Where else?"

"Well, I suppose you could start there if you have your heart set on it, but you probably risk putting the audience to sleep."

I bristle inwardly.

"And you have a better idea?"

"I think so," he says. "I think you open with the fishing boat."

"That's halfway through the book," I complain.

"That's right. It's also an interesting, suspenseful sequence which leads directly into Walt's relationship with Jessie Drummond."

"Okay, but—"

"Joe, try to picture it. Opening credits. Fog. The clang of buoys. The sound of a foghorn. Walt is bundled up in his peajacket. One of the mates hands him a mug of coffee, offhandedly mentions his mother or a sibling, maybe a birthday, and then moves off. The cameras on Walt's face, pushes in, memories flood in, we flashback to his childhood in the foster home in Nebraska. A foster mother who is unloving and distant, foster siblings who come and go, some for a year, some for as little as a month. We're still starting at the beginning but we've opened with an intriguing scene with ominous overtones. Something is going to happen but we don't know what so all the expository childhood stuff is revealed with an underpinning of suspense."

I nod. I see what he's getting at.

"So we tell the first half of the book in flashback."

Stu shakes his head.

"No, just the childhood years up to Walt's leaving home for the Oklahoma oil fields."

"But—"

"Follow me on this, Joe. Suddenly Walt is awakened from his reverie by a fog horn, shouts of danger. Out of the mist the freighter looms, bearing down in the little fishing vessel. Panic. Every man for himself as the boats collide. Walt is thrown into the water, sinks below the surface as the freighter churns above him. He washes up on the beach,"

"This is good, Stu. Very good," I tell him.

"Walt's near death. Along comes Jessie Drummond. She finds Walt, summons her brother, they get him back to their house."

"Wait a minute. What about the hospital?"

"You don't need the hospital," he says. "It's a stall and wastes time. The thing is to get Walt from the beach to the Drummond household as quickly as possible. Jessie's going to nurse him back to health and in the process we jump start their relationship." He hesitates, watching for my reaction.

"Wow," I say.

"Right," Stu says with a smile.

"I can see I have a lot to learn."

"Trust me, Joe, you'll catch on right away. I can tell from the prose how your mind works. It's just a question of keeping things visual and editing out whatever is superfluous."

"And all the material in the oil fields, my relationship with Kitty Falconer, the phony murder charge—"

"You're feverish, close to dying. You're in and out of consciousness."

"And while I'm hanging onto life, more flashbacks."

"Now you've got it," Stu says. "By the way, you've slipped a couple of times and said 'me' and 'my'. Just how much of Walt is really you, Joe?"

"Enough," I shrug.

"Yeah, I thought so. You've had a helluva life, my friend."

"So far," I say.

We chat for another twenty minutes and then we're interrupted by the Assistant Director with some crisis to deal with. Stu gets up, tells me to roll things around in my head and we'll go at it again tomorrow, same time. We shake hands and I start out feeling a lot more confident about this project than I did when I got on the plane in Los Angeles. At the doorway I hesitate and turn back.

"One other thing, Stu. Do you know where I can find Peter Falk?"

He gives me an odd look.

"No. Why, Joe? Are you here on business?

I smile sheepishly.

"A favor for my partner," I say.

"Well, I'll say this. Bertha has good taste. A lot of people have been sniffing around Peter the past few weeks. Agents. Managers," He checks his watch. "He's got an 11:30 call so he's either in his dressing room or across the street at the diner having breakfast or if he's not there, you might try the Salvation Army outlet on the next block."

It takes me five minutes to find his dressing room which he shares with Stuart Whitman, the top billed star of the movie, and David J. Stewart who plays the notorious Lepke, head of Murder Inc. Falk's not there so I cross the street to the diner. Empty, except for two cops at the counter downing coffee and donuts. I head across the street in search of the Salvation Army.

CHAPTER FOUR

As soon as I walk in, I see him. He's in the back of the store, standing in front of a full length mirror wearing a dark blue overcoat and a scruffy fedora which he is fiddling with, wearing it one way and then another. I approach him unnoticed.

"Mr. Falk?" I say.

He looks in my direction.

"Hi. How ya doin'?" he says and then turns his attention back to his hat. He pushes it forward, then cocks it to one side appraisingly. "What do ya think?" he asks.

"About what?"

"The hat. Guys I grew up with, wiseguys, they wore hats like this."

"Did they?"

"Oh, yeah," he mutters, stepping closer to the mirror for a better look. "Yeah, this is good. Very good. Not bad for four bucks."

"The hat?"

"Yeah, the hat. I'm gonna wear it in the next scene." He again stares intently and then like a man who has just remembered his wife's birthday, he looks at me quizzically. "Do I know you?" he asks.

I put out my hand.

"Joe Bernardi."

He smiles as we shake.

"You're the writer. Stu told me about you. I read your book, Joe. A fine piece of literature."

"Thanks. I'm not sure I'd call it literature."

"I would," Falk says. "How do you like the overcoat? Nine bucks at St. Vincent de Paul."

"Do you always get your wardrobe at thrift shops?"

"If I have to. The wardrobe guy, nice fella, but not a clue. If you're gonna play the part, you gotta look the part."

"Makes sense to me. Look, Mr. Falk—-"

"Peter. Call me Peter."

"Sure. Peter. Look, Peter, I know you're shooting this afternoon but how about letting me buy you dinner tonight?"

"What for?"

"To get acquainted."

"What for?"

"So I can learn a little more about you."

"Why? You gonna try to sell me a vacuum cleaner, Joe?"

"Oh, no—-"

"Then what ARE you gonna try to sell me?" he asks.

The smile is still there, his voice is still pleasant and low key but there's steel in his expression. Peter Falk is nobody's fool.

I tell him who I am and about Bertha and about our possible interest in managing him.

"Yeah, I've heard of you guys but I've already got an agent," he says.

"We don't agent, Peter, we manage careers. It's a whole different thing. Why don't you let me tell you about it over dinner."

He ponders that for a moment.

"You on an expense account?" he asks.

"Absolutely," I reply.

"I only ask because this place I'm thinking about, it's—well, never mind. How about I meet you at the Mudhole at six o'clock?"

"Is that the restaurant?"

"No, that's the theater."

"What theater?"

"The theater where I have to meet somebody."

"Okay."

"Then I gotta say hello to somebody."

"Fine."

"You don't mind?"

"Not in the least."

"Then we can eat. You sure you have an expense account?"

"Absolutely."

"That's good. Very good."

At that moment he looks at his watch.

"I'm late," he says as he hurries to the front of the store. I hurry after him. He pays four dollars for his newly acquired hat and dashes out the door, me in his wake. He and I jog down the street toward the studio. Over his shoulder he tells me how to find the theater and then he's climbing the stairs to the studio. I wave after him but he disappears inside without even a goodbye. I have no idea whether we will sign him for a client but I'm pretty sure if we do, it won't be dull. I turn toward the street and begin looking for a cab.

As soon as I enter the Astor lobby I make a beeline for the concierge desk. I tell the guy on duty I need a typewriter brought to my room, I don't care what kind as long as it works. I also need about fifty sheets of plain white paper. I give him my room number and slip him a sawbuck. He says he'll get right on it. Once in my room, I order a burger and a Piels beer from room service and turn on the noon news. Some opinionated sports maven is giving his critique of the Olympic Winter Games which are opening tomorrow in Squaw Valley, California. The USA has no prayer. The Russians and the East Germans will wipe up the floor with us. In annoyance I turn off the set. Of course we'll lose. Our guys and gals are amateurs, the Commies are state sponsored steroid-ridden freaks but I don't need some snotty know-it-all in a fifty dollar haircut to tell me about it.

It's nearly one o'clock when I finally sit down at the typewriter and slip a sheet of paper into the carriage. I stare at the blank page for at least a minute and then cautiously, I type :

FADE IN-SAN FRANCISCO BAY-EARLY MORNING

I lean back and stare at the paper again. This time five minutes go by and I think my brain is going clickety-click. But maybe not. At last I lean forward and start to type.

The fishing boat Tarpon glides slowly and quietly through the water. The fog is thick, Visibility is near zero. A seaman stands on the bridge, eyes searching, listening intently to the sounds of foghorns and clanging buoys. He is wearing a thick peajacket because it is bitter cold and vapor is coming from his mouth and nose. His name is Walt Cannon and he is a man with a past.

I lean back and read what I have written. It doesn't seem half-bad, It might even be good. I lean forward and again start to type.

By five o'clock I'm done. My back is killing me, my fingers are refusing to function and I am developing a monster headache. In four hours I have written three pages. Actually I've written more, maybe fifteen or twenty pages, most of which are in my wastebasket. Start, stop, crumple, start again, re-think, crumple, start again. It's an agonizing process and I have three pages to show for four hours work. I scan them quickly. They're good. They may be very good. Or maybe Stu Rosenberg will think they're crap but I don't think so. One thing I've already figured out, writing a screenplay is not for the slothful.

I get up from the table and go into the bathroom where I slosh cold water all over my face. I pop a couple of aspirin and then go to the phone to call Bunny. 5:00 here means 2:00 in California. Normally she brown bags lunch and eats at her desk so I'm hoping I'll catch her.

"This is Bunny Bernardi," she says, picking up.

Bunny Bernardi. I love hearing it.

"This is your everlovin' husband," I say.

"And well you should be," she says, "I don't roll over for just anybody. How's the Big Apple?"

"Big. Why don't you ask me how the screenplay's coming along?"

"My God," she says, "you're writing already?"

"Three whole pages," I say proudly.

I tell her about my meeting with Stu Rosenberg and my subsequent encounter with Peter Falk. She's intrigued by Stu and amused by Peter. When I ask how things are going on her end, she tells me that her boss, Jim Kelso, is leaving tomorrow morning for a conference of newspaper editors in San Francisco and she's going to be in charge for the next three days.

"Nervous?"

"Why should I be?" she asks. "I didn't sober up just to fall on my ass."

"Good point," I say. "How's the kid?"

"Same as ever. We're practicing makeup by using her old dolls as guinea pigs." I laugh. I can picture it.

"And Jill?" I ask.

There's a moment's hesitation.

"Not so good, Joe. We spent a couple of hours yesterday evening, just gabbing. I think she should go back to Mayo for more tests but she won't do it. She says she feels fine but I know she doesn't."

"What do you think?" I ask.

"Honestly? Nothing good. Whatever's going on, she's in denial."

"As soon as I get back, I'll talk to her."

"Good idea," Bunny says. "I hope she'll listen."

A few minutes later I hang up and for a long time I sit staring at the phone. Seven years ago Jillian Marx and I had a brief and exciting fling and out of that affair came my daughter Yvette. Jill had desperately wanted a child but had little use for the idea of a husband, We had some bad times early on but eventually we worked things out. I'm still not 'Daddy' but I am kindly and lovable 'Uncle Joe' and for the time being, that's enough. Kindly and lovable 'Aunt Bunny' agrees. It's been a good arrangement.

But now I'm worried. For the past year Jill's been losing weight and her energy level is way off. She went to the Mayo Clinic for tests and they diagnosed nothing more dangerous than vitamin deficiency. I'm not so sure they had it right. I contacted Mayo and tried to talk to her doctor but got nowhere. Patient confidentiality and all that and besides, who was I? An old boyfriend? I vow to sit down with Jill as soon as I return home and have it out with her. If there's something seriously wrong, we need to do something about it.

I check my watch. Ooops, I'd better get moving if I expect to get to this little theater by six o'clock. I grab my jacket and hurry from the room.

The sun has been down for at least an hour and when I exit the lobby, I'm hit by a blast of cold Manhattan air. This is when I could really use Peter Falk's nine dollar overcoat but in Southern California, such things are not necessary. I hurry back inside and locate the men's store,. They don't carry overcoats but they do have a cozy cashmere sweater which I charge to the room and slip into under my jacket. Once again I step outside, braving the elements, It's not great but it's better. The doorman grabs me a cab and a moment later I'm heading crosstown to the East Village.

From the outside the Mudhole doesn't look like much, a converted storefront on the corner of the block next to a dry cleaner. A sandwich board by the entrance promotes tonight's offering, "Eulogy for a Ghetto Queen" written by Winston Baxendale and directed by Luther Bascomb. Two glossy photos identify the principal performers, a slick looking guy with greasy combed back ebony hair named Jonathan Harker and a worldly-wise looking babe named Amythyst Breen who, despite the best efforts of a professional re-touching, obviously has a dozen years on her co-star. The bottom of the sign reads "Curtain at 8:00". I check my watch and look around. It's 6:06 and no one is here early in hopes of getting a good seat.

I step inside and find myself in a dimly lit foyer. To my right against the far wall I spot a tiny refreshment bar that features a huge coffee urn and a display case filled with candy bars, cracker jack and pretzels. To my immediate left is a staircase and since Peter is nowhere in sight, I go looking for him. The staircase has eight steps and ends on a landing next to the seating section. I calculate in my head. Six rows, twelve seats to a row. A full house would be 72, all with a close-up view of the small stage a few feet away. There is no curtain and on the stage I see two rocking chairs, a hobby horse and a jungle gym painted red, white and blue. Dominating the back of the stage is a ten foot high photograph of Eleanor Roosevelt. I'm curious about this play but not curious enough to want to see it.

"Excuse me, sir. Are you here to make a reservation?"

I turn at the sound of a soft and sweet female voice. Her face is sweet, too, but she stands at least six feet, weighs well over 250, arms like ten pound salamis and legs like tree trunks. I'm grateful that she's smiling at me.

"No, actually I'm—"

"Plenty of good seats left for tonight's performance."

"Thanks, but I'm supposed to meet Peter Falk here. He's late."

"I know," she says. "I've been expecting him myself for the past twenty minutes."

"Joe Bernardi," I say, introducing myself.

"Portia Justice," she replies.

"Are you an actress?"

"Once in a while. For this production I handle box office and the refreshment stand." I nod. "A couple of years ago I was in a low budget feature called 'Amazons Unleashed'," she says.

"I missed that one," I say.

"So did most people," she replies somewhat sadly.

I look around more closely at the threadbare musty little theater that perhaps had once known better days. Perhaps not.

"Can I presume that business hasn't been all that good?" I ask. She shrugs.

"If you'd seen the play, you'd know why. Don't tell anyone I said that."

"Hello! Anybody? Velma!"

It's a loud voice from the tiny lobby and I'm pretty sure it's Falk. Footsteps galumph up the staircase and he appears, looking slightly disheveled and still wearing his nine dollar overcoat. He looks around and spots us.

"I'm late," he says sheepishly as if we didn't know.""It's four blocks from the subway and it's starting to snow. Velma, how's your mother?"

"About the same, Peter," she says.

Peter grasps me by the elbow and leans in close, speaking quietly.

"Excuse me for a minute, Joe. I gotta talk to Velma."

With that he takes Velma's arm and leads her to the other side of the theater. They stand close, their backs to me and I can't hear what's being said but I do see Peter take his wallet from the back pocket of his rumpled suit. For a moment, Velma, or whatever her name is, shakes her head but Peter seems to be insisting. Then she gives him a hug and hurries away, toward me, with tears in her eyes. She heads down the stairs to the lobby, no doubt to service any early arrivals. Peter approaches me.

"I thought her name was Portia Justice," I say.

"That's her stage name. Her real name is Velma Micklenberger. She's nuts for 'The Merchant of Venice'."

"Never would have guessed."

"Her mother had a stroke a few weeks ago and Velma and her kid sister are taking care of her."

"And money's tight," I say.

"So she needs a little help. What else is new? She was there for me plenty of times a few years back when things were rough. I always pay back, Joe. Always. So listen, there's somebody else I gotta see and then we'll go eat. You mind?"

"Of course not."

"The guy's the playwright. A very bright fella. We used to study together when he thought he was an actor. He wasn't but now he thinks he's a writer. Maybe yes, maybe no. Are you sure you don't mind?

"Not at all," I tell him. "If you like ask him to join us."

"I'll ask him but he won't come. Apples and grapes."

"Apples and grapes?"

"Apples and grapes, that's all the guy ever eats, but I'll ask him. And the expense account? No problem there?"

I raise my hand in a three fingered salute.

"I can handle it."

"Good. Be back in a minute," Peter says and with that he hurries to the stage and through a curtain into the backstage area. I sigh and lower myself into the nearest seat. That's the third time he's asked me about my expense account. I haven't the vaguest idea where he wants to take me but I have a wallet full of cash and a brand new Diner's Club card and a couple of blank checks in my suitcase back at the hotel. I can handle anything.

"Don't you turn your back on me!"

A loud angry voice is coming from backstage. A moment later a young man strides angrily onto the set followed by a heavy set older man. The young guy is the slick article whose photo is posted outside the front door.

"And I'm telling you, mind your business, old man. You may be my director, you're not my keeper."

"And I'm telling you, I don't want that stuff around my theater and I certainly don't want that slimy son of a bitch Finucci hanging out here. Next time I see him, I'm calling the cops."

The young guy laughs.

"Oh, you do that, Luther, and see how far that gets you. And by the way, this isn't your theater. Maybe you've forgotten about Mrs. Grandee."

"I run this theater, not her."

"Well, you don't run me!"

With that the young guy dashes to the staircase and runs down into the lobby and, for all I know, out into the street. The older man stares after him and then turns in disgust and walks backstage. I don't know exactly what I just witnessed but something tells me it was probably a lot more interesting than Eleanor Roosevelt on a hobby horse.

A moment later Peter reappears and hurries in my direction.

"Is he coming?" I ask.

He shakes his head.

"I told you. Apples and grapes. Come on. Let's go. I'm starved," he says.

He flies past me and heads down the staircase. I race after him, into the lobby and out the door into the cold February air.

CHAPTER FIVE

Charlie Wang's Shanghai Cafe is no greasy spoon but it is also no Delmonico's. The decor is gaudy red and gold highlighted by three faux pagodas but the aromas coming from the kitchen are tantalizing and as Peter and I slip into our booth, I can feel my hunger pangs multiply. I open my menu and check out the prices. I can buy a complete dinner for what I'd spend on an appetizer at Scandias but I guess for a struggling actor, this place must seem like top of the line.

"Nice, huh?" Peter says.

"Very nice," I agree.

Our waiter, a pleasant geriatric Chinaman with a grey queue down his back, brings us a pot of hot tea and takes our order without benefit of pencil or paper, a trick only the Chinese have mastered. I sip the tea. It feels good. In fact everything about this place feels good. When we'd emerged from the theater Peter wanted to walk here. Only eight blocks, he'd told me. Since I was already in the grip of my own personal ice storm. I hailed a cab and we arrived safely before hypothermia set in.

"Sorry I kept you waiting back at the theater," Peter says, "but I had to say hello to an old buddy."

"No problem."

"Winnie and I—Winston Baxendale, the playwright—we go back to the days when I was studying with Eva LeGallienne. Winnie wanted to be an actor, too, but I read some of his stuff and you could tell he was a writer. I mean, you could certainly tell it. He had a delicious way with words. This play, it's his first real production, so I had to drop by and tell him how much I liked it."

"It's good then," I say.

"Nah, it stinks. He's got stuff in his trunk ten times better but what am I gonna do, bust his balls?"

"Of course not," I say. "So, Peter, tell me about yourself. Are you married?"

"Not yet," he replies."I think I'm engaged. I'll have to ask Alyce about that. We're getting married as soon as the picture wraps. I guess that means I'm engaged."

"I would imagine so," I say. "Who's Alyce?"

"Great gal. We met at Syracuse maybe six, seven years ago. That was just before I graduated and tried to join the CIA."

"The CIA?"

"They wouldn't have me."

"Your eye?"

"Nah, Marshal Tito and the Merchant Marine Union."

I nod sagely, clueless.

"It's a long story and very boring and by the way, it's the right eye," he says.

"What?" I say sharply, having been caught being blatantly curious and rude in the bargain.

"I can see you staring, Joe. It's okay. I'm used to it. The right eye is glass." He hesitates. " At least I think it is. Sometimes I forget. Wait a minute." He puts his hand over his right eye. "Yeah, I can still see. It's the right eye."

"I'm curious about something, Peter. Harry Cohn. Is that a true story?"

His visage darkens.

"Cohn, that son of a bitch. Yeah, it's true. I'm getting ready to do a screen test for Columbia. A young John Garfield, that's what they're calling me, only I can tell Harry Cohn thinks I'm a young nobody and we get into it pretty hot and heavy and finally he says to me, 'Young man, for what I'd have to pay you, I can get me an actor with two eyes,"

"That was Harry, all right," I say. "Mr. Sensitivity."

"Son of a bitch," Peter mutters under his breath, reaching for the tea pot.

"Pete?"

Suddenly we are both aware that someone has walked up to our table. I look up and recognize him immediately. It's the "reporter" that nearly slammed me down the staircase at the film studio earlier this morning. Peter recognizes him, too, and he's not happy to see him.

"What do you want, Finucci?" Peter glowers.

"Just saying hello is all, Pete," the ferrety little guy says, throwing me a sideways glance. If he recognizes me he doesn't show it.

"Hello. Now beat it," Peter says.

"Aw, Pete, I was just—-"

"Yeah, I know, you were just going to put the touch on me. Shove off, Finucci, and take your junk with you."

"Come on, Pete," he whines. "I'm in kind of a bad way. All I need is a few bucks—"

Peter is steaming now. He looks ready to jump up from the booth and slug the guy.

"You must be deaf. Get away from me, you dumb bastard, or I call the cops!"

Finucci backs away fearfully but even so, there's a sneer on his face.

"Okay, okay. I'm goin'. Big movie star. Didn't take you long to forget your friends. Big asshole, I say."

And before Peter can react, Finucci hurries away. Peter watches him go and then turns back to me.

"Sorry about that," he says.

"An old friend?" I ask

"Used to be," Peter says. "Gino Finucci. We kind of started together here in New York but to tell you the truth the guy's a lousy actor, kind of like Winnie Baxendale only Winnie has brains and this guy Finucci is a certifiable moron. Anyway pretty soon Finucci's selling drugs to make a living. Been in and out of jail for years but he never gives up."

"He was at the studio this morning," I say.

Peter looks up sharply.

"Looking for me?"

"Actually I think he came there to see Harv Jessup."

Peter shrugs knowingly.

"Jessup. That guy. Finucci sells, Jessup buys. They make a nice couple."

"You sure, Peter? I used to know Harv. Not a bad guy. Of course, that was years ago."

"And Finucci was years ago. Come on, Joe, forget those bums. Let's eat."

Our waiter has just brought us four steaming platters of food; moo goo guy pan, cashew chicken, Mongolian beef and fried rice. I start to load up my plate when I realize I'm coming down with a headache and my face feels grimy and sweaty. I slip out of the booth.

"Where's the men's room?"

Peter points.

"End of the hallway."

"I'll be right back."

I toss my napkin onto the table and head for the back of the restaurant. The men's room is surprisingly large and clean with white tile everywhere. There are four stalls, one of which is in use, a couple of urinals and two large sinks. I slip out of my jacket and hang it on a hook and then start to fill one of the sinks with cold water. I start sloshing water all over my face and on the back of my neck when I become aware of movement behind me. I turn just in time to see Gino Finucci lifting my wallet from my jacket pocket.

"Hey!" I yell, lunging toward him but he squirms away and dashes out the door with me right behind him. He races down one of the crowded aisles, slamming into a waiter with a loaded tray and sending chicken and noodles in every direction. I gingerly try to avoid the mess as Finucci races out the front door into the night. By now Peter has seen what's happening and he's out of the booth and tailing me out into the street.

I spot Finucci a half a block away, dodging traffic and I take off after him with Peter at my side and then Peter, younger and in better shape, plows ahead of me and is gaining on the little weasel. Suddenly, my foot hits a wet patch and my feet go out from under me. As I start to crash down onto the rough pavement, I spread my hands to break the fall but my jaw still hits the roadway. I'm rolling over when I see a dead-heading taxi speeding toward me and in the darkness I'm not sure he has seen me. I try to get to my feet and that's when he veers violently to his left just as an old man is riding toward us on a bicycle, hugging close to the row of parked cars. The cab clips the bike, the bike goes down with the old man on it, and I roll away to avoid them both, scraping my face in the process. A car behind the cab slams on its brakes and screeches to a halt.

The cabbie leaps from behind the wheel and hurries to my side. I'm on my hands and knees and I have a stabbing pain in my side. I may have cracked a rib. The old man is trying to disentangle himself from his bicycle and he is either complaining or cursing, I'm not sure which, in something I'm pretty sure is Yiddish.

"Are you all right, buddy?" the cabbie asks, kneeling down beside me.

"I'm not sure," I say. "I think so."

"I didn't hit you," he says hopefully.

"No, you didn't hit me," I reassure him, trying to remain still.

"Well, you hit me, you son of a bitch!" the old man yells as he manages to extricate himself from his bike. The frame is bent and the front tire is twisted out of shape.

"Are you okay?" I call out to him.

"Do I look okay? Does my bicycle look okay?"

By now a crowd is starting to gather and out of the corner of my eye I see an NYPD squad car approaching, lights flashing. It pulls up, double parking, and two uniforms get out and approach. I try to get up. As I wince with pain, the cabbie gives me his arm and I make it to my feet. Just then Peter runs up, waving my wallet at me.

"He ditched this in the gutter, Joe, but the bastard got the money," Peter says, handing me my wallet.

"Thanks," I say. "Too bad you couldn't catch him."

"No chance, Joe. The guy had his car parked around the corner. One of those funny looking toy cars, you know. A Volkswagen."

"A Beetle."

"That's right. A yellow Beetle," Peter says.

By now the two cops are checking out the scene. The taller one is named Ramirez and he fixates on me.

"Okay, what happened here?" he wants to know.

I start to tell it, the cabbie chimes in and a few moments later the old man has limped over to us and is threatening lawsuit. In the past few minutes a couple of dozen people have gathered around. One of them, an obvious tourist, is taking pictures with his Brownie to show to the folks back in Sioux Falls.

By now we're all talking at once and the cop's partner is taking our names and trying to take notes. My teeth have started to chatter. My jacket's back in the men's room and my sweater is helpless against the temperature which seems to be plummeting by the second. I can't stop shivering and I'm aching to find some-place warm where I can sit down. The old man's been bellyaching nonstop for the past ten minutes and finally, to shut him up, I take a business card from my wallet and hand it to him.

"Tomorrow you c-call this number in California. Give them your n-name and address and a replacement c-cost for your b-bike. They'll send you a check that afternoon."

The old man scans the card and then peers up at me suspiciously.

"How do I know this card is any good?"

"Because I s-say so," I snap at him, out of patience.

He shrugs.

"Okay, so I'll take a chance," he says.

"Same for you, my friend," I say as I hand a card to the cabbie. "Do me a favor and take the old fella and his bike wherever he wants to go and then call my office tomorrow and let them know the charges as well as any damage to the cab."

"Forget it," the cabbie says, handing back the card. "I'll give the old man a lift, no charge, and as far the cab goes, we're insured."

"You sure?"

"Positive."

I turn to Ramirez

"Does that settle it?"

"Okay with me if these guys are happy," he says. The cabbie and the old fella nod. They're happy. Five minutes later they're gone and so are the cops and Peter and I are back in the restaurant. I rescue my jacket from the men's room but it doesn't help much. My teeth are still chattering. Our waiter brings back our food, properly reheated, and we dig in, all thought of business talk forgotten. He's just started to tell me about his adventures in Communist Yugoslavia with a girl named Sheila and I have to laugh because the guy's such a great storyteller. He's at a point where's he's describing shoving money into his boots to foil the border guards when Charlie Wang comes over and tells him he has a phone call at the bar. He excuses himself and couple of minutes later he hurries back to the table.

"I gotta go," he says, retrieving his hat from under his chair. "Problems, Joe. I got more problems than brains."

"Can I help?" I ask.

"Naw. Maybe I'll see you tomorrow out at the studio."

"Hey!" I say. "I'm tapped, Peter. You got a ten you can lend me for a cab back to the hotel."

He digs in his wallet for a sawbuck and hands it to me with a grin. "Now I will definitely see you at the studio tomorrow."

With that he's hurrying quickly toward the door. I look at my plate. I can't face one more fried wonton. Right now all I want to do is get back to the Astor and curl up in a warm bed and get some sleep.

And so, after handing Charlie Wang my Diner's Club card, that's exactly what I do.

The next morning my phone rings. Gingerly I reach for the receiver and a cheery voice tells me it's eight o'clock. I mutter a quick 'thank you' and hang up and then nestle down underneath the covers. I do not want to go anywhere. In fact I do not want to move because I have a feeling if I do, my legs will buckle and my arms will fall off. This rebellious act of self-pity lasts about a minute and then I toss back the covers and move to a sitting position at the side of the bed. Very carefully I slip off the edge of the bed and pad my way slowly into the bathroom. The guy I see staring back at me from the mirror looks like hell. His jaw is bruised and he has an ugly scrape on his cheek which is just starting to scab over. My hands are also scraped and bruised and when I submerge them in hot water they sting. I carefully press my hand against my ribs. They're better than last night but they still hurt. Slowly I reach for my toothbrush.

After cashing a check with the hotel, I grab a cab for uptown.

It's already past nine and I find Stu in his office on the phone with some suit in Fox's New York office. He gives my face a curious once over and then gestures me to a seat. Whatever they're discussing it doesn't sound like good news and when he finally hangs up, he mutters something that sounds like an obscenity. I could be wrong.

"Bad news?" I ask.

You might say. The actors may be going on strike."

"When?"

"In two weeks. That is, IF they strike. They talk tough but mostly that's all it is, talk. And what the hell happened to you?"

"It's a long story."

"I love long stories."

I give him the sixty second version and his face darkens. The idea of Peter Falk running around the darkened streets of the East Village chasing some drug dealer scares the crap out of him. The last thing he needs is to have to shut down production because Falk's in the hospital. Then he notices the manila envelope I'm holding in my hand.

"So, Joe, what have you got for me?" he asks.

"A beginning," I say.

He slips my precious three pages from the envelope and starts to scan them. I feel like I'm back in Europe in '44 when my lieutenant would start reading over something I'd written for the next issue of 'Stars and Stripes'. Good reporters got to keep their typewriters and sleep in a warm bed. Bad ones got handed a pad and a pencil and a truck ride to the front lines.

When he finishes, he looks up at me with a smile.

"This is good, Joe. Very good."

That's as far as he gets because at that moment, there's a knock on the door and the frizzy-permed secretary pokes her head in.

"Excuse me, Mr. Rosenberg, but there are a couple of police-men outside—"

The door opens wider and two uniformed cops barge their way into the room. The taller of the two looks from me to Stu and back again.

"Mr. Bernardi?"

"I'm Joe Bernardi," I say.

"Would you come with us, please, sir?" the cop says.

"Where to?"

"Sir, we have orders to pick you up and bring you downtown."

"Orders from who?" I ask. "And bring me where?"

"Sergeant Horvath says if you won't come willingly, we're to cuff you and toss you in the back of the squad car and most importantly, not to share our donuts with you."

Aha, I think. Horvath. A good guy and a good cop. We worked together about five years ago saving Bunny from a homicidal maniac. It'll be good to see him again. Only one thing bothers me. Sergeant Karol Horvath is a homicide detective. So what the hell does he want with me?

CHAPTER SIX

As we drive south in the squad car I figure we're headed for the 9th Precinct which is Horvath's home base but when the cop behind the wheel exits the West Side Highway at 6th Street and cuts across toward Tompkins Square, it looks like we're headed for The Mudhole. I've been trying to pump them for the past fifteen minutes but I know clams who have had more to say than these two guys. Sure enough, we reach Avenue B and pull up across the street from the little theater. Parked at the curb are a squad car, an unmarked Crown Victoria with a whip antenna, a black van with NYPD markings and the coroner's van. My escorts hustle me past the yellow crime scene tape and the gawkers crowding the sidewalk. Once inside they tell me to stay put while they go looking for the sergeant.

I spot Velma over by the refreshment counter towering over a petite woman wearing sweats and sneakers. Velma has her arms around her and is whispering quietly in her ear. The woman nods as Velma starts to gently stroke her hair. Velma is giving her comfort. She may also be intent on giving her something else.

I walk toward them and as I do they turn to look at me. Velma quickly breaks off her embrace. I recognize the babe in the exercise outfit from her photo out front. Without much makeup and in lousy lighting, it's obvious that Amythyst Breen, the leading lady of this opus, all five foot four and a hundred and two pounds of her, is a lot closer to forty than thirty. But even at forty-something she is a very attractive woman with hazel green eyes, thick auburn hair and a face built for come-hither looks

"Good morning," I say to Velma. "Remember me?"

"I sure do," she says. "Peter's friend." She introduces me to Amythyst who barely gives me a glance.

"What's going on?" I ask.

"There's a dead body in the basement," Velma says quietly as if revealing some dirty secret.

"Really? Who?" I ask.

"A man named Finucci. He used to sell drugs but I didn't really know him. What happened to you?" she asks, indicating my battered face.

"I got into a fight with a patch of pavement and lost," I say.

By now Amythyst Breen has tapped a cigarette out of her pack and is looking up at me expectantly, waiting for a light.

"Sorry, I don't smoke," I tell her.

She looks at me in disgust and flounces off behind the counter to rummage for a match. Velma leans in close and whispers quietly in my ear.

"She's very dramatic."

"I can see that," I whisper back. "Why are you here?"

"I found the body but they're bringing in everybody."

"As if I would have anything to do with that lowlife piece of excrement," Amythyst says from behind a billow of smoke. Obviously she found a match.

"Then you knew him," I say.

"We all knew him," she says flatly. "Didn't we, Velma?" Her tone is sharp and accusatory.

"Well, I might have said hello to him once or twice," Velma

says vaguely.

"Good old Gino," Amythyst says bitterly. "Something for every-body. Panaceas to make you forget you're in this lousy theater and performing in this lousy play."

"Bernardi!"

My name has been shouted loudly. I turn and one of the cops is standing by an open doorway which I assume leads to the basement.

"The sergeant wants you downstairs!" the cop calls out.

I nod and excuse myself from the ladies.

The stairs are steep and rickety and even though the lights are on, the basement is a dim foreboding place. I spot Horvath right away, off in a corner, talking to the police photographer.

"Don't touch anything," the cop behind me says. "They're still dusting for prints."

I jam my hands in my trouser pockets just to be safe. The base-ment is dank and musty and crammed everywhere with canvas flats and stage furniture and props of every description filling every square inch of space. Horvath looks up as I approach and while he doesn't exactly smile, he doesn't scowl either. When last I saw him we were on pretty good terms.

"Thanks for joining us, Joe," he says.

"An invitation I could hardly refuse, Sarge."

Karol Horvath's a slim good looking guy in his late 30's, long blonde hair combed back over his ears and high slavic cheekbones. His closest friends call him Kay. He allows me to call him Sarge. I look past him at a crushed and crumpled mass of humanity that once was Gino Finucci, his body splayed atop a lot of cardboard cartons. His face is a bloody mess and it appears that someone has beaten him to death.

Horvath is studying my mangled visage.

"What happened, Joe? You get in a fight?"

"No."

Horvath jerks a thumb in Finucci's direction.

"He did."

"Not with me he didn't," I say and start to tell him about the altercation outside of Charlie Wang's Shanghai Cafe.

"Save your breath, Joe. I read the police report. That's why I had you picked up. Where's your buddy?"

"You mean Peter Falk?"

"No," he says sarcastically. "I mean Yogi Berra."

"He's probably at the Harlem studio. I'm pretty sure he's shooting today."

"He's an actor?" He says it like he's just smelled bovine flatulence.

"Yes, and a pretty good one."

"Never heard of him."

"You will someday."

"Must be one of your clients. Muldoon!" Horvath yells. My friend, the chauffeur cop, hurries over. Horvath looks at me. "What's the address of this studio?" he asks.

"Come on, Sarge," I say, "he's in the middle of shooting and they're on a tight schedule. He doesn't know anything but if you really have to talk to him. I'll bring him around to the Nine as soon as he wraps for the day."

He hesitates, then looks at Muldoon. "Never mind," he says. He looks back at me. "Go upstairs and wait in the lobby. When I'm through we'll go for coffee."

I nod.

"Can't wait."

I turn and start to trudge back up the stairs. Halfway up a figure comes flying through the door and we meet halfway like Robin Hood and Little John fording the stream. I recognize him right away. Jonathan Harker, the play's loudmouthed leading man.

"Horvath?" he says to me.

"Bernardi," I say to him, pointing to the far side of the basement.

He shoulders his way past me, shoving me to one side as he hurries down the stairs.

"Hey!" he shouts, "what the hell is going on around here?"

This is not going to endear him to Horvath who does not endear easily. Horvath looks in his direction with an icy look. I head up the stairs. I want no part of this.

Twenty minutes later Horvath and I are seated across from one another, waiting for two mugs of hot coffee to cool. The White Star Cafe is a greasy spoon diner with delusions of grandeur but it's a block from the theater and cozy inside.

"So, Joe," he says, "what is it with you and dead bodies?"

"Don't start with me, Sarge," I say, half smiling.

He laughs, shaking his head. Five years ago he helped me rescue Bunny from a homicidal maniac who was out to kill her. I've been grateful ever since.

"You know, it's a good thing I know you, Joe," he says. "Any other cop would take one took at your banged up puss and those scabs on your hands and put you at the top of his suspect list."

"You mean you're not going to slap the cuffs on me?"

"Not any time soon," he says. "Now that guy Harker, he's another story. I'm hoping I find a yellow sheet on that arrogant bastard as long as my arm."

"If you're checking under 'Harker' I doubt you'll find much," I say. When he looks puzzled, I say, "It's a stage name, Sarge."

"You sure?"

"Either that or he's a vampire slayer who has switched professions." Horvath still looks confused. "Trust me, Sarge. Run his prints, not his name." I sip my coffee. It's still very hot but drinkable.

"I'll do that. I got a tip that he was one of Finucci's biggest customers. Of course that doesn't mean much. Finucci had a lot of big customers, none of which were actually that big, but the guys in Vice tell me for a small time independent, he did all right for himself."

"What do you mean, independent?"

"I mean, he operated outside the mob. His brother-in-law Sal Rizzo is an underboss with the Gambino family. As a courtesy they left Finucci alone. To the family Finucci was nickels and dimes."

"So Finucci was married to Rizzo's sister?"

Horvath nods.

"Florence. Usually a guy like Rizzo would bring a brother- in-law into the operation but Finucci was such a fuckup, Rizzo wouldn't take the chance."

I nod.

"Well, Finucci may have been doing all right but last night he was broke."

"I don't think so," Horvath says. "We found almost five hundred bucks on him."

"Mostly fifties and twenties?"

"That's right."

"That's what he got out of my wallet. Twenty minutes earlier he was begging Peter for a loan. There was fear in his eyes, Sarge. Real fear. The man was desperate."

"Wonder why," Horvath muses.

I look past him toward the entrance as another familiar figure enters the diner. Mid-50's, white-maned, tall but pudgy and obviously out of shape, he wears rimless eyeglasses. The last time I saw him he was on stage in a pissing match with Jonathan Harker. He looks around, sees us, and approaches.

"Either of you guys Sergeant Horvath?" he asks.

"I'm Horvath."

"My name's Luther Bascomb. I'm the director of the play. You may have heard of me."

"No, I don't think so," Horvath says. "Where have you been, Mr. Bascomb? We sent a car for you over two hours ago."

"I spent the night at a friend's house. I had no idea what had happened until I arrived at the theater about ten minutes ago."

"Uh huh. Why don't you sit down?"

"I'd rather not. I have a lot on my plate this morning," he says, giving me a look, probably wondering who I am.

"Suit yourself."

"Look, Sergeant, we have a performance this evening and one of your policemen told me we probably wouldn't be able to open."

"He was wrong," Horvath says. "We'll be done no later than two o'clock though I don't imagine a day or two closed will have much effect on your balance sheet."

"And what's that supposed to mean?" Bascomb asks irritably.

"Just that you haven't exactly been packing them in, Mr. Bascomb."

"The Mudhole is a house of Art, Sergeant, not of Commerce. The work is everything. The dollars are of no consequence."

Horvath shrugs.

"Maybe so but I would guess that for the foreseeable future you'll be performing to full houses. The murder theater where a drug dealer was mercilessly beaten to death. It's a natural crowd pleaser."

"Your cynicism does not become you, Sergeant," Bascomb says. He starts to leave when Horvath stops him.

"How well did you know the victim, Mr. Bascomb?" he asks.

"I didn't," he says quickly. "I mean, I knew of him. I think he was a friend of Jonathan Harker."

Horvath nods.

"And when was the last time you saw him? Finucci, I mean?"

Bascomb cocks his head in annoyance.

"I'm not sure I like where this conversation is headed, Sergeant."

"Just answer the question."

"I really can't remember. Maybe a week ago. As I said, I really didn't know him that well." Again he sneaks a quick look in my direction as if I were taking notes or something. "And last night

56

I was busy with this new play I'm working on with a friend until maybe two-thirty and immediately afterwards we took a cab and spent the night at his place in the Village. His name is Winston Baxendale and he lives about a block from Washington Square and I can get you his phone number if you need it."

"I'll let you know," Horvath tells him.

"Then I'm free to go?"

"Why not?"

With a look of relief, Luther Bascomb scoots out the front door. Horvath watches him go.

"Helpful old guy. I ask him when was the last time he saw the victim and he tells me his life story, especially his whereabouts last evening as if I'd asked him for an alibi which I hadn't."

"I think he deserves your full attention, Sarge. The friend he was busy with is the playwright of the opus currently being staged at the Mudhole to where all roads seem to be leading."

Horvath cocks his head to one side in mock disbelief.

"You're starting to sound like a detective," he says.

"Me? Not me. Sarge. Not on your life. This beauty is all yours. I'm here on a scouting expedition for new talent and that's it."

"You have no idea how disappointed I am," he says sorrowfully.

"I'm pretty sure you can screw it up without any help from me, Sarge". And on that note I stand up. "Now if you no longer need me—"

"I don't," Horvath says, getting to his feet, "but where are you staying in case we need to talk?" I tell him. "Well, don't leave town for the next couple of days and I'll let you know if I need to speak to this guy Falk."

He walks me out the door. We shake hands and I tell him I hope I don't see him again. He laughs and says he'll do his best to leave me out of it. I hail a cab as he starts to walk across the street to the theater. A couple of minutes later I'm headed north, back to Harlem and the film studio.

CHAPTER SEVEN

It was a few minutes past noon when I reached the studio. The frizzy-permed secretary, whose name I've learned is Madge, told me the lunch break would be close to two o'clock. She was sure I'd be more than welcome if I wanted to pop onto the stage and observe the filming. I thank her and head back to Stage One.

The red warning light isn't lit so they are between takes. I step inside quietly. Gayne Rescher is adjusting a couple of the lights and Stu Rosenberg is speaking quietly to Peter and another actor I don't know. I look around. Off to the side, sitting in his camp chair and observing, is Stuart Whitman, the star of the movie. I recognize him from 'Darby's Rangers', a war flick he appeared in a couple of years back. He's been bouncing around for nearly ten years playing second and third fiddle to the stars. This picture's his big break.

"Again!" the assistant director shouts as Rosenberg moves back to his position by the camera and the actor's resume their positions. There are three people in the scene, Peter and a henchman, and another actor.

"This is picture!", the a.d. calls out. The stage falls silent.

The warning bell rings, the sound man calls out "Speed!", the second assistant places the scene slate in front of the lens and snaps the clacker. "Scene 81A, Take 3" he says.

"And action," Rosenberg says.

My eyes are riveted on Peter, wrapped in his nine dollar overcoat with that silly hat on his head but there's nothing silly about Peter's demeanor in this scene. He is icy and his eyes (even the good one) are dead as a shark's. He is playing Abe Reles, also known as 'Kid Twist', a stone cold killer who is the chief assassin of Murder Inc. The three men are talking. I can't make out the dialogue but suddenly Peter whips out an ugly looking ice pick and plunges it into the third man's belly. He jams it in viciously, again and again and then steps back as his victim falls to the ground dead. Peter Falk may be a funny and charming guy but his idea of Abe Reles is not someone I would care to run into, even in broad daylight.

"Cut! Print!" Rosenberg says and the atmosphere thaws and the chatting and clattering resume. Stu walks onto the set and puts his arm around Peter's shoulder in an affectionate hug. Peter smiles and then excuses himself when he sees me.

"What do you think, Joe?" he asks as he reaches me.

"I think you're a heartless son of a bitch," I reply.

Peter grins broadly.

"Yeah, thanks, I appreciate that," he says.

The grin fades when I tell him about Gino Finucci.

"Aw, Jeez," he says grimly. "I didn't have much use for the guy but this, wow, I don't know, that's a really lousy thing, getting beaten to death."

"I told the police I'd bring you in if you had anything they needed to know."

Peter shakes his head.

"I know what you know," he says. "Last time I saw the guy was last night. I chased him to the next street and then he was driving away. It was only dumb luck I saw your wallet laying in the gutter."

"Yeah, that's what I thought. I'll tell the sergeant. I don't think he'll bother you."

At this point the a.d. comes over and reminds Peter he's got a wardrobe change for the next scene. He hurries off telling me he'll catch up with me later. A moment later I buttonhole Stu who says he doesn't have time for me right now but he's left a yellow pad with a couple of pages of notes on his desk if I want to look them over. Just suggestions, he says. They might be helpful. Meanwhile they'll be wrapping around seven and he can give me at least an hour, maybe two. I thank him and head for his office.

As I approach Stu's office I see the door to the office next to his is slightly ajar and I can hear a voice coming from within. Because I recognize it I hesitate by the doorway.

"Are you sure you haven't seen him?... Look, he's always hanging around this time of day... No, I'm not calling you a liar... Okay, I'm sorry, it's just that, this is important, you know what I mean. I really have to get in touch with him. Do you have any idea where I can find him?... Sure, sure, I understand. Well, if he comes in, you tell him I'm looking for him. Tell him to call me right away... Jessup. That's right. Jessup."

I push the door open and step into the room. Harv Jessup's seated at a desk, phone pressed to his ear, a cigarette dangling from his lips. He looks up as I enter, startled. His face is damp with sweat and he switches gears as smoothly as flipping a coin.

"Okay, honey. I understand... Sure, I'll be home by six at the latest. You make the reservations... Right. Love you."

He hangs up and forces a smile.

"The wife. It's our anniversary. I don't know where we're going tonight but it won't be cheap."

"Harv, I've been standing outside the door for the last minute. I didn't mean to eavesdrop. I couldn't help it."

"Oh." He wipes his face with his handkerchief. "Well, Joe, I wouldn't like you to get the wrong idea."

"He's dead, Harv," I say.

Jessup frowns.

"What? Who's dead?"

"That reporter. The one you tossed out of here yesterday morning. Gino Finucci."

He stares at me in disbelief and I can read his mind. He can think of only one thing. Where can I go now? Who do I know that can fix me up?

"Who else was he taking care of, Harv?"

He shakes his head.

"I don't know what you're—"

"Don't bullshit me, Harv. He didn't just die, he was murdered. Beaten to death."

Maybe Jessup's a good actor because all I see is total disbelief.

"Murder? No."

"Murder, yes, and it won't take the cops long to find you and start asking a lot of questions. Now I know it's none of my business but I'm asking you for your own good, who else was he supplying? A crew member or maybe someone in the cast?"

Jessup's body sags and he shakes his head in confusion, still trying to take it all in.

"Nobody. I mean, I don't know. There could have been somebody but I don't think so." He looks up at me hopefully. "Look, Joe, I know how it looks but I'm no junkie, just a little weed now and then, that's all."

"Have you looked at yourself in the mirror lately, Harv? It's been a lot more than that and Finucci didn't travel all the way up here just to sell you a couple of ounces of marijuana."

Jessup gets up and comes around the desk.

"Look, I have to go," he says.

I take him by the arm.

"Harv, do yourself a favor. Get to a hospital. They can help you."

"I don't need help, Joe," he says, shaking me off. He hurries out the door. I start after him, then stop. He does need my help. So do dozens of people I know back in L.A. just like Harv Jessup but they can't or won't accept it. Like alcoholics they have to hit bottom and when they do they have a choice. Turn it around or die, there is no middle ground.

I go next door into Stu's office and check his desk for the yellow pad. It's sitting on top of a pile of scripts. He's handwritten three pages of notes which I quickly scan. They seem to make a lot of sense. I tear them off the pad and slip them into my pocket. I'll go over them more carefully back at the hotel.

I head down the hallway and then down the stairs and out onto the sidewalk. This area's not deserted but it's not crowded either. A building across the street appears to be abandoned and graffiti has been painted on one of its walls. It's unreadable and looks like a gang signature.

At twenty past twelve it's slightly warmer than it was earlier but it's still cold and like it or not I'm going to have to spring for an overcoat. I decide to stop by Macy's on the way back to the hotel. I look up and down the street hoping to spot a taxi which is when I notice the shiny black Caddy Fleetwood parked across the street. At the same time the Caddy notices me. The driver's side door opens and a T- Rex emerges and starts toward me. He's at least six-three, broad in the shoulders with a pock-marked face, a scar on his neck, and black hair loaded with enough grease to lube the Caddy for the next year. He's wearing a black leather coat and black leather gloves and an expression that would freeze hot bullion.

"You Bernardi?" he asks.

"I might be," I say, backing up a step.

"My boss wants to talk to you."

"Who's your boss?"'

"Follow me," he says starting back to the Caddy. When I don't follow, he turns back to me."You got a hearing problem, pal?"

"Who's your boss?" I ask again.

He moves close to me and peels back his overcoat and his jacket to reveal a shoulder holster into which a chrome-plated .45 automatic has been nestled.

"He's the guy who bought me this for Christmas," the behemoth says.

"Lucky you," I say. I'm always saying dumb things like that in the face of danger but it's the only thing that prevents me from having a urinary accident.

"Wise guy, huh?"

"I try," I say.

At that moment I look up the street and see an NYPD patrol car approaching. I push by the big guy and wave my arms to flag down the cop car. If this guy wants to shoot me, this is his chance but I doubt he's that stupid. I guess right. He hurries to his car and slides behind the wheel. As the squad car comes to a stop in front of me, the Caddy pulls away from the curb. I watch it go and then walk over to the driver side window which has been rolled down.

"What's the problem, buddy?"

"6X-6512. Write it down. It's the plate number of that Caddy that just pulled away from the curb. The guy at the wheel tried to pull a gun on me."

"Yeah?" His expression borders on disbelief.

"Look, I just got a call from Sergeant Horvath at the Nine. I'm kind of a witness in a killing and he wants me down there right away and I can't find a cab so can you guys give me a lift?"

The cop's expression changes.

"To the Nine? Sure, hop in. Wally, call in that plate number."

I get in the back seat and we start heading south. Even though I'm not actually involved in this murder investigation, I think this confrontation is something Horvath should know about. We're flying down Broadway using an occasional blast of the siren to clear out the traffic in front of us. At 34th Street we fly by Macy's and I look at it wistfully through the rear window. Another day without a warm coat.

Horvath is busy.

As soon as I walk in the squad room I see him at his desk talking to a woman wrapped in a coat for which a couple of dozen chinchillas gave their lives. Her makeup's heavy and her bouffant hair looks like a dye job. I put her at 50 minimum, trying to look like 30. Standing stiffly behind her is a slick looking article in a Brooks Brothers three piece suit that costs enough to bribe a Congressman for at least a year. He's tallish, swarthy and with jet black hair turning white at the temples. He reminds me a lot of Cesar Romero.

Whatever the lady is saying to Horvath, she is adamant about it. Every once in a while the guy in the suit leans down and whispers in her ear. She throws him a discreet elbow and keeps talking. After a while Horvath's had enough. He stands. She stands. A final word and then she starts walking toward the doorway where I am standing. The suit follows obediently in her wake. As she passes me, she ignores my virile Mediterranean good looks and strides out the door, fire in her eyes. I look back at Horvath who is waving me to his desk.

"That looked like fun," I tell him.

"Clarissa Grandee," Horvath says, "A patron of the arts. She owns that little hole-in-the-wall theater. She assures me that none of her 'children', as she calls them, could possibly be involved in the death of that dreadful man."

"You believe her?"

"Yeah, like I believe in Tinkerbell."

"The guy in the suit? Husband?"

"Lawyer. Benito Tartaglia, a man with many friends in low places and clients in even lower ones. The lady's a widow with more money than brains. So what's your story?" Horvath asks me.

I pull up a chair and tell him.

"This guy who braced you, he give you a name?"

"No."

"What did he look like?"

I tell him. When I mention the scar on the guy's neck, Horvath gives me a sharp look.

"The scar. Describe it."

"White. Ragged. It ran from just below his ear to the middle of his throat."

"Frankie Fortuna," Horvath says.

"Who?"

"He's a soldier in the Gambino family."

"What the hell does he want with me?" I ask.

Horvath picks up a piece of paper from his desk.

"Black Cadillac Fleetwood, plate number 6X-6512, registered to one Salvatore Rizzo."

I nod as it clicks in.

"Finucci's brother-in-law," I say.

"You seem to have atttracted his attention," Horvath says.

"Why?"

Horvath gives me a patronizing look.

"Why? Because the night Finucci was killed you were chasing him all over the East Village and you have scrapes and bruises all over you and Finucci was beaten to death."

"I didn't kill him."

"I think Sal wants to find that out for himself," Horvath says. "You want me to pick him up?"

"What for? You can't charge him with anything."

"I can deliver a stern warning."

"You think it'll do any good?"

"No, but it's better than nothing."

I ponder that.

"No, let it alone."

"You sure?"

"I'm sure."

Horvath shrugs.

"Your funeral."

I glare at him. The two words I least needed to hear at this particular moment.

CHAPTER EIGHT

I grab a cab and swing by Macy's. They have a nice selection of overcoats, some with eye-popping prices, in particular a great looking cashmere imported from London. I give it one quick look and buy a durable Scottish wool, just as warm at half the price. These days I can afford just about anything but when you grow up poor you have a healthy respect for the dollar and I don't spend ten when five will do. I wear the coat out of the store and feel better already. Let the city freeze someone else's butt off for a change.

Back in my hotel room I sit down at the typewriter and start reading Stu Rosenberg's notes. They're all good, cogent and concise, but I find my mind wandering as visions of Frankie Fortuna and the Cadillac float around my brain. I order lunch and a couple of beers and flip on the television where I find myself watching something called 'As the World Turns'. Some doctor in a white coat is telling this woman that she has a rare blood disease. He's kindly but clinical. She's upset and on the edge of hysteria. I leave the set on as I respond to a call of nature in the bathroom, then answer the door for the room service waiter. I make room on the table for the tray and sit down to eat. Once again I check out the television set. The doctor is still kindly but clinical, she's still got the blood disease and she's still pouring out her fears. The gabbing is ceaseless.

These two are in serious danger of talking each other to death. I lumber over to the TV and turn it off, preferring to eat in silence. After lunch I call Bunny at the office. We chat about this and that but I deliberately neglect to tell her about Sal Rizzo. All she'd do is worry. I report in to Bertha and give her a glowing report on Peter Falk. No, we haven't talked business, not yet. I also don't tell her about Gino Finucci. She believes that I am a magnet for homicidal maniacs and I can't convince her otherwise. Anyway what she doesn't know won't hurt her.

When I hang up on Bertha, I stare at Stu's notes. The room is silent. I've run out of reasons not to get to work but visions of Frankie Fortuna continue to dance in my head. I see myself staring into the business end of Frankie's chrome 45 automatic. I'm begging for my life. I hadn't realized what a wimp I am. To hell with it. I flop down on the bed and fall asleep.

I stir an hour or so later but it isn't an hour. The clock by the bed reads 6:18. I leap to my feet and go into the bathroom where I splash my head and face with cold water. I've got about 40 minutes to get up to Harlem for my meeting with Stu Rosenberg and Manhattan traffic at this time of the evening is brutal. The taxi line outside the hotel entrance is twenty deep and by the time I'm in a cab heading north it's ten of seven.

I needn't have hurried. There was a problem with the camera right after lunch that cost them two hours while they scouted up a replacement. Stu is shooting a scene with Whitman and his female co-star May Britt. When I finally manage to pull him aside between set-ups, he tells me he's looking at a nine-thirty wrap after which he just wants to go home and sleep. He tries to apologize. I tell him not to bother. I've been around the business long enough to know these things happen. I ask about Peter and Stu tells me he was released about three hours ago. He offers to give me Peter's home phone but I tell him not to bother. This has been a lousy day all the way around. We can start fresh in the morning.

I step out of the building into the cool night air. I'm no longer chilly but I have another problem. I doubt that many cabs cruise this Harlem neighborhood at this time of the evening so I start walking toward the nearest cross street some distance away where I see a semblance of traffic. Many of the streetlights on this block are out, their glass globes smashed. Nearby stores are closed up and only a few lights are dimly glowing from apartment windows. Apparently this is a neighborhood that curls up in a ball and hides under the covers when the sun goes down.

On my side of the street cars fill every parking spot. The other side is empty, marked with signs that read "No Overnight Parking" which is odd since at that moment a car parked in the verboten zone halfway up the block flicks on its headlights and starts to slowly approach. I don't like the looks of it. I like it even less when the car passes under one of the few streetlights still operational. It's a black Cadillac Fleetwood and I don't need to see the license plate to know who it belongs to.

I look back toward the studio. No retreat to safety there, I've come too far. The Caddy will cut me off before I've gone twenty yards. I look to my left and just ahead is the entrance to an alley. I have no idea where it goes but if I stay on the street I'm dead meat. I run to the alley and dash into it. It is narrow and pitch dark and I stumble over something and fall, then quickly get to my feet and plunge further into the inky blackness. Suddenly light floods the alley as the Caddy turns in and then stops, it's headlights prob-ing. Now I can see where I'm going but my stomach turns into a square knot when I see the brick wall in front of me. This alley goes nowhere and I'm trapped, caught in the high beams of Sal Rizzo's Caddy.

The driver's side door opens and a shadowy figure emerges and starts toward me. He is back lit so I can't see his features but his size gives him away. Desperately I look around for some avenue of escape, a doorway or a fire escape ladder. There is none. Maybe there's something I can use as a weapon, not that it will do much good against Frankie Fontana's automatic. I spot a length of two by four a few feet away. It is weathered and has a couple of rusty nails protruding from one end. I pick it up and start waving it in front of me like a magic wand. Frankie stops a few feet away.

"Don't be stupid," he says.

"Stay away from me!" I shriek, trying not to sound like a little girl.

"My boss wants to talk to you." Frankie says.

"I'll bet he does."

Frankie shakes is head in disgust and pulls out his pistol.

"I'm not going to kill you, Mr. Bernardi, but if you don't drop that little stick, I will shoot you in the foot and believe me, you will not like it."

Being not very bright and unused to coming up against gorilla-like mobsters, I do a very stupid thing. I step toward him and take a wild swing at his head. Frankie reaches up with his free hand and clamps it around my wrist in a vise-like grip that threatens to break a dozen bones. I yelp in pain and drop the two by four.

"Okay,okay," I say, having no choice to do otherwise.

Frankie smiles and releases his grip, then uses the pistol to gesture toward the car. I start walking.

When I slip into the back seat I find myself face to face with a slick looking article that I have to assume is Salvatore Rizzo. He's thirtyish, well-groomed and smells of Barbasol. He's also wearing a cashmere overcoat which makes me feel a tad shabby. I guess guys in Rizzo's profession are able to throw money around as if it belonged to somebody else.

"You're a hard man to catch up with," Rizzo says.

"Usually my secretary schedules my appointments."

Rizzo smiles.

"Funny. You're a funny guy, Mr. Bernardi."

"So people tell me, Mr. Rizzo,"

"You know me. Good. I like that." He leans forward and taps Frankie on the shoulder. "The river," he says.

"Right, boss," Frankie replies as he backs the car out of the alley. The river. I'm not sure I like the sound of that.

We start driving east toward the Harlem River which is not really a river but a navigable tidal strait that separates Manhattan from the Bronx. Rizzo is silent for a minute and then he says, "So this movie, tell me about it."

The movie? Why is he asking me about the movie? Why isn't he asking me about his brother-in-law?

"Oh, I have nothing to do with the movie," I say.

His eyes turn reptilian.

"Tell me about it anyway," he says softly.

"Well," I say, "it's based on a book by Burton Turkus. He was the Manhattan D. A. back in the Thirties."

"Fucking guy," Rizzo mutters under his breath. He looks up at me. "I was just a kid when he sent my uncle Angie up for thirty years. Fucking guy." He falls silent for a few moments and then once again speaks up. "This picture, it's about Lepke's mob, right?"

I nod and he laughs.

"Murder Incorporated, like Lepke was the president of General Motors or something. Probably some shithead reporter dreamed that one up. Those guys are always writing things and they don't know crap. You think you could get me a copy of the script?"

"I don't know. Maybe," I say.

"I'd like to see what they say. These guys weren't part of the organization, you know. They were outsiders. Wannabes."

"I'd heard that," I say.

"Especially that rat bastard Reles. He's gotta be in the movie. Who's playing him?

"Nobody you ever heard of," I say.

"And Lepke?

"Same."

"Rod Steiger, he'd be perfect for Lepke. You know who I'm talking about? Rod Steiger?"

"Yeah. I actually know Rod Steiger," I tell him.

He looks at me in disbelief.

"Get outta here," Rizzo says.

"It's my business, Mr. Rizzo," I tell him I know a lot of people.

We're approaching the 3rd Avenue Bridge that spans the river. Rizzo points.

"Over there, Frankie," he says, "and cut the engine. We don't want to be disturbed."

We puil up under the bridge in the shadow of one of its concrete footings. It is deadly quiet. Small boats skim by in the water. Street traffic is nearly non-existent.

"I don't like movies like this. It gives people the wrong idea about people in my profession," he says quietly, staring out the window at the river, shrouded in darkness except for the occasional boat coming by. "Aw, fuck it," he finally says and turns to me. "So, Mr. Bernardi, I'm going to ask you this politely but I'm only going to ask you once and I want an honest answer. Did you kill my sister's husband?"

"No, I did not," I say.

"Gino was beaten to death and you look like you've been in a fight."

"I got these scrapes and bruises chasing him through the streets after he stole my wallet."

"Yeah, yeah," he says dismissively. "I read that bullshit police report."

"How were you able to do that?" I ask him.

He gives me a look like do I really believe that Santa Claus could ever get his fat ass down a billion chimneys in one night.

"These cops," he says, "when it comes to guys like Gino or me, they write any damned thing they please. Some of them should be writing comic strips for a living."

"The report is accurate," I insist.

"Yeah, well, maybe it is and maybe it isn't but here's the way it is, my friend. Gino is dead and somebody's gonna answer for it and unless proven otherwise, I'm guessing you're the guy."

"Now wait a minute—"

"Right now my sister Florence is home crying her eyes out. I don't know why because Gino was a no-good, selfish, philandering son of a bitch, but when she says to me, Sally, get the guy who did this and rip his heart out, I gotta pay attention. You see my problem."

"Yes, but—"

"There are no buts, Mr. Bernardi. I'm going to give you a break. Three days that cop gets to find out who did it, assuming it wasn't you. At the end of the three days, if no progress has been made, you are a dead man. It may not be fair but it will make Florence very happy."

"Three days? That's crazy—"

"You know how in all those crappy gangster movies, the guy with the gun is always saying, 'It ain't personal, it's business'? Not this time, Mr. Bernardi. This time it isn't business, it's personal. Monday at six p.m. Mark your calendar. So, can I drop you somewhere? Like your hotel?"

"No, thanks," I say quickly.

He grins.

"I get it. You don't want me knowing where you're staying like maybe the Hotel Astor, Room Ten-Oh-Seven."

I manage to grin back.

"You win. I'll take the lift."

Twenty minutes later Frankie pulls up to the front entrance of the Astor and Sal Rizzo wishes me a pleasant good evening. Happily he does not volunteer to walk me to my room. They pull away as I duck inside and jog to the elevators. Once inside my room I grab the phone and dial the 9th Precinct.

"I was just walking out the door hoping to go home and re-establish a relationship with my wife." Horvath says. "So what's so important."

I tell him.

There is a lengthy silence and then he says, "Eat in your room. Double lock your door and be at my desk tomorrow morning at eight o'clock sharp."

"Then you've had a break in the case?" I ask hopefully.

"No, Joe, just the opposite. I've got nothing."

CHAPTER NINE

"I'm asking you again, Joe, do you want me to pick him up?"

Horvath is leaning across his desk looking me in the eye and there is genuine concern in his voice.

"What for?" I ask. "You've already told me you can't hold him and besides it's my word against his."

"I can make things tough for him," Horvath says. "Maybe scare him a little."

"Come on, Sarge, you know Rizzo doesn't scare and picking him up? That's like jabbing a stick at a hungry tiger. All you're going to do is piss him off."

Horvath leans back in his chair and takes a sip of cold coffee from his carry-out container. A half-eaten cruller sits on a paper plate in front of him, This is Horvath's idea of breakfast. The squad room at the 9th is quiet this time of the morning. The pimps and their chattel are asleep. So are the second story men and the street muggers. Their day starts when the sun goes down and the night shift has to deal with the detritus of humankind that inhabits this area of the city. Now I merely have to listen to low level chatter, the clicking of typewriter keys and the ring of incoming phone calls. A lull in the fight against crime

"Are you sure you didn't do it, Joe? It'd make my life a lot simpler," he says.

"Sorry. Can't help you. Look, Sarge, you've got three days. Maybe you'll catch the killer and the problem solves itself."

"And maybe Houdini will rise from his grave and make Sal Rizzo disappear though I don't think so."

He looks at me and I can tell from his expression, there's something wrong.

"I don't care for that look, Sarge." I say. "What's the problem?"

"Hyman Weiss," he says.

"Never heard of him."

"A high priced lawyer. His brother's a City Councilman in tight with the Mayor. Two nights ago we found his body in an alley behind McSorley's Old Ale House. He had three slugs in the gut and a face full of garbage where somebody had dumped him. I caught the case and everybody from Mayor Wagner on down is all over my Captain and my Captain is all over me."

"I get it. No time for the visitor from California."

"I didn't say that, Joe. I'm working your case. I'm only saying I have a lot of stuff crowding my plate."

"Okay. Have you got anything?"

"Not much."

"What about the crime scene? The lab guys must have found something."

"Yeah, a lot of dust and dirt. That basement hasn't been cleaned out in years. We didn't find any brass buttons pulled from somebody's jacket or a matchbook cover from some nightclub with the killer's phone number written on it or a strand of long blonde hair from some skirt like Jean Harlow. See, Joe, I actually watch some of that crap you guys put out that's supposed to pass for police work but this is the real world, my Hollywood friend, and when I tell you I got nothin', I got nothin'."

At that moment a guy in shirt sleeves and a pulled down tie

comes to the desk and drops a manila envelope on Horvath's desk, barely missing the cruller.

"Guy from the coroner's office dropped this off, Kay. Said you were looking for it."

"Thanks, Mickey," Horvath says as he tears open the flap and takes out the report, two pages typed, single spaced with diagrams. He starts to read. A frown crosses his face. He flips to page two. More frowning before he lays the report on his desk. He looks up at me.

"For the record, Joe, where were you early Thursday morning between midnight and two o'clock?"

"In my hotel room, trying with great difficulty to get to sleep."

"Can you prove it?"

"No."

"That's good enough for me." Horvath says.

"Between twelve and two, is that the time of death?" I ask

"That's what the coroner says. This movie you're working on, Joe, what did you say the name of it was?"

"I'm not working on it. I'm in town collaborating with the director on a screenplay."

"Don't duck the question."

"It's called Murder Incorporated. It's based on a book by a former D.A."

"Real people? Real names?"

"Yes."

"Turkus? Lepke?"

"Yes."

"Abe Reles?"

"Sure."

"Pittsburgh Phil?"

"Who's that?

"Also known as Ice Pick Harry Strauss."

"Not familiar."

Horvath picks up the report.

"According to the coroner, Finucci was severely beaten but it wasn't the cause of death. Somebody jammed an ice pick into his ear." He hesitates, waiting for my reaction. I have none. "For both Strauss and Reles, the instrument of choice was often an ice pick. Tell me about this guy Falk."

"He's an actor," I say.

"He's playing Abe Reles?"

I suddenly see where this is going.

"Oh, come on, Sarge—"

"How tight is Falk in with the mob?"

"He's not."

"He says. Falk knew Finucci and didn't much like him and don't tell me otherwise because I got that from your waiter. Falk chased the guy away from your table."

"Not with an ice pick—"

"And then when Falk saw you running after Finucci through the restaurant he got up and joined in the chase."

"That's right, but—"

"And when you slip and fall on the pavement Falk keeps chasing after Finucci on his own. How far back do these guys go?"

"You're crazy."

"Maybe so, Joe, but right now I want to talk to him. Bring him in as promised or I'll go after him and I won't care if he's in the middle of the death scene from 'Hamlet'."

"Even if I wanted to—-"

"You can go now. Have Falk in here no later than five o'clock this evening."

"I'm not sure I can—"

"I said you can go now, Joe", he says firmly and I realize any further discussion is futile.

I get to my feet,

"You're wrong, Sarge, and I'm going to prove it."

"You're not going to meddle in this case, Joe," he warns me.

"Of course I'm not, Sarge," I lie. "That would be stupid."

I start to walk off. He stops me.

"Joe, one thing. The business with the ice pick. That's going to be a hold back."

I nod in understanding. A hold back is something the cops keep to themselves. It helps a lot in testing the veracity of witnesses and especially in dealing with the usual parade of crackpots who show up after every murder to confess.

"I also think you ought to buy yourself some protection. If you won't let me help, hire somebody who will."

"I can take care of myself."

Horvath laughs.

"Yeah, I remember. You up in Lime Rock getting chased by that whack job in a red pickup."

"I'm still here, Sarge," I say.

"For now. Wake me up when you come to your senses. Now get outta here and stay away until five o'clock when I expect to see you here with your actor friend."

I humor him with a smile and leave.

Of two things I am sure. I am not dragging Peter Falk down here at five o'clock and I most definitely will be sticking my nose into this case. It's my neck on the line, not Horvath's, and I have seventy two hours to redirect Sal Rizzo's suspicions onto somebody else.

My gut tells me that the key to Finucci's death can be found at the Mudhole, either that or someone is trying to throw suspicion in that direction. To find out which, I need a fount of information and I think I know just who it is. I head for the theater in search of Portia Justice, the aspiring actress from Nowheresville, Wyoming, born Velma Micklenberger. I doubt she's there at this hour of the morning but there may be someone around who can tell me how to contact her.

As I walk north on Avenue B towards Tompkins Square, i know a couple of things for sure. Jonathan Harker was a customer of Gino Finucci and Luther Bascomb knew it and didn't approve. Whoever else might have been tied into Finucci remains to be seen. I am also pretty sure Finucci was desperate for money. First he tries to put the touch on Falk and when that fails he steals my wallet. A few hours later he ends up dead, my money in his pocket. Is there a connection there? I intend to find out.

There's a small sign posted at the entrance to the theater. It reads "Closed for Auditions". This is not an encouraging sign but when I try the door knob it turns and I'm able to enter the lobby. Off to my right two attractive young women are seated. Not knowing who I am they smile warmly. This is a sure tip-off they are actresses. Actresses looking for work smile at everybody. I smile back.

Immediately I'm aware of voices coming from the stage as I climb the staircase. There are two people on the cramped little stage. A man is sitting on a folding chair. A woman with half-sheets of paper in her hand is circling around him. She is speaking. He is mostly listening. Sitting in the first row of the audience section is the director, Luther Bascomb. A couple of seats away from him Velma Micklenberg sits with a clipboard in her lap taking notes. I hesitate at the landing while the female anguishes over a pet goat that ran away from home when she was three and then reappeared in a dream wearing a silver crown on the day of FDR's inauguration as President. The guy on the chair looks like he'd rather be somewhere else. So would I.

"Hold it!" Bascomb says getting to his feet. He walks onto the stage and takes the young actress by the arm and leads her a few feet away for a private whispered conversation. I seize this chance to approach Velma.

"What's going on?" I ask her.

"Oh, hi," she smiles. "We're holding auditions for the part of Esmerelda."

"Somebody leaving the cast?"

"Amythyst. She's been signed for three weeks to fill in for Patricia Neway in 'The Sound of Music'."

"Sounds like a big break," I say.

Velma shrugs.

"She'll make the least of it," she says.

"Meow."

Velma shakes her head.

"I'm not really like that," she says, "but you have to know Amythyst. I love her dearly but she works hard to sabotage her career every chance she gets."

"How long do you think you're going to be here? I'd like to buy you lunch."

"I can leave now and let der Feuhrer take his own notes."

I check my watch. It reads 10:32.

"How about noon?"

"Sure. I can last till then."

"Mama Leone's?"

She frowns.

"I'm hungry but not that hungry," she says.

"Luchows?"

"More like it," she smiles.

I look over at Bascomb who is returning to his seat. He sees me and scowls. Since he saw me with Horvath, he probably thinks I'm a cop. Why discourage him? I give him a hard stare and scoot out of there.

The city's warmed up since yesterday and the air is brisk but not cold. My new coat is keeping me toasty. There's something about New York that intrigues me. Everything about it is big except its heart and therein lies its fascination. I've heard the old bromide. If you can make it in New York, you can make it anywhere and it's probably true. But if you are a second-rater, even if you're merely unsure of yourself, this city of towering skyscrapers above and a lacework of subways below will spit you out like a watermelon seed. I wander over to the Village, to Washington Square where I admire the paintings of a few artists who are displaying their work on the sidewalks. None are undiscovered Picassos and none of them seem bothered by it. If there is an ordinance against this sidewalk art gallery the cops don't seem to care. Greenwich Village has a mystique all its own. At quarter to twelve I start hoofing it east over to 14th Street at Irving Place and find Velma waiting for me at Luchow's entrance.

"I wasn't sure if you'd made a reservation," she says, "but even if you had, I've forgotten your name."

I laugh and tell her what it is as we go inside. The maitre'd at his stand asks if I have a reservation. I say no. He sighs and gives me a look that says it all. This is not Schraffts, this is Luchows and we demand respect. I take out my business card and hand it to him. He scans it and a hearty smile forms on his lips. The movie business trumps everything. He quickly grabs two menus and leads us to an excellent table by the window. I thank him with a sawbuck.

As I settle in and start to check out the menu, I look up and see Velma staring at me.

"Just who the hell are you?" she asks.

I tell her, handing her a card as well. She studies it and then tries to hand it back. I tell her to keep it.

"And Peter?"

"I came east with the idea of signing him as a client."

"He's a terrific guy," she says. "And a great actor."

"No argument here," I say.

She falls silent for a moment, then reaches in her purse for a cigarette. I grab a book of matches from the ashtray and light it for her.

"So what do you want with me, Mr. Bernardi?" she asks.

"Why don't we order and then we'll chat," I say.

A few minutes later I watch the departing figure of our waiter as he heads for the kitchen to order up two plates of knockwurst and kraut and a couple of steins of Lowenbrau. I turn to my luncheon companion.

"Portia—"

"Velma. Call me Velma. All my friends do. Portia is a bullshit name for a non-existent career. I'm getting sick of it."

"Okay, Velma, I asked you to lunch for a reason."

"I figured that and I doubt you're looking to get into my panties."

"Correct,"

"So that probably means you're not going to promise to turn me into a big star overnight."

"Two in a row," I smile.

"Doesn't leave much," she says.

"How about saving my life?"

She's surprised by that so I explain it to her: my encounter with Gino Finucci in the rest room at Charlie Wang's, the wild chase through the streets of the East Village, my kidnapping at the hands of Sal Rizzo and his goon and finally the death threat.

She stares at me, mouth agape.

"Holy crap," she says.

"Precisely," I say. "It's my belief, Velma, that Finucci's killer is someone associated with the Mudhole. If not that, then someone who knows enough about the Mudhole people to put the body in the basement to divert suspicion. Either way I need to know all about the people at the theater."

She looks at me thoughtfully and then says, "We'll start with me."

"That won't be necessary," I say.

"Why not?" she says. grinding what's left of her cigarette into the ashtray. "I hated the little shit, not just because he called me a lard-assed porker, I've been hearing that all my life. but because of what he did to Amythyst."

"And what was that?"

"He got her back on the junk. Two years clean and he comes poking around, taking care of Johnny Sverny—excuse me, I mean Jonathan Harker—and Gino must have sensed what she'd been. He gave her some free stuff when she was feeling down and the next thing you know, she's hooked again. Started wearing long-sleeves to hide the needle marks."

"She was into the hard stuff."

"As hard as it gets, "Velma says. "One day on top, the next day—" She leaves it unsaid.

"Tell me about her."

"Not much to tell, Joe. She's a pretty private person. She was born in America, moved to Switzerland with her mother when she was just a baby. When she graduated from one of those snooty Swiss schools for girls, she and her Mom came back to the states. That was like 1939, just before the war broke out. She started studying for the theater, made the rounds like we all did. In '43 she gets the break of a lifetime. the lead in a wartime musical called "Here Come the Waves." She's an overnight sensation. Picture on the cover of Look magazine. She went wild. Booze, then drugs. Her next two shows were flopperoos so she goes out to Hollywood. Small parts in two-bit pictures. More partying, more booze and by 1950, her career was over. That's why she's doing the Mudhole and why the shot at 'Sound of Music' is so important to her. It's her way of getting back on top."

"If she's using she probably won't get there and if she does, she won't stay." I tell her.

"I know," Velma says. "She wants to quit, Joe. She's told me so."

Her eyes darken. "Finucci. That son of a bitch. I could have killed him." She hesitates and then looks me in the eye. "And Joe, believe me, I could have killed him."

"Okay, I believe you, Velma, but let's leave you and Amythyst out of this for the time being. What about Harker?"

"He's an arrogant bastard. Nobody likes him. Just waiting for Hollywood to discover him. Says he's no junkie, just smokes a little weed now and then but I know that's a load of crap. One day I stumbled into the washroom by mistake and Finucci was selling him at least a half a dozen little bags of powder. Even I know horse when I see it."

"Six bags. That's a helluva habit," I say.

"Damned right," she says and then pauses, a strange look on her face. "The only thing is—" She stops.

"What"

"One night last week he was backstage changing into a monkeysuit, you know, bib and tucker, for some fancy shindig uptown. He had his shirt off and he had a pretty good physique but more than that, I didn't see any tracks anywhere."

"His legs?"

"Naw, he was in his jockeys. Unless he was using his ass for a pin cushion, I don't know how he was doing it."

"I'm not much of an expert on the subject," I confess.

"Me, either," she says.

"What about the other cast members?"

"There are none. It's a two character play. It's the only kind Winnie writes."

"That'd be Winston Baxendale, the playwright. Peter's friend. Tell me about him."

"Quiet. Shy. Nervous around women. I don't think he's queer, just intimidated."

"One of Gino's customers?" I ask.

"God no." Velma says. "He's a health nut. His body's a temple, he says. He wouldn't defile it with foreign substances. Sometimes I think it's a chore for him to eat. He's skinny as a straw. Well, you saw him. He was the one reading with that actress."

I remember him. Even though he was just sitting you could tell he was a beanpole. Almost emaciated. Junkies are also skinny. Maybe Velma's wrong about him.

"And the director?"

"No. Luther's a straight arrow. Hates the stuff and people who use it."

"So who else is there?" I ask.

"Leo's our lighting guy. He's at least 60, maybe more. Drinks a lot of beer, smokes cheap cigars but no weed, not that I know of. And besides him there's only Izzy and Adele. They're studying theater at CCNY and they live together a few blocks from here. They handle everything from props to costumes to cleaning up after a performance. We don't pay them so unless they're robbing banks by day, they haven't got two extra nickels to rub together and junk doesn't come cheap."

Just then our waiter returns with our beer and two steaming plates of knockwurst and kraut. The aroma is irresistible. Our waiter wishes us 'guten appetit' and starts to back away from the table. Before he leaves I ask him if he could bring me a small envelope. With pleasure, he says, and a few moments later he returns with a small white envelope bearing the Luchow logo. I take out one of my business cards and scribble something on the back, then seal it in the envelope and write Harker's name on the outside. I hand it to Velma.

"Would you give this to him before tonight's performance?"

"Sure. Glad to."

I smile and lift my stein in a toast. Velma reciprocates and we drink.

"So, tell me about this woman that owns the theater," I say.

"Clarissa Grandee? What about her?"

"The cops were questioning her yesterday."

"Why? She doesn't know anything. She hardly ever comes around the theater. The only reason she bought it last year was to shore up her credentials as a patron of the arts. She's on the board of one of the major museums, she's a big donor to the symphony orchestra and she has a piece of three Broadway shows that I know of. She's a Jesus freak with a steel rod for a backbone and a moral certainty rivaled only by that of Billy Graham."

I look at her approvingly. That was quite a mouthful for a failed actress. Maybe she ought to give some thought to writing instead. With a shove in the right direction big Velma Micklenberger could become the next treasure of the American theater.

"Sorry I wasn't more help," she says apologetically, slicing into her knockwurst.

I smile at her. She has no idea how helpful she's been. Thanks to her, the game is afoot.

CHAPTER TEN

After lunch Velma heads back to the theater on foot. She says the exercise is good for her. I'm headed for the Harlem studio and walking is not an option no matter how good it might be for me. As I stand on the curb looking both ways for a cab I spot a guy sitting on a bench across the way reading this morning's *Daily News*. He's on the short side with red hair turning white and a face full of freckles. He wears a cheap suit and the only reason he catches my eye is, I've seen him before. Like two hours ago in Washington Square as I was browsing the paintings, he always seemed to be hovering nearby, maybe ten or fifteen feet away, trying much too hard not to notice me.

I wave to an approaching cab and as he slides to the curb I slip into the back seat and tell him where I'm going. I glance at the guy on the bench. His eyes lift off the paper and look into mine and then quickly he looks away. As the cab pulls into the street and heads for the next corner, I look back through the rear window. The guy is on his feet and jogging toward a blue Chevy parked about thirty yards away. Obviously Sal Rizzo has me on a tight leash. Or at least he thinks he does. We head north on Second Avenue and when I look back, he's still there, about three cars behind us. I tap my cabbie on the shoulder.

"We're being tailed by a guy in a blue Chevy. Lose him and there's an extra ten in it for you."

"He's as good as lost," the cabbie says as he turns sharply into an alleyway and floors it. For the next five or six minutes, we duck down one street after another, then cut across to Broadway, head south for a couple of blocks, then turn north on 8th Avenue. I check behind us. No sign of him. I tell the cabbie to pull to the curb just to be sure. I give it three full minutes. Still no sign of the Chevy in any direction. Satisfied, I tell the cabbie to head for Harlem.

At ten past two we turn onto 126th Street and pull up to the studio entrance. I get out of the cab and get ready to pay the fare, then look across the street. The blue Chevy's parked at the curb. The freckle-faced guy is behind the wheel, still reading the *Daily News*. I look at the cabbie who shrugs helplessly. I shake my head, bewildered, and pay the fare plus another ten. Then, as the cab pulls away, I take one more look at my shadow. This time he looks over at me and a smile forms on his lips. I am not happy about this. Not happy at all.

Once inside I check in with Madge, the secretary, and learn that Peter is here and shooting on Stage 2. I ask about Harv Jessup. She says the last time she saw him he was in his office. I ask to use the phone and when she gets me an outside line, I dial the local precinct. I'm an out of town executive, I tell them, and somebody has been following me around all day. I want it stopped. I describe the car and give them the address. So much for Sal Rizzo's goon.

I go out into the corridor and walk to the window that looks down on the street. The Chevy hasn't moved. I wait for a few minutes and then a squad car pulls up and two uniforms get out. They approach the Chevy cautiously from both sides. The one on the driver's side unhooks his holster and taps on the window. Freckles rolls down the window. They talk for a few moments and then my shadow pulls out a leather badge holder and flips it open. The cop nods, gives him a tip of his hat and he and his partner go back to their squad car. By now it has become very clear. Horvath. He doesn't want to find my battered blood-stained body in some alley because I know from experience, if there's one thing Horvath hates, it's paperwork. As if things weren't complicated enough, now I have a babysitter.

I walk down the hallway to Jessup's office. Again the door is ajar and Jessup is on the phone. I push the door open and Jessup looks up at me, then waves me inside. This time his call is strictly company business.

"Come on, Phoebe, don't bust my chops. This picture is dynamite, I'm telling you... It is not a remake of the Bogart picture. Bogart's was fictionalized, this is the real deal. Henry Morgan is playing Burton Turkus, the D.A... That's right, Henry Morgan, the comedian, in his first dramatic role. Same for Morey Amsterdam. He plays a Catskill's resort owner... What do you mean no stars? I just gave you two of them... So Whitman's no Tony Curtis, I'm telling you, this is a breakout role for the guy and you get the first interview."

He waves me to the seat in front of the desk as he lights a cigarette even though he's already got one burning in the ashtray. Sweat is pouring down his face.

"Hey, you want star power. Here's one. Sarah Vaughn... That's right. That Sarah Vaughn. Her first movie role... Yeah, she sings. Why would we have Sarah Vaughn if she didn't sing... Look, I'm not going to tell you how to write this story but we've got May Britt playing the female lead... That's right, May Britt, the one that's going to marry Sammy Davis Jr.." He manages a loud but insincere laugh. "That's right, Feebs, first Kim Novak, then May Britt. The little schwartze's got a thing for blondes... What?... Look, I..." He hesitates, then slams the receiver down on the cradle.

"Dumb bitch," Jessup says. "No sense of humor." He takes out his handkerchief and dabs at his forehead. "You ever have days like this, Joe? Trying to get though to some third level editor at some fourth level woman's mag. Jesus, I gotta get out of this business."

I shrug, smiling.

"Tomorrow will be better, Harv. You won't be so strung out."

He glares at me.

"What do you mean, strung out? You're crazy. I'm fine."

"You're not fine," I say. "I think you're still looking for a connection."

"Fuck you, Joe", he growls.

"Tell me about you and Gino Finucci."

"Fuck you again."

"I've been spending a lot of time with Sergeant Horvath who's the lead detective on Finucci's murder. For old time's sake I haven't mentioned your name but I can't protect you forever."

"You don't know what you're talking about," he says.

"Suit yourself, Harv," I say getting up and heading for the door. "Expect a visit."

My hand's on the doorknob when he says "Wait!" I look back. "Sit down," he says. "What do you want to know?"

I sit and he talks. He's been using for over two years and his habit is getting worse. So far it's cost him his job at a major agency and then his marriage and at the moment he's barely hanging on.

"Tell me about yesterday. When I saw Finucci on the stairway he was scared shitless and when I saw you, you weren't much better. What happened?"

"He tried to borrow money."

"How much?"

"Five thousand."

After the restaurant confrontation I'm only surprised by the amount.

"I told him he was crazy, that I didn't have it," Jessup says. "He told me I'd better get it or he'd go to Twentieth and tell them they had a junkie working for them. That's when I lost it. I yelled at him and started out from behind the desk ready to kill him. He knew it, too, because he ran like hell. I got as far as the doorway when I stopped. In my condition I was never going to catch him. Besides, kill him? What kind of melodramatic bullshit was that? I'd be lucky if he didn't kill me."

"Good decision, Harv. He tell you why he needed the money?"

"No."

"Can you guess?"

"Not really."

"That's not a no."

Jessup lights up another cigarette. Now he has two burning in the ashtray.

"When we first hooked up, this was over a year ago, he mentioned he liked to bet basketball. A couple of times he got behind with the bookies. I gathered it wasn't a pleasant experience."

"I imagine not," I say. " So you figured maybe the books were after him again."

"Why not?"

He looks at me nervously, licking his lips.

"Joe, this Sergeant. Do you really have to mention my name?"

Again I stand up to leave.

"Maybe not, Harv. I'll do my best. Meantime, get some help or you're going to end up dead somewhere with a needle hanging out of your arm. I know it. So do you." Before he can reply I turn and walk out of the office.

I hear voices. They're coming from around the corner, near the stairwell. I recognize them both.

Peter Falk is nose to nose with Horvath and he's not happy.

"What are you trying to do, kill me? I'm working here and you drag me off the set to ask me a bunch of dumb questions."

"I'm conducting an investigation, Mr. Falk—"

"And you think I know something about who whacked Finucci? You're crazy! "

"Tell me about Winston Baxendale," Horvath says.

"He writes plays. Can I go now?"

"I'm told he's a good friend of yours."

"So is Cardinal Spellman. Anything else?"

"Last year your friend Baxendale got into a bar fight with a guy twice his size and nearly killed him."

"The lesson here," Peter says, "is never pick on a guy that holds a black belt in karate. Listen, Lieutenant or Sergeant or whatever you are, I've told you a dozen times I don't know anything about who killed Finuccil.Now please, there's a couple of dozen people in there standing around on that stage waiting to go back to work while you're out here flapping your jaw." Peter is steaming.

"Maybe you'd like to come down to the station and answer my questions," Horvath says, just as steamed.

"And maybe you'd like to take a long walk off a short pier. You want to arrest me? Here!" Peter holds out his wrists. "Slap the cuffs on me but you'd better have a warrant."

Horvath looks over and sees me for the first time.

"I thought you were going to bring him in," he says.

"No, YOU thought I was going to bring him in," I say.

Horvath glares at me and then looks back at Peter.

"Look," he says to Peter, more calmly, "I'm going to need a statement, now or later. This case is turning ugly. Your friend here has been threatened by the mob—"

Peter looks over at me sharply.

"Is that right, Joe?"

I nod.

"Afraid so," I say.

Peter looks back at Horvath.

"Okay. I'll be wrapped by five o'clock. I'll see you around six but I'm telling you I don't know anything. Now can I go back to work?"

Horvath nods.

"Six o'clock. Don't be late."

Peter sidles over next to me and whispers out of the side of his mouth.

"I'll meet you there. Afterwards, we'll talk."

He claps me on the shoulder and then hurries off to the sound stage.

"You're wasting your time with him," I say to Horvath.

"We'll see," Horvath says.

"Finucci was up to his eyeballs with the books," I tell him.

"And where'd you get that?"

"You don't need to know that, not yet, " I say. "But Finucci was desperate for money, scared out of his mind and maybe his bookie caught up with him."

"Bookies don't kill deadbeats. It's bad for business and dead men don't pay debts," Horvath says.

"I've heard that once in a while they make an example of some-one, just to keep the clientele in line."

"It happens," Horvath says grudgingly. "But in this case, I don't see it. The bookie, or one of his guys, grabs Finucci and beats the hell out of him. Whoever he was was big and strong and he knew what he was doing. He inflicts just enough damage to make a point. But then suddenly to jam an ice pick in his ear? That makes no sense."

"But it's worth checking out," I say.

"I'll look into it," he says. "Meanwhile, can I drop you some-where?"

"No, I have to talk to the director. I'll catch a ride with whats-his-name in the blue Chevy. By the way, Sarge, what IS his name?"

Horvath gives me a look. A lie is on the tip of his tongue, then he thinks better of it.

"Butch," he says.

"Butch what?"

"Have a nice day, Joe," he says as he turns and goes down the stairs. I watch him leave and then I hurry to Stage 2. I want to grab Stu before the next shot.

I find him off in a corner going over the script. He looks up when he sees me but there's no smile. The man is obviously troubled by something.

"Joe," he says. "My God, man, I am so sorry," he says.

"For what?" I say.

"I drag you across the country and then when you get here I can't find any time for you."

"Not a problem," I say.

"I'm getting it from all sides. We're over budget, we're falling behind and worst of all this picture has to be in the can by March 7. That's the day the writers and actors go out on strike if they don't reach an agreement. March 7. That's sixteen days from now. How the hell am I supposed to finish this picture in sixteen days?"

"Tell the actors to talk fast," I say.

He laughs.

"If only it were that simple. Look, Joe, we won't wrap until midnight so I can't start shooting tomorrow until noon. Come by at nine and we'll squeeze in a couple of hours."

"You're sure? You look pretty beat, Stu."

"Beat but not dead. I'm having more fun with the screenplay than I am with this movie. Humor me."

"Up to you," I say. "See you at nine sharp."

Stu's right about one thing. This screenplay's getting to be fun and if he can make the time and effort, so can I. It'll also be an hour or two when I can completely forget about Sal Rizzo and his simian enforcer, Frankie Fortuna. Stu glances over my shoulder. I look and see Gayne Rescher signal that they're ready for the next shot. Stu and I shake hands and I duck out before the set locks down.

The blue Chevy is still parked across the street. Butch, Horvath's freckle-faced cohort, is no longer making a pretense of reading the morning paper. I jog across the street and open the passenger side door and slip in beside him. He looks at me in surprise. I smile and extend my hand.

"Hi, Butch, I'm Joe," I tell him. "Hotel Astor and don't run any red lights."

CHAPTER ELEVEN

On the way downtown I learn a lot about Butch O'Brien, a veteran of 26 years on the force. At first he regards me with undisguised suspicion but eventually I wear him down with the old Bernardi charm. He's 59 years old, seven years widowed, and came here from Ireland when he was twelve. He's five times a grandfather, walked a beat on Broadway right after the first War ended, raided his share of speakeasies (the ones that didn't grease the local precinct), got promoted to detective in the Thirties, chased after the wiseguys in Little Italy until the second War broke out and then shot up through the ranks as younger, unmarried guys got drafted.

"So what do I call you?" I ask. "Lieutenant?"

"You can call me Butch," he says. "If you wanna get technical, call me Inspector."

I give him a look of disbelief.

"An Inspector, following me around like a rookie right out of the academy?"

"That's right, boyo. This is how it is. A year ago my arches fall so they take me off the street and plant me at a desk. Last month I take my physical and they find a heart murmur so they put me on physical disability. They want to pension me but I tell 'em to fook off. So for weeks I've been sitting around the living room driving my daughter crazy and making life miserable for Kay Horvath when all of sudden, he calls and says do I want a job. Not much pay. Off the books. Whatever he can steal from petty cash. I tell him I don't care about the money, I just want to get back in the game so he says for me to get in my car immediately and come to the precinct which is how I ended up with you."

"Okay," I say, "your feet are flat and your heart's a mess, how's your eyesight and your trigger finger?"

"I can put a hole in a silver dollar at twenty paces, is that what you're asking?"

"Something like that," I say.

"Well, don't you worry about me, boyo. I've been handling those Eye-Ties for many years."

"Who's worried?" I say with a smile. If Butch is buying my bullshit, he gives no sign.

"Now this Sally Rizzo," he says,"he's a miserable piece of work, no better than his dead brother-in-law, God rest his soul, but he's got Gambino's ear so until he fooks up, which he's gonna do, he's dangerous. Stupid people usually are."

"Well, Butch, you've made me feel much much better," I tell him.

He smiles, missing the irony.

"That's what I'm here for," he says.

He drops me off at the hotel and I tell him I'm going to be holed up in my room for the rest of the afternoon. He can pick me up a few minutes to six and drive me to the Nine. He nods and drives off.

Once in my room, I start making phone calls. The first is to a casting agency headed up by a very sharp gal named Wanda Frick who I knew during my Warner Brothers days of semi-celibacy.

"Wanda here," she says.

"Hi, gorgeous, it's Joe Bernardi."

"Ohmigod, what are you doing in town?"

"Business but you were number two on my list."

A momentary pause.

"Joe, I'm married."

"Congratulations. So am I."

"Okay, now that we have that out of the way, let's talk."

We waste a few minutes hashing over old times and then I ask her to get me everything she has on an actor named Johnny Sverny, stage name Jonathan Harker and I need it this afternoon. She says she'll get on it right away. Then I make a dinner reservation and when that's locked in, I call Bunny at her office. I'm not going to tell her what's really going on here in New York just as she is not going to tell me in the unlikely event that the house has burned down. We are both worriers and both convinced that the telephone is an instrument of the devil designed to deliver bad news just when you least expect it.

At ten of six, I'm standing by the hotel entrance when Butch swoops up in the Chevy. I hop in and we head downtown to the Ninth Precinct. To make small talk I mention the movie. He perks up right away. Murder Incorporated? He knows all about those bums, he says. Even put a couple of them away. He asks when the movie's coming out. I tell him at least six months. He says he can't wait.

We pull into the parking lot and even before we come to a stop, Peter is hurrying to the car. He opens the rear door and slides in.

"I hope we're not going anywhere fancy," he says, "I never got a chance to change out of my wardrobe,"

I look him over. Old overcoat, funny hat, rumpled suit.

"As long as you don't pull a gun, you'll fit right in. Butch, this is Peter Falk, Peter, Butch O'Brien."

"How ya doin'?" Peter says,

"Fine," Butch says as he pulls into traffic. He's studying Peter intensely in his rear view mirror.

"How'd it go with Horvath?" I ask Peter.

"Very good," he says. "He busted my chops, I busted his. It was an unproductive meeting."

"He's only doing his job," I say.

"That's what Dillinger used to say when he was robbing banks." He looks into the mirror and sees Butch's eyes still staring at him. "Excuse me, sir, have you got some sort of problem?"

"I do not, sir."

"Maybe I have a piece of spinach in my teeth, something like that?"

"Absolutely not. It's just that—-" He stops.

"Just what, Butch?" I ask

"Your friend reminds me of someone. Can't put my finger on it."

I look back at Peter with a smile. He smiles back and then leans forward, his chin nearly resting on Butch's shoulder.

"Would it help if I was holding an ice pick next to your ear?" he asks ominously.

Butch almost rear ends the car in front of him.

"Jesus, Mary and Joseph," he mutters. "That's it. Except for the smile,you could be the Kid's brother."

"You mean, Abe Reles?"

"Abe Reles. Kid Twist. That's right."

"What about the smile?" Peter asks, "What's wrong with it?"

"Everything. Reles never smiled."

"Never?"

"Never," Butch says.

Peter nods in satisfaction.

"That's terrific," he says, talking to himself. "Never smiles. I can use that. Squint but don't smile." He practices it a couple of times. "Yeah, that's good.That's very good." He claps Butch in the shoulder. "Thanks a lot, pal."

"Don't mention it," Butch says throwing me a look. He has just discovered something that I have known for years, that actors live in a world of their own.

Peter is hungry and so am I. Delmonico's has provided us with a quiet table in the corner where we can talk. I'd invited Butch to join us but when he heard we were going to talk business, he opted for a beer and a sandwich at the bar where he can keep an eye on me. As soon as we've ordered I decide to get right to the point before another unanticipated tragedy befalls us,

"So, Peter, have you given any thought to your future?" I ask.

"Yeah," he says. "Get myself another job as fast as I can after this one wraps."

I smile.

"That's not what I mean."

"I know that. Look, I've got a good agent. Bill Hart takes good care of me and right now that's all I need. I'm a nobody, Joe, and I know enough about you and your partner to know you don't handle nobodies."

"Don't sell yourself short," I say.

"Listen," he says. "If this picture bombs, I'm back doing guest shots on TV shows and the third guy through the door in features. I know it, you know it. So thank you very much. I'm very flattered but no thank you."

"How about if you keep an open mind. Things could change. Next year, the year after, you can call me any time, day or night, and we'll talk."

"Yeah, I could do that," he says. "But meantime, I want to talk about you. What was that the cop was saying back at the studio? You're getting threats from the mob? What the hell's that all about?"

I tell him about my run-in with Sal Rizzo and my 72 hour expiration date. All the while. Peter's shaking his head.

"You know, I don't want to scare you or anything, Joe, but this guy Rizzo, he's a very serious fella."

"Then you know him,"

"Never met him but back in the old days, Finucci talked about him all the time. This is maybe five years ago. Me and Funucci and every other actor in New York are going out for interviews and cattle calls and while you're sitting around, you talk a lot, and Finucci liked to talk about how he was connected because of his wife being Sal Rizzo's sister. Nobody really gave a crap but Finucci kept talking. In addition to being a lousy actor, he also didn't know when to keep his mouth shut. Sal whacked this guy in a florist shop. Sal dynamited another guy's restaurant. Sal took one of Anastasia's guys on a one way trip to the marshes at Sheepshead Bay and left him there for the crabs. It's a wonder Rizzo didn't have Finucci fitted for cement overshoes. Anyway, after a while we lose track of Finucci and then last year he pops up and he's dealing, mostly theater people and mostly in Little Italy and the East Village."

I frown. "But I don't understand something. I thought these guys didn't bother civilians," I say.

"You're not a civilian, Joe. The guy thinks you whacked his brother-in-law, and I'll tell you something else. Florence, his sister, she's a real piece of work. She'll keep busting his balls until he does something which I would say is probably not very good news for you."

"Maybe it's time to pack up and fly back to L.A." I say.

"Terrific thinking, Joe, like Rizzo doesn't know how to find his way to the airport."

"He's not going to chase me all the way to the West Coast," I say.

"He's not? Listen, Joe, back in Ossining I was kind of a street kid and I hung around with a lot of wiseguys, some of them real smart, a lot of them with a screw loose. Believe me, if they want you, they'll get you. It's a matter of honor."

At this point our waiter comes to the table with our appetizers, a plate of fried mozzarella for me. It looks good. It smells good.

And I've totally lost my appetite.

For the next hour I nibble at my food and we chat. Peter does most of the chatting and he does a pretty good job of getting my mind off off Sal Rizzo and his pet bone-breaker. He did a tour with the merchant marine, got fired by the State of Connecticut, traveled in Yugoslavia, got arrested by the Communists in Trieste and as a final resort, decided to become an actor. He's spent several years doing guest shots on television without creating much of a splash and appeared off-Broadway in 'The Iceman Cometh" with Jason Robards. He loves to dabble in art and denies vehemently that he is a chess hustler. He's an unprepossessing guy with the soul of a Renaissance man and I'm fascinated. Despite his reluctance to let us manage his career, I'm going to keep after him.

By nine-thirty I'm back in my hotel room and the Falk distraction has worn off. Once more my brain is flooded with images of Sal Rizzo and I realize that Peter was right. I can't run from this guy. Whatever happens, the situation has to be resolved here and now and I'm pretty sure Horvath won't be able to do it, not in the 48 hours I have left. For the time being Butch O'Brien has my back but in two days, we will both be at risk. I decide to stop whining and start digging and there's no better place to start than the meeting I've set up for ten o'clock in the Astor bar. I can only hope Velma was able to deliver the message.

I needn't have worried. I see him sitting at a table over near the far wall. The place isn't yet crowded. That'll happen when the theaters starting letting out. One side of the oval bar has a lot of activity, well-dressed men enjoying the company of other well dressed men. For years the Astor bar has been a meeting place where the boys of a certain sexual persuasion can congregate without harassment provided they behave with decorum. They dominate their half of the bar and nearby tables, the other half being home to flaming heterosexuals.

As I approach his table, Johnny Sverny aka Jonathan Harker rises with a smile and extends his hand. We shake.

"I'm delighted to meet you, Mr. Bernardi. When I saw you earlier back at the theater I had no idea who you were."

"Well, I'm pleased you could accept my invitation," I say as we sit down.

Johnny Sverny, having discovered my true identity and all that I represent, is nothing like the angry loudmouth I observed on the stage railing at the director, Luther Bascomb. He's impeccably dressed in a tailored suit wearing a muted conservative tie and his hair fastidiously combed. His voice is low key and pleasant. He epitomizes the Manhattan gentleman after dark.

"When I read on your card that you were suggesting the Astor bar, I was afraid for a moment—" He hesitates and casts his glance at the bar.

"I'm happily married," I say. "No reason to fear."

"Of course not," he says. "Some of my best friends move in those circles. Just not me. Shall we order drinks?" he asks, signaling to a waiter.

I order a beer. He opts for a Rob Roy.

"So what do I call you? Johnny? Jonathan? I love your stage name, by the way."

"Either name will do and I chose Harker because literate people don't forget it."

"I would bet not," I say.

"So, Mr. Bernardi—"

"Please call me Joe."

"So Joe, how did you like the play?" he asks.

"Haven't seen it," I tell him.

His face falls, replaced by a look of puzzlement.

"Oh? I'm confused. Your note seemed to indicate—"

"I wanted to sit down with you, Jonathan, because people whose opinion I respect tell me that you are an undiscovered treasure."

"Oh?" He brightens perceptibly.

"For instance your performance as the defrocked priest in "Eating the Eucharist". I'm told you were brilliant and that one of the local underground papers compared you to Richard Burton."

"Better than Burton, actually," he says as our drinks arrive.

"And after that, the one-acter where you played Leon Trotsky on the day of his assassination."

"Brilliant make-up," he says. "I designed it myself."

I shake my head sympathetically.

"I can't understand why you haven't broken out sooner," I tell him.

"Politics," he shrugs, sipping his drink. "I won't play their games."

I nod.

"Look, Jonathan, I'm going to lay my cards on the table. One of the major producers at one of the major studios, I can't say which one, is prepping a major motion picture about the assassination of Abraham Lincoln and I think you would make a perfect John Wilkes Booth."

His face lights up like the star atop a Christmas tree.

"I can do Booth," he says. "Dammit, I was born to play Booth."

"Even if it means shooting Greg Peck?" I smile.

"Gregory Peck playing Lincoln?"

The guy is orgasmic and I almost feel sorry for him until I remember the arrogant prick I saw on the stage of the Mudhole. Anyway with less than 48 hours to go, I haven't got time for pity.

"Well, Jonathan, I want to recommend you but what about your contract with this play."

"Contract? Whoever heard of a contract with off-Broadway theater? I'm lucky I get paid."

"Okay, and then there's the drug thing."

"What drug thing?"

"These people are very straight, very moral. They won't tolerate any kind of drug use and I'm pretty sure you were one of Gino Funucci's customers."

He laughs.

"Come on, Joe. A little weed? I can quit that stuff tomorrow."

"I heard you were into harder stuff."

"That's a damned lie!" he flares.

"You were seen last week buying six bags of heroin from Finucci."

"Not true."

"We're going nowhere if you lie to me, Jonathan. I have a reputation to look out for."

"I smoke pot. That's it. My hand to God." He's almost whining now. Desperate.

I throw up my hands helplessly.

"Well, I'm sorry, I was hoping it would work out." I start to get up from the table.

"Wait!" he says.

Slowly I sit back down.

"I bought it for somebody else," he says.

"Who?"

He looks down into his lap, shaking his head.

"Jeez, man, this is embarrassing," he says.

"Who, Jonathan?"

He looks up at me.

"Between us," he says. "Nobody else."

"Whatever you say."

"Clarissa Grandee."

"The theater owner?"

"Why?"

"As a favor."

"Why?"

He looks up at me in anguish, like a rattlesnake writhing

helplessly, his head pinned down with a forked stick.

"You don't give a guy much room, do you, Joe?" I say nothing, waiting for him to continue. I'm not going to help him. "We're friends. Close friends. Have been for over a year. When I say close, I mean you can't get any closer. Do you get my drift?"

Of course I do and the image of this young stud in the sack with a woman old enough to be his mother revolts me.

"I get it, Jonathan. What I don't get is why you have to buy drugs for her, if in fact that's the truth."

"Oh, it's the truth all right. You know what her name was before she married Oscar Grandee? Clarissa Profaci. That's right. Her father was Vittorio Profaci, a cousin of Joe Profaci, and do you know what would happen to any dealer caught selling drugs to Clarissa? Shall I draw you a picture?"

"Not necessary," I say. "And your attentiveness to Clarissa? Good for your career?"

"It's no crime," Harker says. "She's connected and she's helped me a lot."

I nod.

"And the night Gino Finucci was killed? Where were you?"

His face suddenly darkens and he looks at me with suspicion.

"What's that got to do with anything?"

"Let's just say I'm curious."

"You sound like that cop," he says.

"You're not answering my question."

"It's none of your goddamned business."

"Then we have nothing more to talk about."

I stand and dig into my wallet to pay the tab.

"I was boffing the old lady, all right?" he says angrily.

"Between midnight and two?"

"All night," he says.

"Congratulations to you both," I say with a smile.

"Check with the doorman, he'll tell you."

"I'm sure he will," I say. "So Finucci was trying to blackmail you."

"I never said that," Harker replies.

"You didn't have to. The man was crazed out of his mind, desperate for money. With the your relationship to Clarissa, you made a perfect patsy. One word to Joe Profaci and you were a dead man."

Harker licks his lips nervously.

"I didn't kill him," he says quietly.

"Maybe you did, maybe you didn't but I know one thing for sure, you sure as hell wanted to." I drop a twenty onto the table. "I'll be in touch."

I turn and head for the entrance to the lobby. I can feel his eyes boring in on my back. I make a mental note to double lock my door as soon as I'm safely in my room.

CHAPTER TWELVE

Butch picks me up at 8:30 for the trip to Harlem. I have thought long and hard about sharing what I know with him because Clarissa Grandee's past may be something he knows about. My hesitation involves how much I can trust him because he may be under orders to report back to Horvath and if Horvath finds out I'm poking into Finucci's death on my own, he'll be all over me like DDT on a cabbage patch. If Horvath weren't being stretched every which way, particularly by the Hyman Weiss murder, I'd tell him myself but since I'm pretty sure he really can't help me, I'm just going to have to help myself.

We park at curbside. Butch opts to stay in the car with his *Daily News* so he can read about the whomping the Rangers put on the Bruins last night. I jog up the stairs. It's one minute to nine. I'm right on time.

As soon as I walk through the door I sense there's something wrong. There's an eerie silence about the place. Maybe it's because the call is for noon but even then there would be people around, the sounds of typing, phones ringing. I try the production office door. It's locked. I head down the corridor to Stu's office. That, too, is locked. So is Harv Jessup's. This is more than odd, it's troubling. For want of a better idea I head for Stage One.

I walk through the door and there they are, huddled in conversation in the middle of the apartment set. Peter, Stuart Whitman, May Britt, Gayne Rescher, Harv Jessup and a man I've never seen before. No sign of Stu Rosenberg. Peter catches sight of me out of the corner of his eye and breaks free of the others.

"What's going on?" I ask him.

"Trouble," he says.

"Where's Stu Rosenberg?"

"Out."

"What do you mean, out?"

"Out. Replaced. Fired," Peter says.

"Why? What for?"

Peter looks at me blankly.

"You think they're gonna tell me? I think we're lucky they didn't shut down the picture."

"This is crazy," I say. "Who's directing?"

"The producer."

"Oh, come on," I say in disbelief.

Peter points to the unfamiiar face.

"That's him. Bob Balaban."

"And Rosenberg is where?"

"Nobody knows. Maybe on his way to the coast. Maybe holed up at his apartment."

"I don't suppose you've got a phone number."

Peter shakes his head.

"Maybe Madge in the production office."

"Not here. Door's locked."

"Wish I could help you," Peter says. Then, "Uh, oh, They're waving me over. If I hear anything I'll call you at your hotel."

And then he's hurrying away to join the others. This trip to the East Coast is now showing signs of being an unmitigated disaster. The man who has optioned my book and is helping me write the screenplay has disappeared. A talented and up and coming young actor wants nothing to to with Bowles & Bernardi. And best of all, a Mafia capo is planning to rub me out in less than two days. I wonder if the benevolent God of all creatures has somehow overlooked me.

I find Butch, newspaper in hand, leaning against the hood of the car. Probably tired of sitting. He looks up as I come down the stairs.

"That was quick," he says.

I don't bother telling him my Rosenberg problem. I do tell him I need a phone booth and he tells me there's a diner a couple of blocks away. We drive over and while I'm feeding the pay phone nickels and dimes, Butch is buying a couple of containers of coffee at the register. My first, and I hope only, call is to Wanda Frick, the casting gal who supplied me with the goods on Jonathan Harker. Since Clarissa has a tangental connection to the theater, I figure Wanda may know how I can track her down. It turns out Wanda is a well-informed jewel. Clarissa lives in a posh apartment in a posh building on Sutton Place but short of storming the place with a tommy gun, I won't get to see her. Not there, anyway. The doormen are all ex-British commandos with strict orders to protect the lady's privacy. Happily, however, she is not unavailable. According to today's Trib she's the guest of honor at a charity exhibition of local painters at the Museum of Modern Art. Luncheon at twelve-thirty sharp, by invitation only. I blow Wanda a phone kiss and hang up. I grab Butch and we head for 53rd Street. I have told him where we are going but not why nor have I mentioned Clarissa's name. As I said, because of Horvath, Butch is on a need-to-know basis. At the moment, he has no need to know.

Butch drops me off at the museum entrance and drives to a commercial parking lot at the end of the block. It's early yet but these luncheons are invariably preceded by a cocktail hour where guests and the principals get themselves well lubricated for the ordeal ahead. I follow the sounds of muted laughter ands clinking glasses, passing by colorful paintings which I do not understand nor do I care to. My taste in art involves Rembrandt, Vermeer, and dogs playing poker on black velvet.

I walk into the meeting room, crowded with patrons of the arts and assorted Bohemian types which I take to be the local artists on display for today's honoring. There are two open bars at each side of the room and the booze is flowing like flood stage at Niagara Falls. Through the grey haze of cigarette smoke, I spot Clarissa chatting with a white haired gentleman and a dowdy female in danger of being strangled by the seven strand pearl necklace hanging around her neck. I make a beeline in her direction.

Without apology I burst into the middle of their conversation.

"Clarissa Grandee! I can hardly believe it. What a pleasure this is," I say bubbling over with faux adulation. I look at the gentleman and his lady. "I do hope you don't mind my barging in like this but ever since Larry Olivier told me of this marvelous woman's unselfish dedication to the arts, I have been dying to meet her." Clarissa, momentarily annoyed by my rudeness, now offers me a smile and the other two, bowled over by my aggressiveness, mumble something incoherent. "I do hope you won't mind if I borrow this grand lady for a few minutes.Thanks ever so much." And before they can reply I am steering Clarissa over to the side of the room where we can talk in private. She is dressed in rose-colored silk with long sleeves that end at her wrists. I wonder if that's a fashion statement or something else. A peek at her arms under all that silk would answer a lot of questions.

"Laurence Olivier? " she says. "I'm not sure I actually met him."

"Perhaps not, dear lady. But he knows all about you and the the fine work you do, contributing to many worthy charities, financing the best that Broadway has to offer and in particular, your unselfish devotion to the marvelous work being done by the little theaters off-Broadway."

"Yes, well, thank you, Mr.... I'm sorry, I don't believe I caught your name."

I tell her as well as filling her in on our management company and the dozens of well known actors and directors that we represent. I drop enough names to fill a small town phone book and her eyes widen in envy. There is an impolite name for people like Clarissa whose adoration of movie celebrities borders on obsession.

"My goodness," I say, "that marvelous play at the Mudhole, 'Eulogy for a Ghetto Queen', where did you find such a deep and provacative work? Few people would have had the courage stage it."

"Thank you, Mr. Bernardi. I am quite proud of that production."

"And the cast. Miss Breen and of course, Jonathan Harker, what a surprise he was. A real find. Have you known him long?"

"Well, no, not really. A year perhaps. Of course I knew of his work before we cast the play and I strongly recommended him to Luther Bascomb, our director. I do have an eye for talent."

"Indeed, and I understand that you and the young man have become very close friends."

Her eyes narrow. Her expression becomes flinty.

"Nothing of the sort. We are professional collaborators. nothing more."

"Oh, I'm sorry," I say, "I was led to believe you were more like a patroness, much as the Medicis were in Renaissance Italy."

"That would be lovely if true, Mr. Bernardi. It's not," she says flatly.

"Forgive me, I was misinformed. I was told that on the night that poor unfortunate man was killed in the basement of your theater, you and Mr. Harker were together at your apartment enjoying each other's company."

Her expression has morphed into cold rage and she is now looking past my shoulder into the room, trying to find help.

"I meant only that you were discussing new stage properties to further his career."

"Whoever told you that was a liar, Mr. Bernardi."

"I heard it from Mr. Harker," I say.

"Clarissa, is there a problem here?"

A man's voice behind me. I turn and find myself face to face with Benito Tartaglia, the lady's suave lawyer. I dredge up a smile and stick out my hand.

"Joe Bernardi," I say.

He ignores me.

"Clarissa?"

"Mr. Bernardi is here without invitation, Benito, and he is just leaving," she says.

Tartaglia smiles coldly.

"May I escort you to the door?" he asks.

"I can find my way," I tell him.

"I'll escort you anyway," he says, putting his arm around my shoulder and taking the opportunity to squeeze my neck very hard. I shrug him off and continue toward the doorway. I've found out what I needed to know, that Harker was telling me the truth, not despite the lady's flimsy denials but because of them.

As I near the doorway I realize that Butch is standing there, arms folded across his chest with a hard threatening look on his face. I think for a moment it's meant for me but no, he's looking over my shoulder. I look back. Benito Tartaglia had been following me. Now he has stopped dead in his tracks, turns and walks back inside to join the crowd.

I continue on and as I pass Butch, I hear him mutter, "Nice crowd you hang out with." I head for the exit. He follows me, close behind. Outside I hurry down the steps with Butch now beside me.

"What are you doing hanging around with the likes of Benito Tartaglia and Rissa Profaci?" he asks.

"Socializing," I say.

I walk briskly heading for the garage. Butch stays right by my side.

"I need a better answer than that," Butch says.

"Why?" I ask. "So you can report back to Horvath."

I stop walking and look him in the eye.

"My job's to keep you alive, Joe," he says. "You don't make it any easier getting mixed up with those two."

"But you do report back to Horvath," I say.

"I'm supposed to," he admits.

"You know the deal, Butch. In less than two days, Sal Rizzo is going to have me hit. Horvath can't help me. He's got nothing to go on, no time he can spare and constraints that I don't have because I'm not a cop. Call me selfish but I'd like to live past next Monday. For one thing, I still have two car payments left on my Bentley."

He laughs as I knew he would.

"Not much chance of that if you insist on sticking it to those two birds back at the museum."

"Thanks for the warning. Tell Horvath I paid no attention."

"I'm not going to tell Horvath anything," he says. "You're right. Horvath can't help you. Maybe I can and I've got nothing better to do. Let's find some place to have lunch."

CHAPTER THIRTEEN

Butch bites down on a jumbo-sized cheeseburger, then uses his paper napkin to wipe his mouth of excess ketchup. We're sitting at a cramped table for two in a diner that the health department has apparently been overlooking for the past decade. Maybe it's the ambience or maybe the grease coated walls but the sounds and smells of this wreck of a place are seductive and my patty melt is the best I've had in years. Whether my digestive system will pay for this folly later today remains to be seen.

At this hour, Freddie's Burger Barn is crowded and noisy and even though Butch is leaning toward me he has to raise his voice to be heard.

"You're in enough trouble with Sal Rizzo, boyo. Going after Rissa Profaci borders on suicidal. What's got into you?"

I tell him about my late evening sit-down with Harker in the Astor Bar. He listens intently and when I finish he just shakes his head.

"The man's a fool, diddling a woman nearly twice his age and that one in particular. You know what happens to Harker if her cousin Joe finds out Harker has been feeding her drugs? If he lasted a day I'd be shocked."

"Maybe Profaci got it wrong. Maybe he thought Finucci was

dealing with Clarissa directly."

Butch shrugs.

"Possible. It would explain a lot of things. But I can't see Profaci whacking Finucci without talking to Rizzo first and maybe even asking permission. These guys have a certain code and they like to stick by it. Besides, if Rizzo knows Profaci did it, why is he threatening you?"

"You seem to know a lot about Clarissa," I say.

"All there is." He dips a french fry into a puddle of ketchup in his plate and bites into it with a crunch. The fries here are almost as good as the burgers. "She was a wild kid, always getting in trouble, her old man always having to bail her out. I ran her in for public drunkenness twice. The second time she propositioned me in the back of the squad car. This was before I was married and I was young and horny but I was smart enough to stay away from her. Any guy got involved with Rissa Profaci, especially a cop, was looking for a one-way trip to Sheepshead Bay. Vittorio put an end to it when he married her off to Oscar Grandee."

"Never heard of him," I say.

"He owned a bunch of speakeasies on the east side, two in the Bronx, one in Long Island City. He was very well connected. He was also very old. Pushing sixty. Rissa was 22. She wanted no part of him until her old man explained that Oscar was worth about ten million, had never married and had no family. When he died, she would get it all. She held her nose and married him within the month. For ten years she waited for him to die and I think she finally got tired of waiting. He drowned in his bathtub. The coroner, who was on Joe Profaci's pad, overlooked a large lump on the back of his head and called it accidental. The merry widow went on to lead an interesting and self-indulgent life."

"And the lawyer, Benito Tartaglia?"

"Old Faithful. She keeps coming back to him whenever it ends with the young stud of the month."

"Like Jonathan Harker."

"Only the latest. Won't be the last," Butch says.

"And she never married again?" I say.

Butch smiles.

"Rissa never was much of a one for sharing, her life or her money," he says.

I stick the last bit of patty melt in my mouth and wash it down with the remains of my Dr. Browns' Celery Tonic.

"So let me get this straight. It's possible though unlikely that Finucci was killed by a member of the Profaci family in the mistaken belief that he was dealing drugs directly to Clarissa. Harker might have done it if Finucci had threatened to rat him out to Profaci. Portia Justice, aka Velma Micklenberg might have done it as revenge for reinfecting Amythyst Breen, the actress for whom I believe Velma harbors an unnatural love. And it might also have been committed by Finucci's bookie who was hounding him for payment.."

"Scratch that last one, Joe. Horvath told me to tell you, he tracked down Finucci's bookie and Finucci paid him off in full eight days ago."

I shake my head.

"Then what the hell was Finucci so afraid of?"

"Think, Joe. If he paid off the bookie, he had to get the money somewhere. It's possible he robbed a bank but I think it much more likely he did business with Angie 'The Toad' Lopata."

"Let me guess. The neighborhood lending institution?"

"Bookies by nature are not violent people. Angie Lopata would break off your fingers one by one just to hear the bones crunch."

I think about this for a moment.

"I don't suppose there's much sense in bringing all these suppositions to Sal Rizzo's attention," I suggest.

"None at all," Butch says picking up the check the waiter has left on the table. He holds it up and peruses it carefully, then slides it in my direction.

$2.20 for two burgers and two sodas. I take three dollars from my wallet and leave them on the table. I feel like such a sport.

A funny thing is happening to Butch O'Brien. He's beginning to feel like a cop again and as we drive down toward the East Village he suggests we stop by the theater. Although he's read Horvath's police report he says he'd like to take a look at the crime scene for himself. He asks if I mind. Mind? I'm delighted. The more eyeballs on this case, the sooner we may find the key that unlocks the solution.

We pull up to the curb in front of the theater and the first thing I notice is the new sandwich board by the entrance. It features a giant photo of Amythyst Breen and underneath: "Farewell Performance of Broadway's Own Amythyst Breen. Curtain at 8:00. Limited Seating."

Butch appraises the sign as we start in.

"Harker's not going to like that much," he says. Then he stops and goes back and looks at it again appraisingly. "What do you know about this babe, Joe?" he asks.

Not a lot, I tell him. At one time she made a big splash on Broadway, then her life turned to crap. He grunts, his gaze still fixated on the poster. What the grunt means I have no idea.

We enter the lobby to find Velma with broom in hand sweeping up. She smiles when she sees me but is puzzled by Butch. I introduce him as Inspector O'Brien and he flashes his shield.

"What happened to the Sergeant?" she asks.

"He's chasing after the guy who did Councilman Weiss's brother," Butch tells her. "We're going to look around downstairs. We wont be long."

I lead him to the basement door and he starts down. I start to follow him when Velma asks if there's anything new. I tell her no, not yet.

"Tonight's Amythyst's last performance." she says.

"I know. I saw the sign. Does this mean she's not coming back ?"

Velma nods her head sadly. "The new girl's pretty good but she wasn't interested in a three week fill-in. Luther had a choice to make. He made it."

"She'll still be around, Velma," I say.

"Yeah, I guess," she replies sadly and goes back to her broom.

Butch is standing in the middle of the basement, hands on hips, carefully looking around. There is clutter everywhere but it is organized clutter with dozens of bookshelves holding props of every description. Tables are also loaded with knick-knacks, china, cutlery, pots and pans, glassware and small appliances, all relics of previous stagings, now relegated to storage and awaiting their return to upstairs in some future outing. He looks at the nearby pile of cardboard cartons on which Finucci's dead body had been sprawled and then looks over at me.

"Not right, Joe," he says. "Not right at all."

"What's the matter?" I ask

"Coroner says Finucci died here. Body wasn't moved from someplace else. The guy was involved in a bloody brawl but hardly anything's been disturbed. This table here, five feet from where the body was found, no way it couldn't have been slammed into or knocked over. And where's the blood? I'm not talking about gushers, just random blood spots or spatters. There are none."

"So what do you think?"

"Could be a lot of things," Butch says.

He turns as we both hear footsteps coming down the rickety staircase. When he apperars I see the guy's a skinny beanpole, maybe thirty or so. I recognize him immediately from the audition. Winston Baxendale, the playwright.

"Can I help you fellas?" he asks.

"I don't know. Maybe you can, Mr. Baxendale," I say.

"And you are—?

He lets it hang.

"Joe Bernardi," I say. "A friend of Peter Falk's."

Butch takes out his shield and holds it up for inspection.

"Inspector O'Brien. Ninth Precinct," he says.

"The police were already here on Thursday," he says.

"Well, we're back," Butch says, taking charge. "Baxendale. That would make you the playwright."

"That's right."

"The stiff. Did you know him?" Butch asks callously.

"I knew of him. I'd seen him around."

"Customer?" Butch asks disdainfully.

"Certainly not," Baxendale says indignantly.

I've been around enough cops to know what Butch is up to. Act crass. Annoy the suspect. Throw him off balance. People off balance sometimes say things they shouldn't.

Baxendale's wearing a loose fitting argyle sweater. Butch suddenly grabs him by the wrist and shoves to sweater up his arm past the elbow.

"Hey!" Baxendale cries out.

"Just looking," Butch says examining the playwright's forearm for needle tracks.

And then in a move so quick I almost didn't see it, Baxendale pulls his arm away and with his free arm, spins Butch around and clamps him around the neck.

"If you wanted to look, all you had to do was ask," he says, freeing Butch and shoving him away.

Far from showing anger, Butch smiles.

"Nice move," he says. "You'll have to show me how it's done."

"Don't hold your breath," Baxendale says.

"Before they carted it away, did you get a chance to see Finucci's body?" Butch asks.

"I wasn't here that morning."

"Someone beat the crap out of him. Somebody who knew what he was doing."

"It wasn't me."

"But it could have been," Butch says. "A few months ago you worked a guy over pretty good at the Pink Velvet Cafe."

"I didn't start it."

"I didn't say you did. What happened, the guy call you a nasty name?"

Fury is reflected in Baxendale's eyes.

"Something like that," he says.

"You people have got to learn not to be so sensitive."

"What do you mean, you people?"

"You know exactly what I mean, powder puff," Butch says.

"You've got your head right up your ass, Inspector. I don't diddle with boys or with girls either, for that matter. I'm one of those people who really don't give a damn one way or the other."

"But you hang out at the Pink Velvet."

"I like the company. The men there are able to discuss Nietzsche and Renaissance art and the Industrial Revolution and do so in complete sentences. They have also never heard of Rocky Marciano, Francis, the talking mule, or the New York Yankees."

"And where were you early Thursday morning between midnight and two o'clock?"

"Working on a play my collaborator and I are planning to bring to this theater in the near future. It's from a novella called 'The Unendurable Angst of Sexual Antipathy" by Gerhardt Crumb."

"Never heard of him," Butch says.

"Her," Baxendale responds.

Butch throws me a disbelieving look.

"And your collaborator? The director Luther Bascomb?" I suggest..

"That's right. At two o'clock we go to my apartment in the Village. He sacks out on the sofa bed in the living room and starts to snore. I sit up in bed for about an hour reading 'That Status Seekers' by Vance Packard."

"Never heard of that either," Butch says.

"Of course not," Baxendale says snidely. "It's still in hard cover."

"Besides this Bascomb fella, anybody else vouch for your whereabouts ?"

"My dog Redneck but he fell asleep about quarter to three so theoretically I could have ducked out, offed Finucci, and returned without him knowing I'd left the apartment so, no, I guess I have no real alibi."

Butch fixes him with a humorless stare, then glances in my direction and head nods me toward the staircase.

"If we need you, we'll be in touch," Butch says as he and I head for the stairs and much needed fresh air.

As Butch and I walk out the door, he looks back and mutters, "Wise ass."

"He's a writer, Butch. He can't help it." I reply.

Again, Butch hesitates and looks at the giant photo of Amythyst Breen.

"This photograph makes her look like a kid," he says.

"Believe me, she's not," I say. "My guess is she's pushing forty."

He nods and then we continue on to the car.

Now Butch is sitting in the driver's seat, drumming his fingers on the steering wheel, deep in thought.

"Tell me about her, boyo. The girl in the picture. Everything you know."

"Amythyst? There's not much to tell," I say. I repeat what Velma had told me, about Amythyst's wild days when success had sent her reeling into a world of drugs and booze.

"Why the interest in her?" I ask.

"No reason. Just collecting my thoughts." He turns in my direction. "You know, we're making a big assumption here, boyo. The bookie gets paid off and maybe Funucci got the money from Angie Lopata and maybe he didn't."

"How do we find out?" I ask.

"We ask him," he says as he turns the key in the ignition. A few minutes later he stops at a liquor store to check out a phone book. When he returns to the car he is smiling. He winks at me.

"Bensonhurst," he says.

I am less than thrilled. Even an uninformed California boy like me knows that Bensonhurst is the Mafia capital of the city. I am not sure this is a good idea. I look over at Butch. There's a gleam in his eye. He can't wait. As we cross the bridge into Brooklyn, he fills me in.

Angie "The Toad" Lopata lives in a two story frame house on Stillwell Avenue. It has been the family manse for the past thirty six years. Angie was born there and as the youngest of five children, the only one still living with his widowed mother. At 32 he is unmarried and likely to stay that way, according to Butch. Even the least choosy of the babes who hang around the wiseguys want nothing to do with him. When he opens the door I can see why. He stands about five foot four, stocky and swarthy, with beady cold eyes that stare out from beneath a single eyebrow that spans his forehead. His hair is slicked back, he's wearing a gaudy mustard colored suit and he smells of lavender. It doesn't help.

He greets us amiably.

"What the fuck do you want, O'Brien?" he grunts.

"I came to borrow five large," O'Brien says.

"Don't you know that's illegal? Try a bank."

He tries to shut the door on us. Butch wedges his foot inside the doorway.

"Get lost. cop. I'm getting ready for a date."

"With what?" Butch asks.

A woman's voice comes from within.

"Angelo. who's at the door?"

"Nobody, Ma," he shouts back.

"Invite them in," she shouts. "I'll make tea."

"They don't want tea, Ma."

"I'm making it for your father. I'll make extra."

"Go to your room, Ma."

He steps outside, shutting the front door behind him.

"My old man's been dead nine years, she's stiil making him tea," he says. He seems to notice me for the first time. "Who the fuck is this?"

"Joe Bernardi," I say.

"I wasn't talking to you," he says, turning his attention back to Butch. "So I'll ask you again, cop. What do you want?"

"Gino Finucci."

"He's dead."

"He owed you money."

Lopata shakes his head.

"Like I said that would be illegal."

"I'm not here to bust you for loan sharking, Angie. I want to know who killed him."

Lopata shrugs.

"I hear it was some asshole movie guy from California," he says.

"That would be me," I chime in.

He looks at me and shakes his head sadly.

"Too bad."

"I didn't do it," I say.

"Like I said, too bad."

"Listen, Angie," Butch says. "If you had lent him money,

hypothetically how much would it have been?"

"Hypothetically, six large," he says.

"And you would have made every effort to collect this sum."

"Naturally."

"Including threats to his personal safety."

"It's a matter of procedure."

"And if the threats had no effect?"

Lopata shakes his head in annoyance.

"You seriously think I whacked the guy? Sal Rizzo's brother-in-law? You think I'm really that stupid?"

"But you did threaten him."

"Hell, yes, but I'd have eaten the six grand before I crossed Sal Rizzo. He is a serious man and I would not want to end up seriously dead. So, are we through here?"

"Yeah, we're through. Have a nice time tonight, Angie."

"Yeah, thanks, " Lopata says and then he gives me one last look of pity. "Like I said, too bad," he says and goes back inside.

Butch watches the door close and then turns to me.

"I never realized that Angie has a sympathetic side." he says. "Amazing."

CHAPTER FOURTEEN

It's nearly six o'clock when Butch drops me off at the front entrance of the Astor.

"Stay in the hotel tonight." he says. "Don't go wandering around. If you come looking for me, you won't find me."

"What are you up to?" I ask.

"I'm going to ram a stick down a gopher hole and see what pops up," he says.

"I'll join you."

"No, you won't. This is cop business."

"I don't care—"

"Remember what Bogie said to Bergman at the airport? Where I'm going you can't go. What I have to do, you can't be any part of."

"But—-"

"No buts, Joe. I'm going to pay a visit to Patch, a man of infinite intelligence and an infallible memory. With luck you'll be free of this mess by tomorrow morning. Now go inside and get a good night's sleep."

By now the doorman is holding my door open. Reluctantly I get out of the car.

"Call me in the morning," I say.

"Will do," he says as he drives off. I watch him for a moment and then head inside. I'd give a lot to know what he's up to.

Once in my room I find my message light blinking. I check with the operator. Madge has called me from the film studio. I call the number and when she comes on the phone she reads me a message from Stu Rosenberg: "Everything topsy-turvy. I've been replaced as director. Flying out to Hollywood tonight to get answers. Our project on hold for the immediate future. No one sorrier than me. Stu."

I call Bunny and give her the bad news about the screenplay. Big mistake. She immediately asks if I will be flying back tomorrow morning. I bumble and fumble like a studio vice president caught en flagrante with his secretary, squirming free only when I convince her that I am having dinner this evening with an old buddy from my Europe days during the war and tomorrow the two of us are going to do the town. She buys it, of course. She is a trusting soul. Every time I do this to her I feel bad. Then I call Bertha and tell her that I've struck out with Peter Falk. In that case, she says, she's looking forward to seeing me back at my desk Monday morning. Now I have a major problem. Bertha is not nearly as trusting as Bunny. In fact she isn't trusting at all. Luckily I have spotted a copy of the Broadway theater guide the housekeeper left on my desk. I tell her I have tickets for tomorrow evening at the Broadhurst to see a musical called "Fiorello". The actor playing the lead, Tom Bosley, might be a find for us. Bertha says she knows all about him. He's funny but he's also short and dumpy. Short and dumpy don't have big Hollywood careers. I tell her maybe he's not that short and not that dumpy. I'll give her a report Monday. And I hang up. As I do my eye is caught by the room service menu. My stomach heaves. I can't abide the thought of another meal in the room.

I call down to the Hunt Room to see if I'll need a reservation for dinner. I won't, I'm told, and fifteen minutes later I'm seated at a small table near the entrance, enjoying a glass of Heineken beer, having just placed my order for a rack of lamb, done crispy, with

Lyonaisse potatoes, asparagus and a small Caesar salad in the side. Normally, I hate eating alone in a restaurant. It marks you as a loser but the day has been so fraught with frustration, at the moment I just don't give a damn. I'm staring at a pot bellied old geezer across the way who is being attentive to his dinner partner, a very young and very obvious rent-a-chick. He's prattling on. The smile on her face is fixed in stone.

"Mr. Bernardi," a man says.

I turn and look up at Benito Tartaglia smiling down at me.

"Pardon the intrusion," he says. "Are you waiting for someone?"

Since the waiter has already removed the other place setting, I see no future in lying.

"No, I'm not but I prefer eating alone, quietly and without interruption."

"Good. In that case I'll join you, " Tartaglia says as he slips into the chair across from me. "The front desk told me where I could find you."

"How considerate of them," I say, vowing quick and lethal retaliation against management as soon as I finish eating.

"I'm here to apologize for our little contretemps today at the museum. Mrs. Grandee feels she could have been more gracious and hopes that there are no hard feelings."

"None on my part," I say.

"Excellent. I would like to apologize for my own actions as well."

"Apology accepted," I say

He smiles and at this moment the cocktail waitress comes by. He orders a double scotch, neat. If he's planning to get up and leave, it won't be any time soon.

"That said, however, it is my duty, Mr. Bernardi, to protect Mrs. Grandee from public embarrassment or humiliation."

"Definitely not my intent, Mr. Tartaglia," I say.

"Your behavior today at the museum indicates otherwise, sir.

There are those in her circles who would be disapproving of her liaison with a young man half her age. They would also look askance at her use of drugs and your meddling risks these things coming to light. And even more appalling is the notion, however ridiculous, that Mrs. Grandee had something to do with Mr. Finucci's death."

"I never said that."

"You broadly intimated it," Tartaglia says.

"No, sir, actually my real interest is Mr. Harker who claims to have been spending a romantic liaison with Mrs. Grandee at the time of Finucci's death."

"He was," Tartaglia states flatly.

"Was he?" I respond dubiously.

"He was."

"And you know this how?"

"Because I was there," Tartaglia says with a smile. "Next question."

"Were you a participant?" I ask.

"Hardly. Mrs. Grandee's apartment has four bedrooms, I was in the smallest of the four reading a book and sipping brandy. I'm always on hand whenever the lady has arranged a tryst. A security precaution."

"I see." I say. "So in regards to Mrs. Grandee's whereabouts when Gino Finucci was killed, she and Mr.Harker alibi each other, you alibi them, they alibi you, and who exactly alibis the three of you?"

"On site security."

"Oh, yes, one of the ex-British commandos posing as a doorman who has absolutely nothing to gain by lying."

"Mr. Bernardi," Tartaglia interrupts peevishly. "All the angels in Heaven could swear I am being truthful and all the devils in Hell can swear I am lying and it will make no difference. Either you accept the truth or you don't."

"Well, here's the deal, my friend," I tell him. "I've got about 36 hours left before a shark in a thousand dollar suit is going to have me turned into dog food so if I seem abrupt or direct, it's because I haven't a lot of time to couch my concerns in the politest of terms."

"Yes, I've heard the rumors. Mr. Rizzo is not a man to be dealt with lightly."

"I did not kill his brother-in-law," I say.

"I'm sure you didn't," Tartaglia replies.

"And unless I can supply him with a suitable alternative, I would be unwise of me to make any vacation plans beyond tomorrow evening."

Tartaglia nods sagely.

"Yes, Salvatore Rizzo is a man who is never wrong even when he is wrong. You get my meaning."

"I do."

"And I commiserate with your situation."

"I've been getting a lot of that."

Tartaglia smiles at the cocktail waitress who has just brought him his drink.

"But nosing about in Clarissa Grandee's private life and accusing her or me or Jonathan Harker of murder is not going to avail you a thing."

I shrug.

"Silly me, I got it into my head that if somehow Joe Profaci found out a street dealer was supplying his cousin Clarissa with hard drugs, that dealer would almost certainly end up dead."

Tartaglia smiles and then sips his scotch.

"Silly, indeed, Mr. Bernardi. No doubt you feel that you are well informed but Mr. Profaci knows all about Mrs. Grandee's use of narcotics."

I look at him sharply, unsure that I heard him right.

"Would you mind repeating that?"

"Mrs. Grandee is no longer young and vivacious. She lives alone without family, not even a pet to keep her company. She keeps busy with her collection of charities and meaningless liaisons with men half her age. She does not delude herself that these men care one whit about her. For some like Mr. Harker, she supplies entree to valuable circles. Others are content with gifts of expensive baubles or cash. But make no mistake, Mr. Bernardi, even when there is a young man beside her, Clarissa is in bed alone."

"And cousin Joe supplies the magic to dull the pain of her loneliness." I say.

"In a sense."

"And where do you fit in, Mr. Tartaglia?"

"Mr. Profaci retains me to see that Mrs. Grandee's life is as comfortable and stress free as possible."

"So then you hired Finucci."

"Yes, but Gino Finucci dealt directly with Mr. Harker who then supplied Mrs. Grandee. This was done to protect her and me in the unlikely event that the police started nosing around, So you can see, Mr. Bernardi, that the idea that Mr. Profaci would order Gino Finucci killed is absurd. He was quite happy with my choice of Finucci. Now, unfortunately, we have to find someone to replace him."

"I wouldn't think that would pose much of a problem," I say.

"It doesn't," Tartaglia smiles. "So do we understand each other, sir? I see no reason why you should continue to harass either Mrs. Grandee or Mr. Harker or me, for that matter."

"I suppose not."

"Excellent. I shall inform Mr. Profaci of your cooperation and with the exception of your disagreement with Mr. Rizzo, you may now rest easy." He drains the remains of his drink and stands. "So nice to have made your acquaintance." Without offering his hand, he turns and strides away from the table. I feel myself shiver. Not only am I in Sal Rizzo's crosshairs but now I learn that Joe Profaci has been secretly keeping tabs on me as well. I feel like I'm in the middle of a bad Eddie Robinson movie.

My dinner arrives but either I wasn't as hungry as I thought I was or something is eating at me. The more I think about it, the more I realize it has something to do with that photo of Amythyst Breen outside of the theater. Butch stared at it twice with a certain fascination. I'm positive he's gone to the Mudhole to ask a few questions. I'm only half finished when I put down my napkin and signal my waiter for the check. I know what I was told. Stay in. Don't go out. Sorry, Butch. No can do. The Lord helps those who help themselves and Lord, do I need help.

It's quarter past nine when I exit my cab and hurry into the Mudhole. The play is a one-acter lasting an hour and a half and it will be over in a matter of minutes. I hear Amythyst's voice coming from the stage. I climb the short staircase. Velma is standing on the landing watching the performance as I sidle in next to her. She glances at me, nods with a smile and redirects her attention to the performance. Harker, wearing overalls and a hardhat, is standing with a shovel in his hand next to a pile of papier mache bricks. Amythyst is wrapped in an American flag and spouting some blather about Selma, Alabama, Harpers Ferry and the ghost of Harriet Tubman. I thought this kind of thing died when the war broke out but apparently the spirit of Clifford Odets lives on, at least in the East Village.

Seven minutes later the play is mercifully over. Harker and Amythyst take their curtain calls. She gets a standing ovation from the semi-packed house, all 31 of them. Feigning humility, Amythyst makes a maudlin speech about love of theater and a dozen other well worn cliches. Yes, she is going on to Broadway, to relive the scene of her first triumph, but she will never forget her loyal fans here in the depths of the East Village. Blowing kisses, she disappears backstage. Unable to resist, she reappears and blows some more kisses and then at last, disappears behind the set, this time for good.

As the audience files past us headed for the exit, I ask Velma if she has seen Inspector O'Brien this evening. She tells me that she has not.

"What's the best way to get backstage?" I ask her.

"What for?" she asks.

"I need to talk to Amythyst," I tell her.

She shakes her head.

"Not a good idea," she says.

"It won't take long."

"No, not tonight. She's not feeling all that well."

"I'll keep it short, promise."

"I said no," Velma says sharply as she fixes me with a look that would freeze a charging rhino. I may have mentioned that Velma is at least six feet tall and probably weighs about two-fifty and very little of it is flab. I decide not to argue with her. If she wants to play protector, I won't get in her way. Not at the moment.

"Have it your way," I say as I turn and hurry down the stairs to the lobby. Velma doesn't follow me. Outside the crowd is dispersing and I scoot down an adjoining alley to the back of the little building. I tell myself there's got to be a back entrance and sure enough there is. I try the handle. It turns. I let myself in. I spot one of the stagehands and one of the youngsters who handles costumes and props but there's no sign of Butch O'Brien or Harker or Amythyst. I poke around. There are several blankets hanging from clotheslines and I assume these little pockets of privacy double for dressing rooms. I hear banter between the crew and Harker laughing and then, far more quiet, a gentle sobbing and a soothing voice. I peek around the corner of a nearby blanket. Amythyst is sitting on a chair in front of a makeshift vanity. Velma is rubbing her shoulders.

"I feel so cold," Amythyst is saying. "I can't stop shaking."

"It's okay, baby. It won't be long, I promise."

"Oh, God," she whines wrapping herself in her arms. "Oh, God."
As close as I am and without the American flag to cover her arms,
I can clearly see the needle tracks. Amythyst is strung out. She needs
a fix and without it, she's going through hell. I debate whether I
should interrupt. I'm not sure I can get any rational answers out of
her in this condition and even if I could I'm pretty sure Velma won't
let me try. I decide to wait for a more propitious time.

I return to the rear door and am about to exit when it opens
and a man I've never seen before lets himself in. He's medium build,
chubby and bald and peers at the world through thick-lensed horn-
rimmed glasses. He looks around, lost, and then tugs at my coat
sleeve.

"I'm looking for Velma," he says. I point to the blanketed-off
area I just left. Without thanking me he heads toward it. I go out
the door and into the crisp night air. I came here looking for Butch
and it's pretty obvious he's elsewhere. I'd like to ask Amythyst a few
questions but I'll never get the chance as long as Velma is watching
over her. I hear the rear door open and turn. The bald guy with the
coke-bottle eyeglasses emerges and hurries past me to the street. I
decide I could wait a few minutes on the odd chance that Amythyst
will leave the theater alone. It's a long shot but I don't have much
else. A few minutes later the door opens again and Amythyst comes
out followed immediately by Velma. As soon as Velma sees me,
anger floods her face. She whispers something into Amythyst's ear
and points to a older model car parked about fifty feet away. As
Amythyst walks over to the car, Velma approaches me.

"I thought I told you to leave her alone," she says.

"I would if I could, Velma, but I can't. Someone's out to kill me
and Amythyst might be able to help prevent it," I say.

"Not tonight she won't," Velma says. "We have a little going
away party scheduled at a local pizza joint and you are not going
to spoil it." She's in my face now and I'm trying hard not to back

away but it isn't easy. "You're a nice guy, Joe, and I like you but right now my first concern is Annie. So please, leave us alone and if she's up to it you can talk to her tomorrow. Can you do that? Please?"

I look over at Amythyst who is standing by the car watching me. Her eyes are clear, her head's erect and her attention to me is totally focused. Obviously the bald guy with his little bags of fairy dust has done the job.

"I'll call you before lunch," I tell her and then I hurry away in search of a taxi. Most of the theatergoers have left by now and the street in front of the Mudhole is quiet. I suspect this is not a major trolling spot for on-duty cabs so I decide to hoof it up to 2nd Avenue. I've gone less than ten yards when something belatedly clicks in my brain. I thought I heard Velma say that her first concern was Ammy but now I realize she hadn't said Ammy, she'd said Annie.

And who the hell is Annie?

By 10:15 I'm back in my room and I can do the math. It's 7:15 California time and unless Bunny had a brutal day, she should be home by now. I place the call and a few moments later, a grumpy voice answers the phone.

"Who died?" I ask.

"Who's this?" she asks.

"It's your husband and why are you grumping at me?"

"Oh, Joe, I'm sorry. I didn't recognize your voice, It's been such a crappy day, Advertising's down, circulation's down and Laurel is suddenly leaving to have a baby. Silly me, I thought she was just getting fat."

Laurel is Bunny's indispensable good right hand.

"Sorry, babe," I say, "that's got to hurt."

"I'll live. Trouble is, I'm not sure she's coming back."

"Even worse."

"How's your buddy?" she asks me.

"Who?"

"Your buddy."

"What buddy?"

"Your old pal from W-W-Two. Europe, remember?"

"Oh, THAT buddy," I say.

I hear her sigh.

"Listen, Joe, if you're going to lie to me, you are going to have to remember what lie you told me. Now whether you told me that whopper because you wanted to stay in New York to see a show or a ball game I really don't care but seriously, at your advanced age, if your memory is starting to fail you, take notes."

I laugh out loud. I can't help it.

"You see, Joe?" she says. "You see how open-minded and understanding I can be?"

"You're priceless, darling," I say. "I love you to death."

"Great," she says. "And now Priceless would like to know what was so damned important that you had to go and lie to me."

Busted.

Then at that moment there is a gentle knock at my door. Saved. A least momentarily.

"Hang on, honey," I say. "Someone at the door."

I lay down the receiver and go to the door. When I open it I am greeted by Amythyst Breen, fur coat slung over her arm, her five foot frame clad in a clingy red silk sheath with white silk gloves that reach to her armpits and a crown of tea roses in her hair.

"You probably thought I wasn't coming," she purrs as she slinks by me into the room. I stare at her in mild disbelief. I have known for years that aggressive actresses survive on theatricality, seductive foreplay and wanton sex. Apparently we are already one-third of the way there.

"Excuse me, it's my wife on the phone," I say to her as I cross back to the table and pick up the receiver. "Hi, it's me again." Bunny predictably asks the obvious question. I could easily tell her it was room service at the door but in response to her need for more marital honesty, I decide to give her what she wants.

"A very sexy but unexpected young actress just slithered into the room and I have no idea why she is here. It could be business or she may be unable to resist my blatant Mediterranean charm." I listen carefully. "Sure, why not?" I say and hold the phone out to Amythyst. "For you," I say.

Looking a bit befuddled Amythyst takes the phone from me. 'Bunny', I whisper to her.

"Hello, Bunny?" Amythyst says tentatively. "Amythyst. It's actually a stage name. My real name is Anne... Oh, no, this is strictly business. On Tuesday I start appearing on Broadway in 'The Sound of Music' and I wanted to make sure your husband got to see me in it... Well, yes, it is a little late. I wanted to stop by earlier but the cast of my current show threw me a goodbye party and I really couldn't leave, you understand... You don't? Well, I assure you... Five minutes. Yes, five minutes will be no problem... Uh, yes, and I promise I won't remove anything,not even my overcoat." As she says this she tosses her fur onto my bed. "Certainly. I'll put him back on." She hands me the receiver with a smile. I take it from her.

"Hello, Bunny. I'm back... Hello? Bunny?' I put the receiver back on the cradle and look over at Amythyst. "She hung up."

"Good," she says. "Now we can talk. How about fixing me a drink?"

"Sure," I say. "What do you want? Prune juice? Hemlock? The minibar has just about everything."

"Surprise me," she says, removing her crown of tea roses and shaking out her luxurious auburn air. She tosses the roses on top of the mink.

I pull a small can of V-8 out of the fridge along with a minature of vodka. One Bloody Mary coming up.

"I had no idea who you were, Mr. Bernardi, until Johnny told me about your excellent meeting last night in the bar. Poor Johnny, I feel sorry for him. I can't imagine your coming to see our presentation on his account. His role really is subordinate to mine."

"Uh-huh," I say.

"I already have several Hollywood film roles as part of my ouevre," she says. "A nurse in 'They Were Expendable'. The female lead in 'The Falcon's Alibi' with Tom Conway. I even got to sing with Charles Starrett in 'Bandits of El Dorado' but I'm sure you know all that." She slides effortlessly onto my sofa, tucking her legs and giving me a peek at a healthy expanse of skin.

"Actually, I don't," I say. "I know you made some sort of splash in a wartime musical but not much more." I hand her the drink. She takes it with a smile.

"Nothing for you? I hate drinking alone," she says.

I smile.

"I'm afraid if I have even one drink I won't be able to control myself in the face of such stunning beauty."

"Well, you are a dear, Joe. You don't mind if I call you Joe?"

"Not if I can call you Anne," I say.

"Anne," she says with a giggle, tossing back half her drink. "Little Annie Gamble. Seems so long ago."

"Tell me about it," I say.

"Not on your life, buster. Those days are long gone."

"The Switzerland days?"

She frowns at me.

"Who told you that?" she snarls

"I don't know. Velma, I think."

"Big fat pig," Amythyst says sourly.

Uh-oh, love unrequited, I say to myself. Maybe I'm suddenly not as safe as I thought I was.

"So tell me, Annie, when did your habit start? In Switzerland or after you arrived back here in the States?"

"Habit? What are you talking about?"

"'I'm talking about you and Gino Finucci. I'm talking about him being your connection. I'm talking about you being more strung out tonight than a kite string until your new guy showed up and fixed you."

She sits up straight and lights a cigarette.

"I don't know what you're talking about," she says.

"Did Finucci try to borrow money, or was he more interested in blackmail? Which was it, Annie?"

Her eyes flare angrily.

"Stop calling me Annie! There is no more Annie! Annie's dead! I didn't come here for this."

"What did you come for?" I ask.

"To give you a chance to represent me,." she says. "After Tuesday I'll be back on top again. I was going to bring you along for the ride."

"Well, I appreciate that but I think your comeback's going to be short lived as soon as Rodgers and Hammerstein find out they've hired a junkie."

"You're a damned liar!"

"Take off your gloves," I say.

She turns white.

"What?"

"How long do you think you can hide those tracks in your arms? How long do you think Dick and Oscar are going to let a hophead play the part of a Mother Superior? You'll be lucky to last three days."

She's on her feet now, heading for the door, mink slung over her shoulder.

"Bastard!" she shouts.

"Where were you on Thursday morning between midnight and two a.m.?"

"Go to hell," she says as she goes out the door, slamming it behind her.

I quickly turn the lock in case she changes her mind and comes back. This has been an interesting interlude. I cant wait to tell Bunny all about it which I will do several months from now. If at all.

CHAPTER FIFTEEN

There's a ringing in my ear and it isn't tinnitus.

Dead tired I climbed into the sack last night at a few minutes past ten and proceeded to spend the next three hours tossing and turning, trying unsuccessfully to turn off a brain that was fixated on Monday at six and the hulking presence of Frankie Fortuna.

Ring. Ring.

I open one eye and stare at the alarm clock which I had set for 8:30. It reads 4:22.

Ring. Ring.

Not the alarm. It's the damned phone and I know for a certainty that no good can come of a phone call placed at 4:22 in the morning. I reach over and grope for the receiver.

"Hello," I mumble.

"Joe?"

A man's voice. I feel better. It isn't Bunny.

"Who is this?" I ask.

"Horvath. Are you all right?"

"Of course I'm all right. Why shouldn't I be?"

"It's Butch, Joe," Horvath says. "He's been shot. I'm in the emergency room at Belleview."

My head clears instantly and I sit up, swinging my legs off the bed.

"How bad?" I ask.

"Bad enough," he says.

"I'm on my way," I say getting to my feet.

"It's not necessary," Horvath says. "I was checking to see where you were."

"I'll be there quick as I can," I tell him and hang up.

On the way to the bathroom I pick up the crown of tea roses from the floor and toss it into the trash.

The cab drops me off at the Emergency entrance just as an ambulance is off-loading a guy on a gurney with tubes plugged into every part of his body. I think I hear the driver say something to a hospital orderly about a three car pile up and a drunk driver. I follow the gurney inside. Despite the fact that it's five o'clock in the morning, the place is still crowded in the aftermath of a typical Saturday night on the lower East Side of Manhattan. Shootings and knifings are commonplace and it's obvious that this ward is under-staffed. Doctors and nurses scurry about while family members anxiously await news of a loved one's condition. A heavy-set older woman sits in the corner of the waiting room weeping uncontrol-lably while a young man tries hard to console her. For this woman, the news was not good.

I spot Horvath by the water fountain. He and a woman are talk-ing to one of the doctors. Horvath nods a couple of times and then the doctor retreats back into the treatment area. As I approach his expression is grave.

"Sarge?" I say.

"He's the same, Joe" Horvath replies. "Unconscious, barely hang-ing on. They're moving him to ICU. This is Martha O'Brien, Butch's daughter. Martha, Joe Bernardi."

She nods at me. I smile. She's somewhere around thirty, a red-head like her father with freckles and Irish greeneyes, not unattract-ive but no beauty either. What many people would call substantial and down to earth.

"I'm sorry for your trouble," I say, a favorite expression of the Irish in times of grief.

She nods but says nothing, then turns to Horvath.

"I'm going to sit down," she says.

"Sure."

He watches her as she finds an empty seat close by and sits, ramrod stiff, staring straight ahead.

"This is rough, Joe. He's all she has. She's been taking care of him since she was twenty years old. Her brothers and sisters, all married, all raising families of their own. She got the short stick."

"Maybe she likes it that way."

"Maybe. All I know is, right now, she's scared to death."

"So what happened, Sarge?"

" It was just before three o'clock.They were waiting for him outside his apartment building. The shooter pumped two slugs into him, one in the chest, one to the neck. The neck shot was a through-and-through and they were able to dig out the slug in his chest." Horvath shakes his head in disbelief. "He never even pulled his weapon, Joe. That's how quick it happened. The guy on the ground floor, a fireman ready to go on duty, he heard the shots and ran outside. Butch was lying there on the sidewalk next to the open door of his car."

"The fireman, he see anything?"

"Yeah. Taillights disappearing around the corner. What happened tonight, Joe? Where'd he go? What was he doing""

"I don't know," I say.

"He was under strict orders. Drive you around. Protect you. But that was the extent of it. No playing detective. That's what he was doing, wasn't it, Joe? Playing detective."

"Yeah," I say. "You could say that. When he dropped me off at the hotel he told me—"

At that moment a nurse appears carrying a bulky white plastic bag. "The Inspector's been taken to ICU, Sergeant," she says. "These are his clothes and personal effects."

"Can we see him?"

"No, but there's a waiting room outside the unit. Third floor. You're welcome to wait there."

"I don't suppose he's conscious," Horvath says.

"Not yet," the nurse replies as she goes back into the treatment area.

"Come on, let's go," Horvath says to me as he looks over at Martha and beckons her.

The ICU waiting room is deserted except for an old man sitting quietly staring at the floor. His clothes are a motley assemblage and on his feet are his bedroom slippers. I suspect he dressed quickly and blindly.

The three of us sit on chairs in an empty part of the room as Horvath pulls out the contents of the bag and places everything on a table. Mostly it's Butch's clothing along with his watch, his wallet and a gold Claddagh wedding band.

" Martha," he says, "I'm going to go through your Dad's things. It may help us discover where he was tonight."

She nods her assent and Horvath starts going through Butch's clothing, finding slips of paper, a pack of matches, a stub of a pencil, car keys, loose change. He examines everything meticulously but in the end comes up empty. He shakes his head at Martha. She nods in understanding.

"Are you sure you don't know where he went tonight, Joe? He must have said something," Horvath says.

"He did say something, Sarge. I was going to tell you earlier but we got interrupted. Just before he left me he said he was going to check something out with a man named Patch."

"Patch? Who is he? I never heard of him."

"He didn't say. Just that he was very smart and had a good memory."

"Martha?" Horvath asks.

She shakes her head.

"Sorry. I don't recognize the name," she says.

At that moment, a nurse emerges from the ICU. Horvath gets to his feet and intercepts her. They talk quietly for a moment and then he returns to us.

"There's no change. He's resting comfortably. He's hooked up to every device they could think of and his vitals are satisfactory."

"Any idea when he'll be awake?" I ask.

"An hour from now," Horvath says. "or maybe next week. There's no way to tell. The surgeon's in there now checking x-rays in the event they have to operate."

"What for?"

"Internal bleeding. Something vital might have been nicked by the bullet."

We sit in silence. It feels like an hour. I check my watch. It's been eleven minutes. Horvath picks up a six month old copy of National Geographic. He scans it, then puts it aside. Martha is fingering her rosary beads, her lips moving silently as she repeats the mantra 'Holy Mary, Mother of God...'. I get up and stand by the window looking out over 23rd Street. New York is the city that never sleeps but this neighborhood is dozing. Traffic is light, businesses are closed, few lights shine from nearby apartment windows. An ambulance approaches slowly and quietly. If there is some poor soul within, chances are he is now beyond help.

The elevator dings. I look over as a uniformed policeman steps out and sees Horvath. Horvath moves to him and they talk quietly for a minute or so. Horvath goes to Martha's side, speaking quietly to her. She nods and then he walks over to me.

"I have to go, Joe. It looks like we caught a break in the Hyman

Weiss case. A patrol car came across Weiss's sister-in-law running around the streets in her nightgown, dead drunk, telling the world she killed her husband."

"Not a problem," I say. "Me and Martha will be right here."

"I'll be back as soon as I can," he says, putting his hand on my shoulder and squeezing it. Then he strides toward the elevator. The uniformed cop is holding the door for him. I watch as the door closes. Once again the waiting room is eerily silent.

"Mr. Bernardi?"

I look over and Martha is calling to me quietly. I go over and sit by her side.

"The man called Patch. I know who he is but I couldn't say anything in front of the sergeant. His name's Petie Donnelly. Many years ago he was Dad's partner right up until the war broke out. Dad got promoted and Petie got left behind. Dad said he was one of the brightest guys he'd ever known but he didn't know when to keep his mouth shut. He'd alienated too many higher-ups. About ten years ago he went on a raid to bust a drug operation and he got shot. He pulled through but lost an eye and they put him on permanent disability."

"And Horvath doesn't know about Donnelly?"

"Dad never talked about him. You see, Petie's been working at a lot of jobs the past few years but if the department found out about it, he'd probably lose his disability check. I know. It makes no sense. Nobody can live on a disability check so everybody cheats but the department has its rules and they don't change them for anybody."

"I understand," I say. "And how do I contact this Petie Donnelley?"

"I have his number at home but he's in the book. He lives in an apartment house on Canal Street."

"I'll check him out," I say.

"You needn't stay on my account, Mr. Bernardi. I'll be fine."

I glance at my watch. 5:35. Not a fit time to be contacting

anyone. I'll wait an hour or two. The time passes slowly and then, a few minutes before seven, a doctor emerges from the unit with good news. Butch is doing better. His vital signs are improving and he won't need surgery but he's far from safe, not yet. No, we can't see him. He's in a deep sleep. Perhaps around noon if he's awake. I check my watch and Martha tells me to go. She's as anxious as I am to find out who did this to her father. I tell her I'll keep her posted on anything I learn and with her blessing, I leave. It's obvious she is staying until she gets a chance to see Butch even if it means camping out here in the waiting room for days.

I skip breakfast and fifteen minutes later I'm in a cab pulling up to a weathered townhouse on Canal Street that long ago had been chopped up into small apartments. I could have called ahead but decided not to. I have no idea what I'm going to run into but with Butch in the hospital fighting for his life, anything is possible and whatever Petie Donnelly knows or doesn't know I want to look him in the eye when I talk to him. I tell the cabbie to wait and bound up the stairs to the entrance. The name on the mailbox tells me the Donnellys live in 1B which I find at the rear of the building. I knock once, then twice and finally the door opens and I find myself staring at an older woman in a starched white uniform with 'Sylvia' stitched over her heart. She is just slipping into her overcoat.

"Yeah?" she says.

"My name's Joe Bernardi. I'm a friend of Butch O'Brien's and I need to speak to your husband."

"He's not here," she says.

"Where can I find him?"

"You gotta excuse me," Sylvia says, stepping out into the hallway. "I'm late for work."

"Was Butch O'Brien here last night?" I ask.

"Mister, I haven't got time," she says locking her door.

"It's a simple question. Yes or no. Was he here?"

She glares at me.

"Look, I don't know you and when people I don't know start asking me questions, I don't answer. Now step out of my way."

"Butch was shot last night," I tell her. "Ambushed. He's at Belleview barely hanging on."

I see the shock in her face. Almost immediately she tries to cover up.

"Not my problem," she says. "Now move or I call the cops."

"I have a better idea. Suppose I call the cops and we can have them down here asking about your husband's job which he's not supposed to have while he's collecting disability."

"You bastard," she says.

"Yes, ma'am," I reply pleasantly. "Now where's your husband?"

She tells me.

I find Pete Donnelly working as a watchman at a furniture warehouse on Houston Street. It's a few minutes before eight and the workers are starting to drift in. Two large vans have backed up to the loading dock and an important looking guy with a clipboard in his hand is walking around giving orders. Donnelly is off to one side watching the activity and no doubt on the alert for troublemakers or hijackers. He's tall, slim with thick white hair and appears to be close to 60. His uniform has a shoulder patch which reads Harmon Security. He also has a name tag on his shirt which I am not close enough to read but I don't need to. The black patch over his left eye says it all.

He looks at me curiously as I approach him.

"Mr. Donnelly?"

"That's right."

"My name's Joe Bernardi. I'm a friend of Butch's."

I put out my hand and we shake.

"Nice to meet you," he says. "I was talking to Butch just last night."

"I know," I say and then tell him what happened. His face darkens.

"Damn. I told him it wasn't a good idea. He wouldn't listen."

"What wasn't a good idea?"

"Chasing after Mary Beth Breen."

"Better go slow. I don't know much." I tell him about Butch's fascination with Amythyst Breen's photograph.

He nods and then says, "I've got coffee brewing in the office." He starts off and I follow him.

He's not only got coffee but a half dozen sugar donuts. He offers me one. He doesn't have to offer twice.

"So tell me about Mary Beth Breen," I say.

He takes a sip of his coffee, collecting his thoughts.

"She was just a kid when I knew her. Sixteen, maybe seventeen, kinda wild, hanging around with the wrong crowd. Her folks ran a newspaper stand by the Prince Street subway station. Nice people but they couldn't control her. She didn't hook, nothing like that, but she was in tight with the wiseguys and then one day she just disappeared from the streets. Her folks reported her missing for all the good it did. We couldn't find her. There was a rumor going around that she'd been knocked up by one of the wiseguys. Butch thought maybe she'd been whacked by the baby's father but now it seems that's not true. After a while we just forgot about her. In those days life was cheap. Maybe it still is."

"And Butch thought what? That Amythyst Breen was related? That maybe she was the kid that everybody'd rumored about?"

"He said he saw a resemblance. I wouldn't know. I never saw the photo."

"So, specifically, what did you mean when you said, I told him it wasn't a good idea?"

He looks at me quizzically.

"I'm not sure I should be telling you any of this," he says. "Do you know how to keep your mouth shut?"

"I do."

"My friend's near dead. I don't want the same thing happening to me."

"You can trust me, Mr. Donnelly."

"I hope so. You could be dead yourself if you're not careful."

"Meaning what?"

"Meaning Mary Beth Breen may have reappeared but if so there are those who'd rather this fact not be known."

"I'm listening."

"I'll tell you what I told Butch. What you do with this is your affair as long as my name is not mentioned."

"It won't be."

"I got it from a friend from the old days who may be mistaken but he wouldn't lie about it. There's a place in New Rochelle. Mayfield Manor, a very swanky sanitarium for people with a wide assortment of ailments, chief of which is drug addiction. However they also treat patients with mental and emotional problems which is apparently what they are treating Mary Beth for under the alias Mildred Gamble. My friend who was in the D.A.'s office in those days says a mob lawyer he knew said he actually saw her a year ago and he was positive it was Mary Beth. Anyway that's what Butch asked me about and that's what I told him and then he left and what happened after that, I have no idea."

"That's it?"

"That's all I know," Donnelly says. "Now give it to me straight. How is he?"

"Better than he was. He hasn't regained consciousness but all his vital signs are good and the doctor's optimistic."

"How's the girl holding up?" he asks.

"Martha? She's good. A strong young lady," I say.

"That she is. Maybe after I get off I'll go over and hold her hand."

"I think she'd like that," I say.

I finish my coffee and doughnut and duck out. My cab is waiting where I left it and my driver whose name is Lorenzo, is watching the foot traffic on Houston Street, specifically the secretaries and receptionists who are scurrying to work in the nearby office buildings.

My stomach is growling. The coffee and doughnut didn't do it. "I'm starving, Lorenzo. I need breakfast. Want to join me?"

"I ate," he says. "You want to stop for breakfast? Your tab's already thirty bucks with all the wait time." He's not the pleasantest of guys and he's really starting to annoy me.

"I'm good for it," I tell him.

He shrugs. "I'm just saying."

"Find me a decent hash house with a phone. I'll order something to go."

Ten minutes later I'm on the phone booth calling Horvath. Lorenzo's at the counter getting toasted bagels and coffee for the two of us. I've already looked up the address for the Mayfield Manor in New Rochelle. Now I'm placing a call to Horvath to pass on this lead but what it's a lead to I'm not quite sure. The voice on the other end of the line tells me that Horvath is in with the Precinct Commander and probably won't be available any time soon. I thank him and hang up. I consider waiting until I can talk to the sergeant but discard the idea right away. I'm running out of time.

Outside Lorenzo hands me my bagel and coffee and I climb into the back seat of the cab.

"Where to?" he asks as he slides behind the wheel. When I tell him New Rochelle, he turns and looks at me like I've suggested Forbes Field in Pittsburgh. "I don't think so," he says.

"What's your problem?" I ask.

He taps the meter which now reads $31.90.

"New Rochelle's at least another twenty and if I have to deadhead back it's a lousy proposition."

"You'll be bringing me back on the meter," I say.

He shakes his head.

"I don't think so," he says. "Thirty-one-ninety and grab yourself another cab." He puts out his hand.

Lorenzo's not a lot of fun but I don't want another cab. He's a good driver, the cab is brand new and the heater works just fine. I dig into my wallet and take out three twenties.

"On account," I say as I hand them to him. He takes them with a nod and fires up the engine.

"New Rochelle," he says as we pull out into traffic.

CHAPTER SIXTEEN

My watch says 12:38 when we pull up to the entrance to Mayfield Manor which is situated on Webster Avenue on the outskirts of New Rochelle. Two imposing stone columns stand on each side of the driveway and the wrought iron gate is wide open though apparently most times it is not. At the bottom of the sign that identifies the hospital is a notation in smaller lettering: Visitation Sundays Only—Noon to 4 p.m.

We climb the long winding driveway to an imposing building at the top of the hill. Halfway there I notice an ambulance following us closely. At the top of the hill we pull into a small asphalt section marked 'Visitors' but at the moment it's empty. Either business at the Mayfield is lousy or the loved ones of Mayfield's patients have better things to do on a Sunday afternoon. The ambulance continues past us and takes the driveway around to the rear of the building.

I get out of the car and look around. It's obvious that at one time this had been a private mansion but for whatever reason it has fallen into the clutches of commercialism. The facade is stone, the windows leaded, the landscaping impeccable. We appear be sitting on at least twenty acres of land, most of it wooded except for the broad expanse of lawn that reaches down to Webster Avenue. This is no rehab clinic for the underprivileged which leads me to wonder how Mary Beth Breen, devil-may-care party girl of the Roaring Twenties, could afford to end up in a place like this.

I go inside while Lorenzo waits by the cab. The foyer and lobby are airy and tastefully furnished. To my left is a reception desk, unattended. An archway to my right opens onto a large room with a dozen or so stuffed chairs, several sofas and a giant stone fireplace built into the far wall. This appears to be where visitors are encouraged to meet with the patients. In addition to being dimly lit, the room is also deserted. I check my watch. 12:50. The crowds are running late.

I walk over to the reception desk and pop the little bell that says 'Ring for Service'. After a moment a woman appears from a back room. She is dressed in a white nurse's uniform and her face reflects total confusion as if her quiet domain had just been invaded by a door-to-door salesman.

"May I help you?" she asks.

"I believe so," I say. "I'm here to visit Mildred Gamble."

She freezes in her tracks like a deer caught in the headlights of an oncoming tractor-trailer. Seems like I'm her surprise of the day.

"I—uh—I'm not familiar with that name," she finally manages to get out. Her little name tag reads Vera Hyde, R.N. It should read L.L. for lousy liar.

"Odd," I say, "since she's been under your care for at least the past year."

She fakes a smile.

"Let me call the doctor," she says.

"No need to put yourself out, ma'am. If you'll just tell me where I can find her—"

"No trouble at all. Please take a seat in our Greeting Room. I'm sure the doctor will be with you shortly."

She picks up the phone at her side as I stroll into the Greeting Room and flop down into one of the overstuffed Greeting sofas. I get a closer look at the furniture. It's all heavy with thick upholstery and dark wood. The floors are covered with oriental carpets and the windows are partially blocked by heavyweight drapes. What little light manages to get in dances around the walls casting eerie shadows. I half expect to hear baroque organ music suddenly filling the room. I also half expect that the doctor who has been summoned by Nurse Hyde will be named Jekyll.

He isn't. His name is Chase, William M. according to the brass name plate affixed to his suit pocket and he is the director of this facility.

He smiles warmly as he puts out his hand. We shake.

"Bill Chase. So nice to meet you. I'm afraid Nurse Hyde didn't get your name."

"Joe Bernardi," I say.

"And you are a relative of Miss Gamble?" he asks.

Uh-oh. Trap question. Relatives only? Perhaps so.

"Yes, her cousin," I say.

Chase frowns.

"Sorry, I wasn't aware of any cousin," he says.

"Very distant," I tell him. "I work in Albany in the Office of the Speaker of the Assembly and I'm down here for one day on holiday so I thought I'd drop in to see the old girl."

Chase was holding his own until I mentioned Albany and then his expression changed to one of a man who has just swallowed a prickly pear.

"Well, I feel absolutely awful about this," Chase says, "but we just gave Miss Gamble a sedative and she'll be sleeping soundly for at least the next six hours. I'm sorry you had to come all this way for nothing." I look past him toward the reception desk. Nurse Hyde is on the phone in an animated conversation with someone. Since she keeps looking in my direction I assume I'm the topic of conversation.

"Not a problem." I say. "I'll be delighted to wait."

He plasters on that smile.

"I'm afraid that won't work out, Mr. Bernardi. By the time she awakens, visiting hours will be over."

"Wait a minute," I say, raising my voice. "Let me get this straight. I come here to visit my cousin. You put her to sleep with a sedative that will keep her out for hours and then tell me I can't see her because she slept through visiting time, is that it?"

"I wouldn't put it exactly that way," Chase says.

"Then how would you put it, Doctor?"

By now Nurse Hyde has gotten off the phone and she approaches us.

"I hate to interrupt, Doctor, but the floor nurse tells me she gave Miss Gamble a very light sedative. She may be awake in an hour or so."

A look passes between them that I see but cannot quite translate, somewhat like two cannibals jollying the local missionary while out of sight behind the nearest shack, a huge cast iron pot of water is coming to a boil. Chase turns to me, the smile back in full bloom.

"Well, there you are, Mr. Bernardi. An hour's wait at most. Make yourself comfortable and I'll notify you when your cousin Mildred is awake."

At this moment a burly guy who looks like an orderly enters through the front door. He has a blonde buzzcut and exudes all the arrogance of an Army M.P. He glances in my direction and his gaze settles on me for an instant too long before he disappears down a nearby corridor.

"I could do that," I say, "or I could take a short trip down to the village for some lunch and return in, say, an hour."

"No need to do that," Chase says, taking me by the arm. "We have plenty to eat here. Come into the kitchen and we'll fix you something."

He starts to lead me past the reception desk and what appears to be the facility's dining room. We go through a swinging door and into a very modern looking kitchen. A heavyset man is at a large double sink cleaning up stacks of luncheon dishes. Another man is at the mammoth grill, cleaning it meticulously.

"On Sundays we feed our patients brunch at 11:30 in advance of visiting hours," Chase says. "We're just not equipped to handle our own people as well as their guests."

Who seem to be crowding through the doors like shoppers at a New Year's white sale, I think.

Chase grabs a chair and pulls it up to a nearby table. "Ramon," he says to the guy at the grill, "Mr. Bernardi is our guest for lunch. Anything he wants."

"My pleasure," Ramon says.

Everybody here is so accommodating I can hardly stand it.

Chase leaves and I look around. We had walked through a dining room that was pristine and this tells me that brunch was not served there. Therefore I conclude that the patients probably ate in their rooms. I also eyeball the dirty dishes and quickly compute that no more than twelve meals were served although this place clearly has ample room for three times that many patients. I was leery of this place to begin with. Now I am downright suspicious. This is no place for a nice Italian boy from Southern California.

"Ramon!" I call over to the grill guy. "Men's room?"

He points to a nearby door.

"Down at the end. Last door on the left."

I thank him and push through the door. At the end of the corridor is another door which opens to the outside. I skip the men's room and try the handle of the exterior door. It's unlocked. I step out into fresh air. To my right is the ambulance parked in front of double doors marked "Emergency Only". To my left is the corner of the building and the driveway that leads out to the main road.

Quickly I turn the corner and jog around the side of the building toward the parking lot. Mildred Gamble will just have to wait. I can't get away from this place quick enough. But when the parking lot comes into view I see that it's empty. The cab's gone and so is Lorenzo. I look to the left and right. No luck. I've been abandoned.

"Mr. Bernardi!"

Someone's calling my name. I turn. It's the burly orderly I saw come in the front door just a few minutes ago. He strides toward me.

"What are you doing out here?" he asks.

"My cab was supposed to wait for me," I say.

"I guess he got tired of waiting. Come back inside. Your lunch is getting cold."

He takes me by the elbow and starts to steer me toward the entrance. His grip is strong. Very strong.

Ramon has prepared biscuits and a bowl of vegetable soup. It might even be chicken soup because there are a couple of things floating among the celery that could be chicken. I can't be sure. I take a bite. I still can't be sure.

Unwilling to leave me alone, the orderly is sitting at another table nearby munching on a drumstick while he labors over the TV Guide crossword puzzle.

"I Love... blank," he says to no one in particular. "Four letters."

The kitchen help stare at him without a clue. I have a clue but I'm not interested in helping out the dumb ox. I know one thing. He is standing between me and escape and I am more and more convinced that if I don't run for it, I'm dead meat. Butch came around here asking questions and they shot him for his trouble. What makes me think I'm going to fare any better?

I try one more spoonful of the barely edible soup and then I stretch my arms and get up from my chair.

"Sit down," the orderly says.

"I thought I'd check to see if my cousin's awake yet."

"She isn't," he says, turning the page in search of the puzzle solution.

He is basically sitting with his back to me. Mounted on the wall near my hand is a huge cast iron frying pan. Even though I'm terrified I know I'll never get a better chance. I grab the pan with two hands, take two loping steps toward him and slam the pan down on the back of his head as hard as I can. I hear an ugly 'thock' as he falls face forward and then slips onto the floor, unmoving. I may have split his head open. I don't care. I look at the two men who are staring at me wide-eyed. I wave the pan at them and they instinctively back up a couple of steps. Then I dash toward the door and down the corridor to the rear entrance. Once out into fresh air I turn right and sprint toward the ambulance which is still parked in front of the Emergency entrance. I pray to God that the driver is a careless jerk.

I slip into the driver's seat and reach under the steering wheel. Bingo! The keys are in the ignition. I start the engine and throw it into reverse. It behaves like a groggy whale but at least I have it moving. I shift into first and head for the driveway. At that moment the driver emerges and starts yelling at me. He gives chase but when I smooth it into second I leave him behind. I start past the parking lot just as a strange car glides to a stop and the driver gets out. I have to look twice to make sure I'm not seeing things. The newcomer is Frankie Fortuna. I recognized him immediately. I'm pretty sure he recognized me.

Picking up speed I start the long winding descent down the driveway toward Webster Avenue. The gate is in sight when I am suddenly gripped by an icy fear. The gate is starting to close and there's no way in hell I am going to get there before it shuts. I'm sitting on a substantial hunk of metal and I've got a lot of horsepower under the hood but that gate's not made of tinfoil. What the hell. I have no choice. I floor the accelerator. The gate looms closer and closer and then it clicks shut. I brace myself as the front end slams into wrought iron. I shouldn't have worried. The gate was no match for my vehicle but now I have another problem as I go screaming onto Webster Avenue, narrowly missing a Chevy coming from my left and a Dodge from my right. I hit the brake and turn the wheel and pray I don't flip over. I skid sideways and I can feel the left side of the ambulance leave the ground for what seems an eternity before it settles back on four tires. I come within a whisker of sliding into a roadside ditch, then straighten out and start down the road toward the town.

I take a quick glance into my side mirror and spot the car trailing me. Frankie Fortuna is on my tail. I would love to floor it but I realize I am running up the backs of a parade of Sunday drivers out for an afternoon spin even as Frankie is running up my rear end. I scan the dashboard and find the switch marked 'Siren" and flip it on. The cab is instantly filled with an earsplitting wail and in front of me, I watch as the cars blocking my way duck to the shoulder to let me pass. Unfortunately they are also permitting Fortuna to pass and he is tight on my tail only a car length behind. I jam on my brakes, hoping he will be caught napping and ram my rear end. I'm not worried about the ambulance but serious front end damage might disable Fortuna's car. I'm not that lucky. He barely taps the back of the ambulance and then drops back a couple of car lengths.

I'm getting worried. As I get closer to town the traffic becomes heavier and I don't know how to shake this guy. Then, at that moment, fate intervenes. I speed past a sign which reads "New Rochelle Police Department 1/4 Mile Ahead". From here I can see the building and when I reach it I speed into the driveway and cross into the parking lot before applying the brakes and coming to stop only feet from a couple of squad cars. I look out my window. Frankie had slowed. Now he picks up speed, continuing down the road.

I leap from the ambulance and race up the steps into the building. A uniformed cop with three stripes on his sleeve sits behind the information desk and he looks up as I reach him.

"My name is Joe Bernardi," I say. "I just borrowed an ambulance from Mayfield Manor and I need to speak to Sergeant Karol Horvath of the Ninth Precinct, New York City, now." Emphasis on the NOW.

CHAPTER SEVENTEEN

For the next hour I stay safely within the confines of the headquarters building. The sergeant tries to pump me for information but I tell him I'd rather wait until Horvath arrives before going through my story. The Chief is away for the day fishing with his grandson so the sergeant calls in the Deputy Chief whose name is Haggerty. I repeat my position. Wait for Horvath.

A few minutes past three, he pulls up in his unwashed unmarked beatup Crown Victoria and when he walks in the door he looks far from happy. He grabs me by the arm and pulls me aside.

"Okay, Joe," he says, "what have you gotten yourself into now?"

Nothing bad, I assure him. In fact I may have uncovered something that reflects on the Finucci killing but we have to bring the local cops in on it.

A few minutes later we are seated around the Chief's desk while Haggerty eyes me with both annoyance and skepticism as I narrate my close call with the people at Mayfield Manor. Horvath, too, is wondering what this is all about until I mention Frankie Fortuna and then he moves forward to the edge of his chair, listening intently.

"Well, this is all very interesting, Mr. Bernardi," Haggerty says, "but you know, those folks at Mayfield, we've never had a problem with them. They keep to themselves and mind their own business."

"And what business is that, Chief?" I ask. "Are you sure you really know?"

His eyes narrow into unfriendly slits.

"I'll tell you what I do know, young fella, is that you stole their ambulance and here in New Rochelle that's a serious matter."

Haggerty is fat, sixty and bald which is why he thinks of me as a young fella. I think of him as something of a dunce.

"Have you asked yourself why they haven't reported their stolen ambulance, Chief?" I say. "Maybe it has something to do with keeping to themselves and minding their own business."

Horvath jumps in before I open my mouth one time too many.

"I think, Chief, you might have a better appreciation of the situation if you knew who Frankie Fortuna is. He works directly for a man named Salvatore Rizzo who is an underboss in the Carlo Gambino crime family."

Haggerty's face darkens.

"That so? Got no use for those big city Eye-talians here in New Rochelle."

"Well, you just might have a nest of them right up the road," I suggest.

He looks from me to Horvath and back again.

"And what do you think I should do about it?" he asks.

"For starters," I say, "we could go back and check out Mildred Gamble whom they very adamantly do not want me to see."

"Not to mention returning their damned ambulance," Haggerty adds.

"Just what I had in mind," I say glancing over at Horvath who subtly nods his approval.

We caravan back to Mayfield Manor, me in the lead driving the ambulance followed by Haggerty and a uniformed deputy in a cruiser with Horvath bringing up the rear.

The wrought iron gate is completely off its hinges and lying by the side of the road as I drive between the two stone pillars. At the top of the hill we park and go to the front door. Even before I can ring the doorbell, the door swings open and Nurse Hyde invites us in.

"We were all very concerned about you, Mr. Bernardi," she says. "Dr. Chase in particular. I'll tell him you're here."

I'm sure he already knows but I let her go through with her little charade. I'm looking forward to seeing how Chase is going to characterize the day's earlier events.

Haggerty has wandered off into the Greeting Room to admire the furnishings while Horvath has pulled me aside.

"Tell me again about this business with the Breen girl and the woman who is staying here under the name Mildred Gamble."

I go through it again. Amythyst Breen, the actress at the little theater, had been one of Finucci's customers. The woman known as Mildred Gamble is probably Mary Beth Breen and if so, is likely to be Amythyst's mother. How all this fits together I'm not sure but with Frankie Fortuna involved, there is a very strong connection somewhere. All we have to do is find out what it is.

"That's your job, Sarge. You're the detective, not me."

"Well, I'm pleased to see that fact has finally sunk in," Horvath says with a wry smile.

I look past Horvath to the stairs as Dr. Chase descends quickly and approaches us, that smile plastered on his face and that hand again outstretched.

"Mr. Bernardi, so good to see you. We were all very worried. Are you all right?"

"Why shouldn't I be?"

"Well, your bizarre behavior, I was afraid you had experienced some sort of episode."

Oh, here we go. Psychiatrist attempting to weasel out of jam by alluding to me as some sort of head case.

"Not bizarre at all, Doctor. Just good old-fashioned survival instincts. Say hello to Detective Sergeant Horvath of New York's Ninth Precinct."

Never losing the smile, Chase shakes Horvath's hand.

"A little far afield of your neighborhood, aren't you, Sergeant?"

"I am," Horvath smiles back. "That's why we brought along Deputy Chief Haggerty of the New Rochelle Police Department."

Haggerty strolls into our midst.

"Sorry to be intruding, Doc, but I had to make sure Mr. Bernardi here brought back your ambulance. A few scratches and dents here and there but no major damage."

"I'm grateful for your help, Chief," Chase says.

"As to why he took it, he said he had the feeling he was being kept here against his will."

Chase drags up a wellspring of indignation.

"Why, that's ridiculous. We were careful to treat him like a valued guest. Unfortunately, his cab driver left him stranded which no doubt angered him but we had nothing to do with that."

"Not even that beefy orderly with the blonde buzz cut?" I ask.

Haggerty glares at me for interrupting.

"He also says he came to see his cousin, a Miss Gamble, and you prevented him from doing so."

"Absolutely untrue," Chase says. "At the time she was asleep and in no condition to be awakened. I merely asked him to wait."

"And while Mr. Bernardi was waiting," Horvath says to Chase, "did you make a phone call to a man named Frankie Fortuna?"

"I did not. I don't know anyone by that name."

"Odd that he would show up here just as Mr. Bernardi was leaving in your ambulance."

Chase is starting to lose patience.

"I wouldn't know anything about that."

Haggerty nods sagely.

"Tell you what, Doctor," he says, "I think we can clear up a lot of this by letting Mr. Bernardi here see his cousin. What do you think?"

"I'm afraid I really couldn't permit that," Chase says.

"Oh? And why is that?"

"Her condition is precarious."

"And just what is her condition?"

"I wish I could tell you, Chief. I can't. Doctor-patient confidentiality."

Haggerty looks thoughtfully at me, then at Horvath and back to Chase.

"Well, how about if you just show me her admittance form."

"Can't do that either, Chief. Same reason. Those forms are confidential."

"I see," Haggerty says. "Well, Doc, here's how it is. Judge Fisk lives five minutes from headquarters and I am now going out to my car and radio my sergeant to get over to the Judge's house and have him sign a writ of habeas corpus which will allow us to see this Mildred Gamble and I am also going to have him authorize a search warrant which will enable us to look not only at Miss Gamble's admission form but the forms for every other patient in this place because I've always held that if you see more than one gopher hole in your lawn, chances are good there's more than one gopher. I'm sure you get my drift."

With that Haggerty turns on his heel and strides toward the front door. I take it all back. He's still fat, sixty and bald but he's far from a dunce.

"Wait!" Chase cries out. Haggerty turns back. "No need to go to all that trouble, Chief. I'm happy to cooperate." He turns to me, "Come, Mr. Bernardi, I'll take you to your cousin."

"I think we'll all go," Haggerty says.

Chase starts to object, then thinks better of it. The four of us start up the staircase to the second floor.

"She has her good days and bad," Chase says. "Today has not been particularly good."

It is very quiet as we reach the landing and start down the corridor. There are ten doors, ten rooms. A couple of the doors are open. We can hear the muted sounds of television sets but no conversation. Whoever these people are, they are isolated, at least on a Sunday afternoon and common sense dictates it doesn't get any better the rest of the week. Horvath is walking directly in front of me and as he starts to pass an open door he looks in and then stops short. After a moment he continues on. As I pass the doorway I, too, look in. A stout man with black hair just starting to turn grey is sitting in his undershirt in a chair watching a golf tournament. He looks up at me with mild curiosity, then turns his attention back to the TV set.

Chase has stopped at the last door on the left hand side. The door is open. He puts out his hand and bids me enter. As I do I immediately realize that this room is at least twice the size of the room I just looked into. It is tastefully decorated in muted pinks and yellows. The furniture is white. Plush pink and white carpeting covers the floor. A large 17″ TV rests on a table in the corner and next to it is the open door to a private bathroom. Finally, against a far wall is a canopy bed and in the bed is a frail looking woman, propped up by pillows, but made to look even smaller by the size of the bed. This is Mildred Gamble. It may even be Mary Beth Breen. She is staring straight ahead and, for the moment at least, she doesn't seem aware of our presence. Well, I have accomplished what I came for. I am face to face with this mysterious woman and now I have to deal with her while not looking like a complete fool. I decide that boldness is the best policy.

I walk over to the bed and take her hand in mine and smile down at her.

"Hello, Mary Beth," I say. "It's cousin Joe."

Her eyes look up into mine and she smiles.

"Hello, Joe," she says.

"And how are you today?"

"Why I'm fine," she says. There's a certain blankness in her response, some sort of disconnect, as if she's been drugged or, perhaps worse, in a constant state of detachment from reality.

"You have it wrong, Mr. Bernardi," Chase harrumphs. "Her name is Mildred. Mildred Gamble."

"Is that right, Mary Beth? Is your name Mildred?"

"Well I don't know," she says. "I suppose it could be. I'm really not sure."

Horvath and I share a quick look.

"Annie sends regards," I say. "She's thinking about you."

"Sweet child. She should be getting home from school any minute now."

I sit on the edge of the bed, still holding her hand,and look at her closely. Like Amythyst she is small and somewhat frail. They also share the same auburn hair and hazel green eyes. I'm pretty sure this is Amythyst's mother and I am pretty sure she is living in a non-threatening world of her own making.

"Are they treating you well, Mary Beth?"

"Oh, yes."

"Is there something I can do for you? Something I can get."

"No, I don't think so. I wish I would hear from my brother Arthur. It's been such a long time. I worry about him over there, fighting those huns. Mother is worried too. The letters just stopped.Do you think you could find out about that, Joe?"

"I can try," I say.

"I would be ever so grateful," she says, squeezing my hand.

"I promise, Mary Beth. Now why don't you lie back and try to get some sleep."

By the time we have returned downstairs Dr. William M. Chase has broken into a cold sweat.

"I don't understand any of this," he says. "I was told specifically that her name was Mildred Gamble."

"It appears that's not the case, Doc," Haggerty says. "Let's take a look at her admission form."

"That won't be much help," Chase says.

"Let's see it anyway," Haggerty insists.

We go into Chase's office where he opens a drawer in a filing cabinet and riffles through the folders, finally extracting one. In the folder is a single sheet of paper. Haggerty looks at it while I peer over his shoulder.

It is a comprehensive form but very little has been filled in. Name: Mildred Gamble. Address: 127 Avenue de la Harpe, Laussane, Switzerland. That ices it for me. No question now that this is Amythyst's mother. The only other piece of information on the form is an emergency call number: 212-434-2333. Every other spot has been left blank including date of admission, name of closest relative, date of birth, social security number, and perhaps most important of all, name of financially responsible party.

I look hard at Dr. Chase.

"Unless that woman upstairs committed herself voluntarily, which I find hard to believe, someone brought her here and that someone is paying the bills. Who is it?" I ask.

"I don't know," Chase says.

"That kind of answer's going to get you nowhere, Doctor," Haggerty says.

"It's the truth. Years ago a man I'd never seen before and haven't seen since showed up with two associates and the woman upstairs. He said he wanted her taken care of in comfort. He opened up a brief case one of his people had been carrying and dumped one hundred thousand dollars on the dining room table. That was to pay for a year's care in advance. Each year, he said, on this date, someone would appear with another hundred thousand dollars. In between, without warning, he said, someone would appear to make sure that I was holding up my end of the bargain."

"This man," Horvath says. "Can you describe him?"

"Middle-aged, expensively dressed but pretty ordinary looking. It was the only time I ever saw him. Since then many different men have come here either to check up on the care we're providing or to make the annual payment. They don't say much and they don't stay long."

By now I have slid over to the side of Chase's desk and I turn the telephone toward me. I lift the receiver and dial the number. 212-434-2333. After three rings, a man answers.

"Trattoria Venezia."

Quickly and quietly I hang up.

By now Horvath has been handed the admission form for Mildred Gamble. He peruses it and then looks toward Chase.

"I'd like to see the admission form for Tony Caprizzi," Horvath says.

"Who?" Chase says with a puzzled expression.

"Tony Caprizzi. Middle room upstairs, left hand side. Pot belly from too many pizzas and too many beers."

"Mr. Mallory," Chase says.

"Call him whatever you like. Ten weeks ago we were looking for him in connection with the shooting of a Colombian diplomat outside of the U.N. Plaza. We thought he'd skipped the country. Apparently not."

"I don't know anything about that," Chase says.

"Of course you don't," Horvath says, elbowing him out of the way and starting to sift through the file folders.

"You can't do that," Chase says angrily.

"Check me out, Doc. I'm doing it." Horvath says as he pulls a single sheet of paper from the file drawer. "Mallory, John J. Joe, what's the emergency contact number on the lady's form?"

I tell him.

"Same number," Horvath says.

"It's an Italian restaurant," I tell him.

Horvath nods.

"They have to start catering to a better class of people."

Twenty minutes later we leave. Officer McKay remains behind as Chief Haggerty returns to headquarters. Horvath has told him to call Sergeant Royce at 17th Precinct. Royce caught the squeal on the UN slaying. He also gave him the number of FBI headquarters and the Special Agent in Charge Lou Novak. One or both of them should soon be descending on Mayfield Manor like snow on Aspen in the middle of January.

As for me and Horvath we will be leisurely driving back to Manhattan and to the Ninth Precinct where the Sergeant will lay on me his own special brand of hell for sticking my nose where it doesn't belong.

CHAPTER EIGHTEEN

I was wrong. Eventually we are going to get to my dressing down but first we swing by Belleview. Horvath has called ahead and learned that Butch is awake and lucid. He's also radio'ed the 17th to make sure Sgt. Royce is on his way to collect Tony Caprizzi from Mayfield Manor. SAC Lou Novak of the FBI has also been contacted to be certain the Feds are rounding up the rest of that crowd. Novak assures Horvath that a task force has just crossed the Triborough Bridge on its way to New Rochelle.

A few minutes before six we pull into Belleview's parking area and make our way to Butch's private room. He's sitting up, watching the local news on television. When we enter a a broad grin crosses his face.

"And just when I thought you'd forgotten all about me," he says.

"Fat chance of that," Horvath says. "If you'd died I'd probably lose my badge. I still might. I give you a cushy job off the books playing bodyguard for my friend and you get yourself knee deep in mob trouble. Jesus, Butch, what were you thinking?"

"I was thinking maybe we'd get them greasy bastards before they got us." He looks over at me. "And how are you doing, boyo?"

"Just fine, Butch, and where's Martha?" I ask.

"Just left to feed the cats. Said she'll be back in time for Ed Sullivan."

"Shouldn't you be resting?" Horvath asks.

"Plenty of time for that," Butch says. "So, you went out to that phony hospital. What happened?"

"You first," Horvath says.

Butch nods and takes us back to Saturday evening when he dropped me off at the hotel and then went in search of Petie Donnelly.

"It was a year or two ago and me and Petie were tossing back a few and reminiscing about old times and Mary Beth Breen's name came up and we all knew her, of course, and then when she disappeared, we just figured she was dead, the rumor being that some wiseguy had knocked her up, maybe a married wiseguy who didn't want any trouble. But Petie, he'd said no, she wasn't dead, that a mouthpiece from the old days said he'd actually seen her not more than a couple of years ago. And when I saw the picture of the woman at the theater, last name Breen, I got to wondering if there was a connection which is why I went to see Petie, to see if he could tell me anything more or maybe give me the name of the lawyer who said he saw Mary Beth alive."

He coughs and then reaches for his water pitcher. I grab it for him and pour him a glass of water.

"Damned medicine, makes you real thirsty," he says.

He drains half the glass and puts it on his tray.

"Where was I?" Butch asks

"The lawyer," I say.

"Oh, yeah. A real loser named Phil Donatello, mobbed up to his adam's apple, but it turns out I didn't need him because Petie remembers the name of the place where Donatello says he saw Mary Beth which, of course, was Mayfield Manor. So I thank him and off I go and it's about seven thirty when I drive up to the entrance just as this flashy looking Continental is waiting for the gate to open and when it does I drive right through on his tail and at the top of the hill, we both park and we head for the door. Right away I recognize the guy who was driving the Continental. Lou Terranova, a muscle guy in the Gambino organization, and he's got a grip on this kid, maybe sixteen or seventeen and spaced out so bad he can hardly walk and I'm figuring if anybody could use some help from a hospital like this one, it'd be the kid. Anyway the door opens, they let the two of them in and I slide right in with them because maybe they figure I'm extra muscle."

"Yeah," Horvath says. "You and your Irish face."

"Did I say these people were smart? Anyway I make my way to this reception desk and I tell the nurse I'm here to see Mary Beth Breen. She looks at me like I just asked to see the Pope and says there's nobody here by that name. I flash the badge and ask for the admissions records which is when she calls over this doctor who reminds me of an aluminum siding salesman."

"Bill Chase," I say.

"That's the guy. Anyway he gives me the same bullshit story and pretty soon we're talking search warrants and trespassing and two goons built like Sherman tanks come out of the woodwork at which point I think it's probably a good idea to leave. But just then I spot Carmen Stefano."

"Who?" I ask.

"Carmen Stefano," Horvath says. "Married to Nunzio Stefano. He went away three years ago on a prostitution beef and she would have gone with him but just before the end of the trial, persons unknown broke her out of Rikers and she disappeared."

"Right into Mayfield Manor," I say.

"You've got it, boyo. Anyway I make like I didn't recognize her and I leave threatening to come back with the Third Army to back me up and I drive straight back to the city to look up Phil Donatello to make sure he actually saw Mary Beth at that place two years ago."

"And?" Horvath says.

"Came up empty. I look everywhere. His house, his office, the usual bars where the wiseguys hang out. Nothing. So after two hours finally I give up and go home. I park my car at the curb, I open my car door and—" He shrugs. "Two flashes from the shadows. For an instant I know I'm hit and that's all I remember."

"You never saw the shooter," Horvath says.

Butch shakes his head.

"They must have figured I recognized Carmen. Had to be. These guys are real careful about shooting cops."

"Well, you're lucky you caught a guy who couldn't shoot straight." Horvath says. 'By the way, you missed Tony Caprizzi, He was upstairs in his shorts watching Dow Finsterwald make hash out of Doug Ford at the L.A Open."

Butch shakes his head.

"Caprizzi, too? What is that place, a rest home for the FBI's most wanted?"

"So it appears."

"I hope you're shutting the bastards down," Butch says.

"Even as we speak, Butch," Horvath says. "Even as we speak."

It's past seven-thirty when we finally get back to the Nine. We're both starved and looking at a long night so Horvath phones out for pizza while he catches up. With Haggerty's blessing the NYPD sent three additional units to Mayfield to back up Deputy McKay and sometime before midnight those seven "patients" who have outstanding warrants or are missing witnesses or otherwise fugitives from the justice system will be transported back to the city for incarceration.The twelve actual patients like Mary Beth will remain until they can be relocated to a more legitimate facility.

Horvath and I are sitting across from one another at his desk when the pizza arrives at five past eight. Three minutes later we are both digging in when Sal Rizzo arrives accompanied by two burly uniformed cops who have him by his arms, pinned between them. They plop him down in Horvath's other visitor's chair.

"What the hell is this, Horvath?" Rizzo demands to know, seething. He glances at me. It doesn't help his mood.

"What's the charge, Ryan?" Horvath asks.

"Resisting arrest, Sarge," one of the cops says.

"The hell you say!" Rizzo fumes. "These two goons walk up to me and say I'm wanted for questioning. The big guy grabs my arm, I shrug him off. That's all. I just shrug him off and all of a sudden I'm under arrest."

"Sounds like a misdemeanor to me," Horvath says. "Did he call his mouthpiece?"

"Never had a chance."

"Good. Wait downstairs if something rancid slithers in the door that even smells like a lawyer, divert him in another direction."

"Will do."

The two uniforms head out to the front room to take up their vigil.

"You can't do this, Horvath," Rizzo says only slightly calmer.

"Of course I can't. Sal. How's your old pal Lou Terranova?"

"Haven't seen him in months," Rizzo says.

"No surprise. Lou's on probation. He's prevented by law from fraternizing with undesirables and I can't think of anyone more undesirable than you, Sal."

Horvath picks up a big slice of pizza and chews off half, relishing it.

"Mmm. This is good. Great mozzarella. Say, my boys didn't interrupt your dinner, did they, Sal? I hope not. That would have been rude."

Rizzo says something harsh in Italian, knowing Horvath doesn't speak it. At the last second he remembers me and looks over at me nervously. I give him a grave look and shake my head reprovingly from side to side. I don't speak Italian either but Rizzo doesn't know that. He slinks back in his chair.

"The thing about Lou is this, Sal." Horvath says. "He's going back in the joint. Yeah, he made the mistake this afternoon of doing his friend Arnie Waltz a favor by taking his spaced-out junkie of a kid to Mayfield for treatment and in doing so found himself rubbing elbows with some of those undesirables I was talking about. Can you imagine his shock when he finds himself face to face with Carmen Stefano? Very sad. Terribly unfair. I think he's probably looking at another three, maybe four years before he gets another shot at the outside."

"Heartbreaking," Rizzo says.

"I only tell you this to make a point. My friend Joe here, for example, a fine upstanding citizen, minds his own business, pays his taxes, and yet he tells me that his life has been threatened. Threatened! Can you believe that, Sal? Here in America, a law abiding gentleman like my friend Joe Bernardi has had his life threatened by a disgusting, slimy, bottom feeding, foul and contemptible excuse for a human being. Now, forgetting for a moment that I am a police officer, what do you think I should do about that?"

"I don't know what you're talking about," Rizzo mumbles.

"Sal, didn't I just tell you a very interesting story about how the little things we do, even the well meant ones, can get us in a whole lot of trouble. I'm sure Lou Terranova never thought for a moment that today's good deed would end up with him going back to Sing Sing for another stretch,. You see, it's those little things that'll get you, like making wild threats against a man with friends in high places all over this country, friends who would squash a gunk-sucking cockroach like you without a second thought if they thought it would help a friend."

"I'm happy your friend is connected," Rizzo says."He is not alone in this regard. I, too, have generous friends willing to intercede on my behalf should the occasion arise."

"I'm still waiting for a response to my question, Sal. What do you think that I, as a private citizen, should do about this creep that has threatened my friend's life? If, for example, I were to come across him in a dark alley without my badge but with my gun. What should I do? Help me out here, Sal. You wiseguys always seem to have the answers."

Rizzo stares at him for a moment and then at me.

"First of all if this shadrool says I threatened him, he has a hearing problem, or he's a liar, Either way it isn't true. And besides that, Horvath, you're a gasbag. All this tough guy bullshit when everybody knows you're a straight arrow by-the-book flatfoot, always were and always will be. And finally the only way this pal of yours winds up dead after six o'clock tomorrow evening is if he steps in front of a city bus. Okay?"

Horvath looks at him levelly.

"Actually, Sal, it's not okay. You see, nobody around here said a word about six o'clock tomorrow evening." Rizzo freezes momentarily and that ophidian smile disappears from his lips. "What do you want me to do? Roust your boss and drag him down here to answer for your stupidity. Carlo Gambino does not suffer fools gladly, Sal, and he's not going to be happy with either of us, particularly you."

After a moment, Rizzo gets to his feet and straightens his coat.

"I'm going now, Horvath. The only way you can make me stay is to arrest me. If you do that I get my phone call and I promise you I won't be here long. Up to you."

Rizzo waits for a reply. Horvath looks over at me and with great exaggeration, raises his eyes to heaven.

"Blow, Rizzo. Get out of my sight," Horvath says reaching for another slice of pizza.

After he's gone I say to Horvath, "What do you think?"

"I think he's too stupid to be scared. You still have to watch your back." He looks me in the eye. "I can't help you, Joe. The Captain's already ripped me up and down over Butch."

"What do you suggest I do"?"

"Wait. Maybe I got through Rizzo's thick Italian skull, maybe not, but either way, he gave you until six tomorrow evening. You should be okay until then."

"You don't know how good that makes me feel," I say.

Horvath looks around the squad room until his eyes fall on a skinny bald guy laboriously typing a report one finger at a time.

"Mueller!" Horvath calls out. The guy looks up, wide-eyed, as if the headmaster was about to rap his knuckles. "Take my friend Mr. Bernardi to the Astor. Do not stop for any reason even if he begs you. Drop him at the entrance and make sure he goes inside. Then wait five minutes to make sure he does not come out again. If he does, arrest him."

"Yes, sir!" Mueller says getting up quickly from his desk and slipping into his suit jacket.

Horvath looks at me sternly.

"There are a limited number of things I can do to protect you from Sal Rizzo. There is nothing I can do to protect you from yourself. I do not want to receive a phone call telling me that you are toes up on a slab at the City Morgue and do you know why I do not want to receive this phone call, Joe?"

"Because you hate paperwork?" I venture.

"Precisely," Horvath says with a smile.

CHAPTER NINETEEN

Alone in my hotel room, I have never felt more isolated. I feel chilly and I'm starting to shiver even though the wall thermostat reads 71 degrees. Tomorrow morning when I awaken I will have less than 12 hours to deal with Sal Rizzo who seems determined to appease his sister Florence with my innards. Months or years from now when the truth finally comes out, I'm sure he will utter the word "Ooops" with great solemnity.

I stare at the ceiling in a sea of befuddlement. Someone at the Mudhole beat the living crap out of Gino Funucci and then applied the coup de grace with an ice pick to his ear. It has all the earmarks of a mob hit but I don't think it is. I think the ice pick is a diversion. Leaving out Jonathan Harker, who is alibied up to his nose hairs, that leaves only two possibilities. One is the playwright Winston Baxendale who, despite his scarecrow frame, has demonstrated enough karate know-how to deck Ingemar Johannson without raising a sweat. What his motive might be, I have no clue. The other possibility is so abhorrent to me, I don't even want to think about it.

At that moment the phone rings. I check my watch. 9:33. That would be 6:33 California time. I lift the receiver expectantly.

"It's me," I say playfully.

"I certainly hope so," comes a man's voice. "Otherwise I have the wrong number."

"Who is this?" I say.

"Is this Joe?"

"Yes, this is Joe," I say slightly annoyed.

"This is Peter. Peter Falk."

I relax.

"I didn't recognize your voice. How are you doing?"

"Never mind me, how are YOU doing?"

"Fine, I guess," I say.

"How can you be fine when you got a guy like Sal Rizzo coming after you? Joe, I checked with some people who know some people who know some people and they tell me Finucci wasn't kidding. This guy Rizzo is very bad news."

"He is, Peter. Absolutely."

"You gotta stay clear of him, Joe. I mean it."

"I'm trying."

"I spent a couple of hours this afternoon, calling around, like I said, talking to to people who know people who know people."

"Gotcha."

"I was trying to find somebody who could talk to this Rizzo guy and maybe call him off."

"Not going to happen," I say.

"So I found out," Peter says. "You alone over there? You want me to come by?"

"No, I'm okay. Thanks for the offer. But listen, Peter, can I ask you something?"

"Sure, whatever you want."

"Velma. How long have you known her?"

"I don't know. Three, maybe four years."

"Tell me about her."

"What's to tell? She'd like to make a living as an actress but that isn't going to happen. Not too many parts for a gal her size. She lives with her mother in a crummy apartment about three blocks from the theater. The mother's an invalid. I think I told you that."

"You did."

"Any other family?"

"Just the kid sister. A real dodo."

"And the sister, she watches the mother when Velma's working?"

"The sister, a neighbor, someone's always looking out for her. And Velma's only five minutes away if they need her."

"Girl her size," I say. "I bet she can take care of herself."

I hear him laugh.

"Are you kidding me? She's as tough as nails. Quiet, almost shy, but if you get her mad, look out. I remember, maybe three years ago right after New Years we're all sitting around in this bar and this tough looking guy with tattoos up to his armpits, says something to her about her weight, like for a hippo she ain't all that fat and he starts to laugh. Velma takes one step toward him, decks him with a right and knocks him off the barstool. Then she grabs him by the shirt, drags him to the front door and throws him out into the snow."

"Tough girl," I say.

"Only when she has to be."

"She got anything going, I mean, like a boyfriend?"

"She never mentioned anybody," Peter says.

"She seems awfully fond of Amythyst Breen,"

"Yeah? I wouldn't know."

"Do you think it's possible Velma's more interested in females than she is guys?"

There's a moment's silence as Peter mulls over the enormity of what I've suggested.

"Do I think what, I mean, are you saying—-? No, absolutely I wouldn't know anything about that. No, that kinda stuff, that's not my business."

"Sure, I understand," I say, "and thanks, you've been a big help."

"No, Joe, if I'd caught the guy before he got into his car and drove away, now that would have been a big help."

"If you say so,"

"I gotta hang up now. Jessup's got me doing an interview with *Women's Wear Daily*. What the hell do I know about women's wear that I can talk about in public?"

"Well, good luck."

I wait for him to click off. He doesn't.

"Peter?"

"Joe?"

"Still here."

"Just one more thing," he says. "I think maybe in a few months I'll be coming out to Los Angeles. Everybody's leaving New York. The work's drying up. The job's are in Hollywood. Anyway, that invitation to talk to you and your partner, is that still open?"

"Absolutely," I say.

"Then I guess I'll be seeing you," he says and with a click he's gone.

I stare at the phone. Something is starting to itch at me. Maybe I'm hungry, Two slices of pizza isn't much of a supper. I glance over at the fruit bowl sitting atop my TV set. Even though I haven't eaten any of it, they change the bowl every day. A large pineapple surrounded by two apples, two bananas and a bunch of grapes. I have no idea why they keep sending a pineapple since there's nothing in the room to cut it open with. Maybe it's the same pineapple and they just keep sending it back day after day. Maybe a couple of years ago they bought a few dozen pineapples and haven't had to buy any since. I think about the bottle of Piels beer in the mini-bar and wonder how it would taste with a banana. And then it hits me.

The car. Finucci runs to his car to make his escape and two or three hours later he shows up at the Mudhole where he is introduced to the Big Sleep in a very malicious way. But where's his car? It should be parked on the street or at least it should have been. Probably towed away by now.But what if it wasn't? What if he'd gotten a ride to the theater? If so, by whom? Or maybe a cab but where did the cab pick him up? And in any case, where the hell is the damned car?

I peel a banana and try to wash it down with the beer. The beer tastes great, the banana tastes like crap. I toss away the banana and rip open a bag of stale potato chips. They taste slightly better than the banana. Twenty minutes later, still hungry, I slip under the covers and manage to get to sleep.

The next morning I opt for breakfast in the room, parked in front of the television set, watching unenthralled as Dave Garroway interviews a precocious 9-year-old who is playing 'Sissy" on one of the network's new lame-brained sit coms. It's morning's like this that I miss J. Fred Muggs, the studio-wrecking chimp that often drove Garroway up a wall. But at least Muggs was fun to watch. I find nothing fun about this tot's views on world peace.

I had phoned the Nine at eight o'clock and asked for Horvath. Not there. Left my number. Called again at nine. Still not there. Now it's nine-thirty and I'm fed up. I'm not hanging around this hotel room for eight and a half hours waiting for six o'clock to come. I'm going to take Rizzo at his word and assume I am safe until six. I have to. There are places I need to go and people I need to see.

The doorman hails me a cab and I head for the Mudhole. At ten o'clock on a Monday morning I have no expectation of finding it open but if I have to, I'm going to break in and find Velma's address. She and I need a face-to-face and I can't put it off any longer. We pull up to the front entrance and I pay the cabbie off. I watch him drive away. The fewer people around the better to witness what I have in mind.

There is a new sandwich board propped up out front. This one features Harker and the new girl. Curtain at 8:00. Seating Limited. I go to the front door and grasp the handle, expecting resistance. To my surprise it gives and the door swings inward easily. I step into the lobby and the first thing I'm aware of are voices coming from the stage. Shrill voices, female, angry and combative. I climb the stairs and look down onto the stage. Three women in bikinis are sitting on folding chairs holding sheets of paper and obviously rehearsing a play. From what I can gather, they are discussing male genitalia, the parties attached to said equipment and the levels of performance in utilizing them. Bascomb and Baxendale are sitting in the front row paying strict attention. If they are looking for a way to pack the theater every night they couldn't have picked a more intriguing subject. Certainly it's a lot more provocative than Eleanor Roosevelt and her hobby horse.

Suddenly one of the girls spots me on the landing and lets out a shriek, throwing an accusatory finger in my direction. The two men whip their heads toward me and glare.

"The theater is closed!" Bascomb shouts.

I come down the stairs and when I do, Baxendale recognizes me.

"Mr. Bernardi," he says.

"Yes. Sorry to interrupt but I need a couple of minutes of your time," I say.

"We're busy," Bascomb says.

"Fine. I'll be back in about twenty minutes with Sergeant Horvath and we'll see if you're too busy to talk to him."

I start back up the stairs.

"Wait!" Bascomb says. He looks over at his actresses. "Take ten backstage, girls. I'll let you know when we're ready for you."

The ladies give me one more collective fisheye and then they disappear behind the black curtains. I start back down to stage level.

"'That girl in the red bikini seems a little high strung," I say.

"They all are," Baxendale replies. "This is a closed rehearsal. No onlookers, In the last five minutes of the play the girls take off all their clothes and perform the rest of the play in the nude."

"Oh, I see. So this is sort of an undress rehearsal," I say, unable to resist. I'm right about packed houses. If they do this right they're in for a run that may last until 2000.

Bascomb gives me a pained look.

"At the risk of appearing rude, Mr. Bernardi, whatever you have to say, get to it. We have no time to waste."

"Thursday morning between midnight and two a.m. someone lured Gino Finucci into the basement of this theater, beat the hell out of him and then killed him. You, Mr. Baxendale, are at the top of the list."

Baxendale laughs.

"Why, for God's sake? I hardly knew the man."

"Maybe, maybe not, but you are one of the few people around with the physical skills to inflict that kind of beating."

Bascomb shakes his head.

"You may remember, sir, that I told that policeman that I was with Mr. Baxendale that evening. We were working on this play, in fact."

"And I believe I told you the exact same thing, Mr. Bernardi," Baxendale says.

"Yes, exact. Almost too exact making me wonder if maybe you two are lying to protect one another, especially with this gold mine of a production in the offing."

Now it's Bascomb's turn to laugh out loud.

"Bernardi, you don't know what the hell you're talking about."

"I know this much, Mr. Bascomb, that when large amounts of money are involved, anything is possible and everyone is a suspect including the gardener, the butler and the downstairs maid. And while we're at it, whatever happened to your House of Art where making money was a mortal sin?"

"You imply that our new play is unworthy, Mr. Bernardi, without even bothering to read it. Had you done so you would have been quick to grasp the subtext and the overriding commentary on modern day warfare between the sexes."

"Well, you've got me there," I admit. "Now as to your whereabouts on the morning of the murder."

Bascomb sighs impatiently.

"At the risk of repeating myself, after Wednesday evening's performance Winnie and I went over to a very small casting studio on Canal Street where we met for three hours with a dozen bikini clad ladies of the evening who claimed to be aspiring actresses. Nine were not. The three backstage were chosen. Maybe you'd like to speak to them."

I stay quiet for a moment and then I clear my throat, finally managing an apology. It is accepted none too gracefully and I can't wait to escape this House of Commerce that is turning hookers into successors of Katherine Cornell. Before I leave I ask if either of them knows Velma's address. Baxendale tells me there is a cast and crew list in the drawer at the back of the refreshment counter. I thank him humbly and slink away. My options are narrowing and heading inexorably in the one direction I'd rather not go.

Fifteen minutes later I've walked three blocks to a rundown apartment house on 5th Street near 2nd Avenue. Velma Micklenberger lives in a two bedroom unit on the ground floor at the rear of the building. It's times like these when I wish Horvath were with me to ask the ugly questions I would prefer to go unasked but Horvath is not available and my watch tells me I have less than six hours to get to the bottom of things.

I rap on the door and hear stirring coming from within. After a moment the door opens and Velma peers out at me. She smiles.

"Joe," she says. "What a surprise."

"Mind if I come in?"

"Of course not," she says, "but try to be quiet. I just got Mom to sleep. We had a terrible night."

"I'm so sorry," I say as I walk into the tiny apartment. A bedroom door is open and I can see an elderly woman, also of substantial size, propped up in bed, apparently asleep. Velma goes over and shuts the door. "Around midnight she was awake and trying to tell me something and when I touched her forehead she was burning up. I started rubbing her down with alcohol and finally around two, the fever broke and she was able to fall back to sleep. I was afraid of a recurrence so I sat up in a chair in her room until dawn."

"And your sister, she wasn't able to help?"

"Audrey wasn't here, " Velma says. "She comes. she goes. I can't keep track. I know I can't count on her so I don't bother. No, right now, it's just me and Mom. Without me around I don't know what she'd do."

Now I feel like a real creep.

She gestures to the sofa.

"Sit down, please. Can I get you something? Coffee, soda, a cup of tea?"

"No, thanks", I say.

She plunks down in an easy chair across from me and lights up a cigarette.

"Well," I say, "as difficult as it is, at least here you're away from the murder investigation that's swirling around the theater."

"Then they still don't know who did it."

"No, not a clue. About all they can figure so far is the killer is a big guy, good with his fists and with a pretty good motive for wanting Finucci dead."

"Probably a lot of people fit that description," Velma says.

"Not as many as you'd think," I say. "The killer would also need access to the theater basement, either a key or someone to let him in. That narrows the list considerably."

"It certainly does," Velma says thoughtfully. "Are you sure I can't get you something?"

"No, I'm good, thanks. Wednesday evening, Velma, after the performance, did you stick around the theater or did you come straight home to look after your Mom?"

"Oh, I had to come home. Audrey was out somewhere, God knows with who. Mom was by herself."

"I imagine that happens a lot," I say. "With Audrey, I mean."

"You have no idea."

"Do you ever get a helping hand from Amythyst?" I ask casually.

"No, why should I?"

"You two seem like very close friends," I say.

"We are but I don't involve her in my problems with mother. She has enough problems of her own without taking on mine."

"But I'm sure there isn't anything you wouldn't do for her if the need arose."

"Probably not."

"And was Gino Finucci one of those needs, Velma?" I ask.

"What?"

"You said it to me over lunch at Luchow's, remember? You hated Finucci for what he had done to Annie Gamble."

"How do you know her name—?"

"I know a lot of things, Velma, and some things I don't know and one of them is, did you kill Gino Finucci because of what he had done to your friend?"

"No, Joe," she says, "you're wrong."

"You say you came back here to an empty house except for your mother who maybe was aware of your presence but in no position to verify it or to report that you had later gone out, back to the theater—"

"That's crazy. I was here the whole time. In fact she had an episode. I almost had to take her to the hospital."

"In which case you almost had an alibi." I know I sound harsh but I have to be. I have to shake her up if she's lying and make her slip up so I can somehow get to the truth. "It's plain to see how you feel about her, Velma, and that's no sin but murder is, no matter how loathsome the victim might have been."

"But Joe, I wasn't here alone with Mom. I had someone with me. When she started fighting me, trying to talk when she couldn't, trying to climb out of bed, swinging wildly at me when I tried to calm her, I did the only thing I could think of. Even though it was late and past dinner time, I called Charlie Wang's restaurant to try to find Peter Falk. He told me that's where he'd be eating if I needed him. I couldn't believe it when he was still there. As soon as he heard what was happening, he rushed right over and stayed with me until nearly four in the morning."

I stare at her, flabbergasted, and relieved that she is innocent. Apparently she mistakes my expression for one of doubt.

"I'm sure there must be someone who was at the restaurant that night who can corroborate my story," she says.

I smile and take her hand and tell her not to worry about it. She has a real good alibi. Unbreakable, in fact.

CHAPTER TWENTY

Gamblers have an expression. When they are down to the cloth, it means they are out of chips. That's me. I'm tapped out. I had high hopes for either Bascomb or Baxendale or both but a trio of hookers has taken them off the board. I was sickened by the thought that it might have been Velma who did in the slimy drug dealer but, no, she has a pretty good alibi. Me. I was with Peter Falk at Charlie Wang's restaurant when Velma called him in need of help at home with her invalid mother.

I have nothing left. Sal Rizzo has made it clear he's not afraid of me or Horvath or the entire NYPD for that matter. The one straw I still have clasped in my clammy fist is Finucci's little Volkswagen which may mean absolutely nothing. It's just seems odd that it isn't around. I'm smart enough to realize that I can't race around Manhattan on the hunt for one yellow Beetle but the police can if they are motivated enough. I grab a cab and head for the Nine where I will forcefully try to persuade Karol Horvath that my life is worth saving.

My skills of persuasion will have to wait. He isn't here. I take up space on a wooden bench usually reserved for friends and close relatives of muggers, hookers, car jackers and other leading lights of the East Village. It's not as much fun as a dentist's waiting room where one can always thumb through a year old copy of 'Better Homes and Gardens' but I make up for it by closing my eyes and pretending I'm sunning myself at Zuma Beach with Bunny and Yvette at my side. The ruse almost works but the clatter of typewriters, the ringing of phones and the raised voices of perps and police alike eventually spoil the illusion.

Horvath rolls in shortly after noon. I've learned he's been in court all morning where Hyman Weiss's sister-in-law, no longer bombed out of her mind and wandering the streets outside her townhouse in a lace negligee, sedately informed the judge that she was not in the least responsible for the three bullets that terminated her husband's life. Her attorney seconded her assertion and because she was and is very good friends with key politicians in the city hierarchy, she was allowed to post one million dollars bail to stay out of jail. She immediately wrote a check and her attorney accompanied her back to her house. Another example of the even-handedness of the American justice system.

"I'm glad to see you're still alive," Horvath says as he flies by me and heads for the staircase to the second floor squad room. I follow close behind. He settles in at his desk and slips an official looking form into his typewriter. Uninvited I sit in the chair across from him.

"Why are you here, Joe?" he asks. "You should be back in your hotel room where it's safe."

"Then I take it you haven't arrested Finucci's killer," I say.

He just glares at me and starts to type, one finger at a time.

"What about the car?" I ask.

"What car?" he asks back.

I tell him what car and why it may be important and what the hell, he hasn't got anything else so shouldn't he be looking into it? All the while he's typing like he's not hearing a word I have to say and then he stops, staring for a long time at his official looking form and then he looks over at me.

"It probably doesn't mean a thing," he says.

"Probably not," I say.

He looks back at the form, thinking, then reaches for his phone and dials a number.

"Yeah, this is Sergeant Horvath at the Nine. Have you guys got a yellow VW beetle there? You might have picked it up on Thursday, Friday at the latest. East Village… Uh, huh… Check it, will you?…" There's a long wait. He stares at me. I stare back. Finally, "You do, huh? Did you check the plate number…" He picks up a pencil and slides a piece of paper toward him, ready to write. "Finucci. Right. That's the car. Got an address?" He writes it down. "I'm coming over. Don't let anybody near it till I get there."

He hangs up and gets to his feet.

"Let's go, Sherlock," he says as he heads for the door, me right behind him.

The Tow Pound for the Borough of Manhattan is located at Pier 76 at 38th Street and 12th Avenue. It looks like a graveyard for a couple of hundred junkers but most of these cars are fairly new, merely victims of the city's strict towaway enforcement. We pull up to the entrance and are let through. The guy in charge is a Sergeant named Wolfe. He points down one of the rows. Toward the end on the left. he tells us. The door had to be jimmied to get it open but other than that, no one's been near it.

We walk down the aisle passing cars of every age and description. Some of these cars will cost fifty bucks to redeem, others three hundred or more. The owners will be notified more than once. Eventually, if not claimed, most of these vehicles will be sold at auction. Such are the joys of owning a car on Manhattan Island.

We find it tucked in beside an old Buick Roadmaster. It needs a wash but there are few dents or scrapes and it appears to be fairly new. Horvath goes to the front door and using a clean handkerchief, opens the door.

"Look, don't touch," he says as he leans in and peers at the interior of the little car. Carefully he pops open the glove compartment and sifts through the contents. A couple of old traffic tickets, the registration, an All State insurance card and a half-eaten Three Musketeers bar.

Finally he steps back.

"We're going to need the lab guys down here, Joe. There's blood all over the place."

I look inside. He's right. It's dried up now and brown but it's blood, all right. On the seat, the floor, the steering wheel, just about everywhere.

"Come on," he says as he starts back toward the entrance. At the little shack by the gate he calls the crime lab. They promise to get technicians on site within an hour. We climb back into his car and head back toward the East Village. As he drives he is grim-faced.

"I let it get by me, Joe. Too many cases, especially the Hymie Weiss debacle and little things start to slip through the cracks. We found his car key on the key chain in his pocket and I didn't follow up. Sloppy. Careless. Stupid. I'm not even sure we interviewed his wife. I sent one of my best guys to get her statement and I don't remember reading it. That's how screwed up I am. I need a damned vacation."

"Maybe you need a new vocation," I say.

He looks over at me and then laughs.

"Who'd have me?" he says.

Twenty minutes later we're back at the Nine having picked up ham and cheese sandwiches from the deli next door. I've rustled up two mugs of coffee while Horvath is going through the Finucci file.

"She's here," he says. "I just overlooked it. She didn't have much to say except that cops are generally stupid and useless and that if we can't get the guy who killed her Gino, her brother will. My guy ended the report by describing her as intransigent. That's a fifty dollar word we include in our reports from time to time and is a synonym for a four-letter word beginning with the letter C which we are prohibited by department policy from using."

"I get the picture."

"You want a lift back to the hotel?"

"What for?"

"It's going to be at least two or three hours before we hear from the lab and then they may have nothing."

"I'll stay," I say. "I've got nothing better to do."

So for the next three hours I do my best not to make a pest of myself and fail miserably. At five-fifteen, the call finally comes through. The dried blood matches Finucci's blood type. There are no extraneous fingerprints anywhere in the car. Strike three and yer out.

With no leads to follow up on and no one to question, Horvath drives me back to the Astor and drops me at the entrance.

"We've had a guy tailing Rizzo all day." he tells me. "but that's no guarantee he won't order someone to do his dirty work." I nod in understanding. "Go to your room, Joe. Stay there. Tomorrow we'll try to work something out."

"I'll stay put. I'm dumb, Sarge, but not crazy," I tell him.

He grins and drives away as I walk into the hotel lobby.

I'm halfway to the elevator well when I hear a female voice call my name.

"Joe! Joe Bernardi!"

I turn. She's hurrying toward me, a broad smile on her face. Dark haired, petite, and gorgeous, she's carrying a large purse and a rolled-up copy of this afternoon's Journal-American. Though I suspect she may be an aspiring actress I really have no idea who she is.

"Joe, I can't believe it," she squeals with delight. She's right on top of me, smile still plastered on her face when she lowers her voice to a near-whisper. "I have a gun wrapped in this newspaper and if you don't do exactly what I say, you and maybe a lot of other people are going to get hurt." To make her point she jabs me in the stomach with the newspaper. What she's holding inside of it feels considerably larger than a fountain pen.

"Whatever you say," I croak.

"44th Street exit," she says, nudging me that direction. I don't resist. She could be bluffing but if she's not, I could start a bloodbath. When we walk through the door onto 44th Street, I find a familiar looking Cadillac parked at curbside. The driver who is opening the rear door for us is also familiar looking. Frankie Fortuna hasn't shrunk much in the past couple of days. The babe climbs in first. I hesitate, glancing at my watch which reads 5:32.

"I still have twenty-eight minutes," I tell him.

He throws an elbow into my side and I stumble into the back of the car. The babe does not help me up. A moment later we are pulling into traffic.

Darkness has already fallen and the lights that illuminate the heart of Manhattan are already on display. We crawl along Seventh Avenue, mired in traffic, passing a host of theaters and restaurants, the iconic landmarks of New York's theater district. I suspect our final destination will not be quite so glamorous. Frankie edges over to the left, then turns toward the west and a minute later we're heading north on the West Side Highway, leaving the colorful neon of Broadway far behind us. At the exit for the George Washington Bridge we turn off and head east into the bowels of the Bronx. Here the lights are dimmer and shadows abound in the narrow streets of a once proud borough which has been deteriorating for decades. Frankie is constantly checking his rearview mirror for signs of an unwanted tail and several times he makes unnecessary turns, doubling back on his route, just to be sure. At last he makes one final turn onto a darkened street. Ahead there appears to be a solitary restaurant with lights aglow. He pulls up to the front door and stops. Immediately, I notice two things. There is a sign posted on the glass of the doorway which reads: Closed for Private Party.

Above the doorway is the name of the restaurant, Trattoria Venezia.

Frankie knocks twice on the door. The curtain pulls back and a swarthy looking man peers out. The curtain falls back into place and the door opens. Frankie enters first. I'm next. The little gal with the big gun is right behind me. As advertised, the restaurant is closed to the public but it is not empty. Two men sit at a table to my left, watching me intently. Another sits at the end of the bar. A fourth man is seated at a table with a clear view of the room as well as the doors that lead to the kitchen. A fifth man is stationed by a corridor that leads to the rear of the building, perhaps to an exit. All five men have two things in common. They all wear well-tailored expensive Italian silk suits. All five boast a bulge under their jackets by their left armpits.

At the far side of the room is a sizable banquette at which two men are sitting. In the middle is a man I have never seen before. The other man is an old acquaintance. Sal Rizzo. Frankie takes my arm and guides me to the banquette. The man I do not know nods and smiles.

"Thank you, Frankie. You may go sit down now."

Frankie nods, backs up a step, then turns and goes to a nearby table. The man then looks to my female captor, says something pleasant to her in Italian, blowing her a kiss. She smiles and then goes to sit at the bar. The man turns his attention to me.

"Good evening, Mr. Bernardi. Thank you for coming. Please, sit down."

He gestures to the empty seat across from Sal Rizzo. I look around the room for the cop who's supposed to be tailing Rizzo. I don't see him so I slide in.

"You have me at a disadvantage, sir," I say. "I don't believe I caught your name."

He smiles,

"You may call me Carlo," he says with a gracious smile.

CHAPTER TWENTY ONE

Carlo Gambino proves to be a gracious host. He pours me a glass of an excellent aged Sagrantino which I accept and then offers me an expensive Cuban cigar which I decline. He signals to his minion by the kitchen door. The minion disappears inside and emerges a moment later with the chef in tow. The chef stands before us quietly writing down our dinner order, nodding in approval as Gambino selects each dish without benefit of a menu. Gambino stops and turns to me.

"Do you care for calamari fritti, Mr. Bernardi?" he asks.

I don't like squid any more than I like French snails but I smile and nod because I am going to do nothing to upset this,so far, congenial man. If I had my druthers, I'd prefer to select my own last meal, but who knows, when it comes to Italian cuisine, Carlo Gambino may be a man of impeccable taste.

As our chef scampers away to prepare dinner I give Gambino a closer look. I suspect he's at least sixty with a thin frame, a slim face and piercing eyes that seem to miss nothing. He speaks softly with an Italian accent and could easily pass for a banker or an accountant. Now and then he flashes a gentle smile but there is no smile in his eyes. Here is a man who has committed murder many times over, was an underboss to Albert Anastasia until three years ago when he ordered a hit on Anastasia who was subsequently gunned down in the barber shop of the Park Sheraton Hotel. For the past three years he has headed the Gambino crime family, one of five that rule New York as part of the syndicate or the Mafia, whichever term you prefer.

My eyes shift from Gambino to Sal Rizzo. When he catches me looking at him, he looks away. Gambino notices the byplay.

"I have not introduced you to my associate Mr. Rizzo because I understand you already know one another," Gambino says.

"In a way," I say.

"Salvatore, who is a cousin to my cousin Mario, is invaluable to me, Mr. Bernardi, my good right arm. My business dealings would be a great deal more difficult without Sal to intervene on my behalf. In some ways he is like a son to me."

Uh-oh, here it comes. You seem like a nice guy, fella, but family is family and blood is blood so enjoy the ravioli while you can.

"However, like many young people, he can be impetuous and from time to time act unwisely. I believe that this is what happened in your case, Mr. Bernardi. Goaded by his sister Florence, a beautiful and sensitive woman who sometimes displays the manners of a screech owl, Salvatore threatened your person, something he should not have done. I have chastised him for this and he has apologized profusely to me. I am satisfied. However I asked him to join us this evening, Mr. Bernardi, in the event that you, too, would like a personal apology."

I look over at Rizzo who is giving me a hard look, daring me to humiliate him. No, thanks. I don't need any more trouble from this guy.

"Unnecessary, Don Carlo. I am satisfied."

Gambino smiles. Rizzo smiles. I breathe a sigh of relief. Horvath will be delighted. The man's hatred of paperwork is monumental.

At this moment a waiter brings us a platter of antipasto. Gambino scoops some into a small salad plate and digs in. I follow suit as does Rizzo.

"Even though he was Salvatore's brother-in-law, I had no use for Gino Finucci," Gambino says, chomping on a pepper. "He was a stupid, mean spirited man involved in a disgusting business. He was slowly poisoning my niece to death and I believe if it had gone on much longer, I would have taken care of Mr. Finucci myself."

Without visibly flinching, I do a double-take. He slid over it so quickly I'm not so sure I heard him right.

"You say Finucci was poisoning your niece?" i ask.

"Of course he was, Mr. Bernardi, as you must well know by now, considering the many questions you have been asking of anyone and everyone connected with this unfortunate occurrence."

"Amythyst Breen," I say.

"A silly name," Gambino says. "There was a time, I have been told, when Anna was silly and amusing and full of youthful fun but that was many years ago."

"Anna?"

"Anna Gambino. She was fathered by my brother, Gaspare, although he and the mother were not married."

"The mother being Mary Beth Breen," I say.

"Yes, I am aware that you have visited her. A pitiful sight. God has not been good to her. She was once a vivacious young woman but very free-spirited. Too much so. When her pregnancy was discovered, there was momentary talk of abortion but Gaspare wouldn't hear of it, even though he was engaged to another woman at the time. I made arrangements to send the Breen woman to Switzerland where the child would be born and raised without the Gambino family name. Mary Beth Breen became Mildred Gamble, the child was christened Anna Gamble and when she was old enough she was enrolled at the Chateau Mont-Choisi school for young ladies in the city of Lausanne. From time to time I would receive letters describing her progress. I continued to pay the bills while Gaspare stayed out of it. His wife knew nothing of Anna. In 1939, with Europe going insane, Mary Beth returned to the States bringing Anna with her. At age 19 she had an aptitude for theatrics and began to study as well as make the usual rounds. Then in early 1943, a producer who I knew slightly was putting together a patriotic wartime musical and needed backing."

"Which you were delighted to provide," I suggest, beginning to get the picture.

Gambino smiles.

"My brother Gaspare who was never a part of my business dealings made a decent living but he was in no position to help. I was. I secretly offered my producer friend $75,000."

"With only one string attached," I say.

"Just the one but he jumped at it because he envisioned a show with many chorus numbers featuring men in uniform. The leading female role was actually quite small but then in rehearsal, when Anna started to sing and dance, her part became larger and larger and, well, you know the rest, Mr. Bernardi."

"The toast of Broadway, darling of the critics, a Tony nomination—"

"Yes. All of that," Gambino says dolefully. "Late night parties, booze, promiscuous affairs with men whose names she couldn't remember the following morning. It came so fast and disappeared just as quickly and by 1950 she was stranded out in Hollywood, unable to make a living, attaching herself to any man who would pay her attention, sometimes only for a month or two before the stench of scotch on her breath became too much for them."

Gambino falls silent because at this moment our waiter reappears, his tray piled high with steaming dishes of pasta which he places before us. "Buon appetito, Don Carlo," he says as he backs away.

Gambino scoops a hefty amount of shredded parmesan onto his dish and then twirls the linguini with his fork. He takes the bite and nods at me with satisfaction. I follow suit.

"And then eventually she comes back East and takes advantage of her new opportunity off-Broadway," I say, trying to regenerate the conversation.

Gambino smiles at me.

"And do you suppose that this opportunity one day magically flew in her window like a butterfly looking for a place to alight?"

"I see," I say. More behind the scenes help from Uncle Carlo. "And her new found opportunity in 'The Sound of Music?" I ask.

"No, no, my influence doesn't reach that high. This three-week replacement part, this she got on her own."

"Good for her," I say, "and maybe it will lead to something bigger and better if she can just stay away from the Gino Finuccis of the world."

Gambino shrugs.

"Perhaps. Perhaps not. There is something in her bloodline, the same seed of irrationality that has put her mother under constant medical care. Anna cares for no one but herself, thinks of nothing but her own desires. Gaspare washed his hands of her years ago. I did not give up because I prize the family name even though she is still unaware she secretly bears it. But I, too, have lost all patience, Mr. Bernardi. She is what she is, she will be what she will be." For a moment I think I see a look of regret cross his face. "I should have let Gino be. I should have known I could not change the inevitable."

This is the second odd thing he has said to me this evening and even as I am wondering what he meant he looks over at me and sees the curious look on my face.

"Mea culpa, Mr. Bernardi," he says. "But for me you never would have become involved in this tragedia familia, this family tragedy."

"I don't understand," I say.

"In one final attempt to protect Anna, I ordered Frankie Fortuna to administer a severe beating to Gino along with a final warning to stay away from Amythyst Breen. For obvious reasons I did not involve Salvatore in this request because of the family involvement. Unfortunately Frankie did his job too well. These things happen. He came to me, sick at heart, not knowing what to do or what to say to Salvatore. I told him we would keep the matter between ourselves. But now the truth has come out and like myself, Salvatore understands that Gino's death at Frankie's hands was unfortunate but not deliberate."

I look over at Rizzo who nods in agreement. Throughout dinner he has said very little, a testament to the respect he holds for the man he calls Don. He and Gambino have laid everything out in the open, believing they have answered all questions. They haven't.

"Just out of curiosity," I ask,. "where exactly did this beating take place?"

"Behind a bar on Second Avenue. Gino did a lot of business there," Rizzo says.

"So Frankie beat him and then just left him there in the alley?" I say.

"It's what he told me," Rizzo says.

Maybe this makes sense to these two guys and yes, the revelation that Gino was beaten by Frankie Fortuna answers a big question. Everything seems to fit except for one minor thing. He was found dead in the basement of the Mudhole, sprawled on some boxes, with a puncture from an ice pick in one ear.

Perhaps I should be confounded by this latest development. I'm not. On the contrary, suddenly all the pieces have fallen into place and I know who killed Gino and why.

CHAPTER TWENTY TWO

As soon as I awaken the next morning, I retrieve the cast and crew list which I filched from The Mudhole and check for an address. It's located on Mott Street near Canal at the northern edge of Chinatown. I'm going to grab a bagel and coffee and then head over there. If I'm lucky I will find her in and finally put an end to this madness. I have thought long and hard about bringing Kay Horvath along and decided against it. I need answers and dragging the police into it at this point will only shut her down. Besides, what proof do I have? I mean, the kind of proof that would allow Horvath to make an arrest. None. And yet I am totally convinced that Amythyst Breen murdered Gino Finucci. It can't be any other way.

It's twenty past ten when my cab pulls up to the address listed on the Mudhole's cast list. The number coincides with an oriental tourist trap trying to pass itself off as a Gift Center. Then I notice that the two floors above ground level appear to be apartments. I also notice the doorway just to the left of the Gift Center. I pay off my cab and make for the door. It opens easily and I step into a tiny alcove which features four mailboxes. 3A belongs to Kohl/Breen. The name Kohl is a new development. What is it with this woman?

I look for an elevator, silly me, and not finding one I trudge up the stairs to the third floor where I find the door to 3A just to the left of the staircase. I knock. No response. I knock again. This time I hear someone approaching. The door opens to reveal a scrawny half-naked young man with disheveled straw-colored hair and in bad need of a shave. He could also use a shirt and trousers not only for the sake of modesty but because his dirty undershirt does nothing to hide the track marks on his arms.

"Yeah?"

A surly and suspicious greeting.

"I'm looking for Amythyst," I say.

"Not here," he mutters trying to shut the door on me. I wedge my foot in the door jamb.

"Where is she?"

"Who the fuck are you?" he glowers.

"The guy who's looking for Amythyst."

"Cop?"

"No," I say. I reach in my wallet and produce a business card which I hand to him. He brings it up close to his face and squints at it, then checks me out.

"You're the Hollywood guy."

"Right."

His attitude softens.

"Yeah, she told me you guys had a great meeting. She was real excited. Annie needs a break, she really does. You want to come in?"

"No, thanks. I can't stay."

He puts out a limp hand and smiles.

"I'm Charlie Kohl. I pay the rent,"

I shake Charlie Kohl's hand. It's not only limp, it's cold and clammy. I look at him more closely and realize he's young. Very young. Early twenties maybe.

"I gotta tell you, she sure is excited about going back to California, especially with you and your partner behind her. All she needed was that one break to get back on top, that's what I kept telling her."

I think back to my encounter with Amythyst. It was nothing like what Charlie Kohl is describing. I knew from the first that Amythyst was a troubled woman. Now I realize that she is also delusional.

"I'm going to miss her," Charlie says. "She's like my muse. I paint, you know. I haven't had an official showing yet but I'm getting there."

A sidewalk Picasso. They're all over the place working as dishwashers or busboys or, more likely, getting money from Mom and Dad to chase the dream before they finally slink back home and morph into insurance agents.

"Do you know where I can find her, Charlie?" I ask, anxious to get away from this guy as fast as I can.

"She's at the theater."

"The Mudhole?"

"No, no. 46th Street. The Lunt-Fontanne. Dress rehearsal. She opens tonight."

I nod. Of course. I should have known. I thank him and start to go. As I start down the staircase he stops me.

"Listen, if you talk to her, tell her everything's okay. I was on the phone with Felix and he'll be by before supper."

I nod again and keep going down the stairs. Finucci's dead but Felix is alive so all's right with the world. I almost feel sorry for these two sad pathetic people.

At eleven o'clock I enter the foyer of the Lunt-Fontanne through one of the doors that open onto the street. I immediately head for the double doors that lead into the auditorium, ignoring the objections of the clerk in the ticket booth. He won't chase me. He has tickets to sell

As soon as I step inside, I see her. She's up on the stage, dressed in the habit of a Mother Superior talking quietly to a man I presume is the Stage Manager. If the show were just opening, the director,

Vince Donehue, would be staging the scene but Donehue is long gone. That puts the Stage Manager in charge of folding newcomers into the ensemble. I look to the left as an actress enters from backstage wearing workout togs and carrying a mug of coffee. Out of costume and wlthout much makeup Mary Martin still looks like a million bucks. She acts like it, too. A lot of stars wouldn't be bothered showing up for a replacement cast member's dress rehearsal but Mary's a pro and always has been.

As I walk down rhe aisle I see a solitary figure sitting in the middle of Row M. I think I recognize him so I edge along the row of seats toward him.

"Mr. Rodgers?"

Richard Rodgers turns and looks up at me, momentarily blank.

"Joe Bernardi," I tell him.

Recognition replaces confusion as he gets to his feet, extending his hand.

"Joe, how are you? My God, man, it's been years."

"Nine at least," I say. "The party at Gertie Lawrence's apartment after the opening of 'The King and I'."

"I remember. Two of the king's wives got falling down drunk, Brynner almost broke a leg trying to do a cossack dance, and Noel Coward showed up half in the bag and couldn't remember the words to any of his songs. What a night that was."

"Well, when it comes to all night debauchery, Broadway has it all over Hollywood any day of the week."

"I think I'll take that as a compliment," Rodgers says, sitting back down. I sit beside him. "So what are you doing here?" he continues.

"I thought I'd catch the rehearsal," I say.

"Oh? Do you know Amythyst?"

"We've met. How do you know her, Mr. Rodgers?"

"Dick," he corrects me.

"Dick," I say.

"I met her years ago, Joe. Oscar and I had just opened 'Oklahoma' at the St. James theater and right across the street Amythyst was knocking them dead at the Majestic in "Here Come the Waves". I remember sneaking over there a half a dozen times to watch her sing and dance as perky Daisy Darling, sweetheart of the Navy. God, was she terrific. Oscar and I seriously thought about her for Julie Jordan in 'Carousel' but she was out in Hollywood making a picture for John Ford then and wasn't available. Then a couple of weeks ago I saw a little ad for her off Broadway show the same day Pat Neway said she needed three weeks off. Seemed like a good idea at the time. Still does."

"By the way," I ask, "where is Oscar?"

"At fhe farm in Pennsylvania," Rodgers says, his face darkening slightly.

"How's he feeling? I mean, one hears rumors."

He's gives me a gentle smile.

"I know that rumors are your stock in trade, Joe, but this is one I'd rather not get into."

"As you wish. Say hi for me, will you? Tell him I'll be thinking of him."

Rodgers smiles.

"I'll tell him. He'll appreciate it." Then, looking at the stage, he squeezes my arm. "They're ready to go," he says.

Onstage, the Stage Manager signals to the lighting technician as the house lights dim and a couple of spots hit the actresses. There's some dialogue about Maria being torn between the church and her newfound responsibilities at the Von Trapp home. And then the pianist in the pit hits an arpeggio and Amythyst begins to sing the inspirational 'Climb Every Mountain'. I am startled by the full bodied voice that comes from that tiny frame. Her command of the song is strong and sure. I sense Rodgers leaning forward in his seat and when I look over at him, he is transfixed. When the song ends, he gets to his feet and applauds. The Stage Manager gives him a thumbs up and Amythyst favors him with a playful curtsy. Rodgers turns to me with a smile.

"Well?"

"Stirring. There won't be a dry eye in the house," I tell him. I haven't the heart to tell him why I'm really here.

We chat a moment or two more and then he leaves by way of the lobby. I walk down the aisle and hop up on the stage and go in search of Amythyst Breen, conceived a Gambino, renamed Anna Gamble. If she is having trouble figuring out who she is, I am not surprised.

I find her sitting at the vanity in Patricia Neway's dressing room. She has removed the nun's habit and is now wearing a long sleeved white cotton sweater as she removes her makeup with cold cream. She looks in the mirror and spots me standing in the open doorway. She smiles.

"Mind if I come in?" I ask.

"Please do. I thought tnat was you sitting next to Dick Rodgers. I couldn't be sure."

"Dick and I go back many years," I say.

"And how was I?" she asks.

"You know how you were. You don't need me to tell you."

"A girl always likes to hear pretty things," she says coquettishly. "What did you think?"

"Honestly, I think you've made a terrible mess of the past seventeen years of your life. I think you've thrown away a God-given talent. And worst of all I think that five days ago you ruined any chance of redeeming your career and your self-respect."

"You're talking in riddles," she says.

"Early Thursday morning you murdered Gino Finucci, Annie, and because of that, you are probably going to spend the rest of your life in prison."

She laughs.

"Don't be ridiculous. The man was beaten to death. Do you really think I could have done that kind of damage to him? Look at me, for God's sake."

"No, Annie, he was already half-dead when he drove himself to the Mudhole. What happened? Battered and beaten, did he ask you for help, was that it? Did he beg or was it something else? Did he threaten you? Maybe he'd been threatening you all along. Did he threaten to tell the producer, Leland Hayward, about your drug problem? Maybe he threatened you with the newspapers. Junkie plays nun in Sound of Music. Nice headline. Winchell would have run with it. They all would have."

She shakes her head violently.

"You're wrong," she says. "Jonathan Harker—"

"Jonathan Harker was in a boudoir on the Upper East Side servicing the owner of the Mudhole. Velma was at home trying to deal with her sick mother and her alibi is 24 karat. Me. And as for Luther and Winston, they were auditioning hookers for their next production. No, it was you, Annie. It had to be you who shoved that ice pick into Gino Finucci's ear."

She looks up at me sharply, caught, fantasy no longer a response to reality.

"No," she says quietly, shaking her head.

"Yes," I tell her. "Why don't you tell me about it?"

She looks at herself in the mirror and then uses a Kleenex to wipe away a last vestige of cold cream from her chin. She tosses the Kleenex into her wastebasket and lights up a cigarette.

"Sure, why not? It was just past midnight. I was exhausted after the performance and I'd fallen asleep on a sofa backstage. I woke up when I heard someone stumbling around in the basement. I turned on the lights and went down the stairs. He was sitting on an old bench by a pile of boxes, head in his hands, covered with blood. He looked up at me, half dead. He threatened me. He said he had to. He was desperate. He owed six thousand dollars to a man who had threatened to kill him. He would have said anything, done anything to get that money. I told him I didn't have any money to give him and no way to get it. He just laughed and said something obscene. He tried to stand but he couldn't. He fell backwards onto the boxes. That's when I saw the ice pick on a tray of knives and forks. I knew the stories. I knew how these gangsters operated. I never thought twice about it. The cops would think he was just another slimy drug dealer who crossed the wrong person. I jammed the ice pick into his ear. He never even moved."

"You committed murder."

"He was filth," she says. "Anyway I had no choice."

"You could have gone to your uncle," I say.

"Oh, God," she says quietly. "Is there anything you don't know?"

"Then you know about Carlo. I wasn't sure."

"I know. I've always known," she says bitterly. "My mother told me right before I went into rehearsal for 'Here Come the Waves'. She said I had a right to know, that I needed to know. Men like Carlo Gambino come with a price, she said. When you put yourself in their debt, they will find a way to collect and you will never know what or when that time will come. I didn't listen because I didn't care. The bright lights, the fame, that's all I wanted and if there was a price I'd pay it."

"And was there a price?" I ask.

"Not the kind you're thinking about. He never approached me, never said a word, never acknowledged my heritage. He still doesn't know I know. I kept waiting for the day when he'd come to collect, It never came. I boozed my way through two flops while my mother was losing her mind. Quietly he stashed her away in a sanitarium and I never heard from her again. I have no idea if she's alive or dead."

"She's alive," I say.

Amythyst looks at me and nods.

"I thought she might be. And?"

"She's not unhappy, Annie. She lives in a world of her own and she's been well treated."

"Then I guess I owe him that much."

She looks at herself in the mirror.

"I've come a long way from Daisy Darling, haven't I, Mr. Bernardi?"

"You have."

"You know, I got this part all by myself. I didn't need his help for this one."

"Yes, Dick Rodgers told me."

She smiles at me in the mirror.

"It's going to be a marvelous three weeks, isn't it?"

I shake my head.

"You know it isn't, Annie. I'm sorry."

She looks at me in pain and averts her gaze. Her defenses are down. She has nothing left to protect herself from the truth and I am starting to feel sorry for her. Born out of wedlock into a family of gangsters, shipped overseas to grow up in a foreign country, raised by a woman suffering from mental disorders, and beholden to a cold-blooded man for a career that turned out to be short-lived and destructive. When she looks back up at me there are traces of tears in her eyes.

"Would it be too much to ask you to wait until after tonight's performance to notify the police?" she asks. I hesitate. "I have no place to go, Mr. Bernardi, and no place to hide. I would be most grateful."

I look at her face in the mirror. Gino Finucci is not worth this woman's heartbreak. I place my hand on her shoulder. I nod and she reaches up and takes my hand and squeezes it.

It's quarter to nine. Kay Horvath and I are sitting in two unsold seats in the back row of the orchestra. A squad car is parked out front, another is out back by the stage entrance. He's not happy with me but he understands. True to her word, Amythyst is performing and she is brilliant. At the end of her song she gets a standing ovation. Finally, the curtain rings down. The cast appears for curtain calls. When Amythyst emerges, the audience once again gets to its feet paying her a well-deserved homage. Her face is aglow as she acknowledges their plaudits. Theo Bikel and then Mary Martin take their bows. They come back twice and then it is over and tonight's crowd begins filing out. When the theater has pretty much thinned out Horvath and I walk down to the stage and start to mount the steps. An usher blocks our way until Horvath displays his shield. As soon as we get past the curtain I start to lead the Sergeant toward Amythyst's dressing room.

At that moment a distinguished looking gentleman intercepts us.

"Is one of you gentlemen Sergeant Horvath?"

"I am," Kay says.

"I'm Leland Hayward, the producer. I was told you would be in the audience this evening and that there seems to be some problem involving Amythyst Breen."

"There is, sir," Horvath says and quickly and concisely explains the situation. Hayward pales, shaking his head.

"My Lord, this is devastating. That poor woman."

"None of us are happy about this, sir. Now if you would direct us to her dressing room."

He points. Horvath thanks him. Out of the corner of my eye I spot two uniforms entering the stage door. We find her dressing room. The placard that this afternoon read Patricia Neway has been replaced by one reading Amythyst Breen. Horvath knocks. There is no answer. He knocks again. When there is still no answer, he tries the door. It is locked. He pounds loudly.

"Miss Breen! Open the door! Police!"

Silence. He looks at me scowling, then spots a nearby security guard and holds up his badge.

"Open it up," he says.

The security guard unlocks the door and opens it wide. Horvath and I walk in. The room is overflowing with baskets of flowers from well- wishers and at first we don't see her. Then I spot her. She's lying on a small sofa against the far wall of her dressing room. She is still. Very still. As I get closer I see the pain frozen on her face. She did not die peacefully but she did die quickly and I suspect she wanted it that way. No last minute heroics to save her for forty years of prison life. No, none of that for Amythyst Breen. As I kneel down beside her I spot a glass vial on the carpet. I sniff at the contents. I'm no expert but I guess strychnine. I stand up and look around for Horvath. He's already on the phone calling for the coroner's van.

THE END

Author's Note

For over twenty years I had the privilege of being an off-again, on-again friend and colleague to Peter Falk. I worked as a story editor for one year on Columbo, eventually producing one two-hour episode. In the interim I wrote a dozen scripts leaving my name on most of them. During this time I got to know a little about this highly intelligent Renaissance man with interests and talents far beyond the acting profession. When he died on June 23, 2011, he left a hole in the heart of Hollywood. He also left behind a legacy that will live as long as there are television sets, DVDs and movie theaters. This novel, like those that have preceded it, is fiction but the movie "Murder Inc." is not. It was Peter's big break and he made the most of it, receiving a nomination from the Academy as Best Supporting Actor. Otherwise the picture opened to so-so notices and did tepid business. The picture was shooting right up until the March 7th deadline when the strike by the actors and writers went into effect. The murder of Morey Amsterdam's character, planned for the Catskills, then at a closer-in section of Westchester, was finally filmed on the street in front of the studio only moments before midnight while a union representative held a watch in his hand to make sure that strike rules weren't violated. The picture did little for Stuart Whitman's career but the following year Whitman was nominated for a Best Actor Oscar for his role in "The Mark". Stuart Rosenberg returned to television directing, finally getting his big break in 1967 when he helmed the iconic Paul Newman feature, "Cool Hand Luke". Nine months after 'The Sound of Music' opened on Broadway, Oscar Hammerstein II died of stomach cancer at his farm in Pennsylvania. The lights of every Broadway theater were dimmed for a minute in his honor.

ABOUT THE AUTHOR

Peter S. Fischer is a former tele- vision writer-producer who currently lives with his wife Lucille in the Monterey Bay area of Central California. He is a co-creator of "Murder, She Wrote" for which he wrote over 40 scripts. Among his other credits are a dozen "Columbo" episodes and a sea-  son helming "Ellery Queen." He has also written and produced several TV mini-series and Movies of the Week. In 1985 he was awarded an Edgar by the Mystery Writers of America. In addition to four EMMY nominations, two Golden Globe Awards for Best TV series, and an Anthony Award from the Boucheron, he has received the IBPA award for the Best Mystery Novel of the Year, a Bronze Medal from the Independent Publishers Association and an Honorable Mention from the San Francisco Festival for his first novel.

Available at Amazon.com

www.petersfischer.com

PRAISE FOR THE HOLLYWOOD MURDER MYSTERIES

Jezebel in Blue Satin

In this stylish homage to the detective novels of Hollywood's Golden Age, a press agent stumbles across a starlet's dead body and into the seamy world of scheming players and morally bankrupt movie moguls.....An enjoyable fast-paced whodunit from opening act to final curtain.

—Kirkus Reviews

Fans of golden era Hollywood, snappy patter and Raymond Chandler will find much to like in Peter Fischer's murder mystery series, all centered on old school studio flak, Joe Bernardi, a happy-go-lucky war veteran who finds himself immersed in tough situations.....The series fills a niche that's been superseded by explosions and violence in too much of popular culture and even though jt's a world where men are men and women are dames, its glimpses at an era where the facade of glamour and sophistication hid an uglier truth are still fun to revisit.

—2012 San Francisco Book Festival, Honorable Mention

Jezebel in Blue Satin, set in 1947, finds movie studio publicist Joe Bernardi slumming it at a third rate motion picture house running on large egos and little talent. When the ingenue from the film referenced in the title winds up dead, can Joe uncover the killer before he loses his own life? Fischer makes an effortless transition from TV mystery to page turner, breathing new life into the film noir hard boiled detective tropes. Although not a professional sleuth, Joe's evolution from everyman into amateur private eye makes sense; any bad publicity can cost him his job so he has to get to the bottom of things.

—ForeWord Review

We Don't Need No Stinking Badges

A thrilling mystery packed with Hollywood glamour, intrigue and murder, set in 1948 Mexico.....Although the story features many famous faces (Humphrey Bogart, director John Huston, actor Walter Huston and novelist B. Traven, to name a few), the plot smartly focuses on those behind the scenes. The big names aren't used as gimmicks—they're merely planets for the story to rotate around. Joe Bernardi is the star of the show and this fictional tale in a real life setting (the actual set of 'Treasure of the Sierra Madre' was also fraught with problems) works well in Fischer's sure hands....A smart clever Mexican mystery.

—Kirkus Reviews

A former TV writer continues his old-time Hollywood mystery series, seamlessly interweaving fact and fiction in this drama that goes beyond the genre's cliches. "We Don't Need No Stinking Badges" again transports readers to post WWII Tinseltown inhabited by cinema publicist Joe Bernardi... Strong characterization propels this book. Toward the end the crosses and double-crosses become confusing, as seemingly inconsequential things such as a dead woman who was only mentioned in passing in the beginning now become matters on which the whole plot turns (but) such minor hiccups should not deter mystery lovers, Hollywood buffs or anyone who adores a good yarn.

—ForeWord Review

Peter S. Fischer has done it again—he has put me in a time machine and landed me in 1948. He has written a fast paced murder mystery that will have you up into the wee hours reading. If you love old movies, then this is the book for you.

—My Shelf. Com

This is a complex, well-crafted whodunit all on its own. There's plenty of action and adventure woven around the mystery and the characters are fully fashioned. The addition of the period piece of the 1940's filmmaking and the inclusion of big name stars as supporting characters is the whipped cream and cherry on top. It all comes together to make an engaging and fun read.

—Nyssa, Amazon Customer Review

Love Has Nothing to Do With It

Fischer's experience shows in 'Love Has Nothing To Do With It', an homage to film noir and the hard-boiled detective novel. The story is complicated... but Fischer never loses the thread. The story is intricate enough to be intriguing but not baffling....Joe Bernardi's swagger is authentic and entertaining. Overall he is a likable sleuth with the dogged determination to uncover the truth.... While the outcome of the murder is an unknown until the final pages of the current title, we do know that Joe Bernardi will survive at least until 1950, when further adventures await him in the forthcoming 'Everybody Wants an Oscar'.

—Clarion Review

A stylized, suspenseful Hollywood whodunit set in 1949....Goes down smooth for murder-mystery fans and Old Hollywood junkies.

—Kirkus Review

The Hollywood Murder Mysteries just might make a great Hallmark series. Let's give this book: The envelope please: FIVE GOLDEN OSCARS.

—Samfreene, Amazon Customer Review

The writing is fantastic and, for me, the topic was a true escape into our past entertainment world. Expect it to be quite different from today's! But that's why readers will enjoy visiting Hollywood as it was in the past. A marvelous concept that hopefully will continue up into the 60s and beyond. Loved it!

—GABixlerReviews

The Unkindness of Strangers

*Winner of the Benjamin Franklin Award
for Best Mystery Book of 2012
by the Independent Book Publisher's Association.*

Book One—1947
JEZEBEL IN BLUE SATIN

WWII is over and Joe Bernardi has just returned home after three years as a war correspondent in Europe. Married in the heat of passion three weeks before he shipped out, he has come home to find his wife Lydia a complete stranger. It's not long before Lydia is off to Reno for a quickie divorce which Joe won't accept. Meanwhile he's been hired as a publicist by third rate movie studio, Continental Pictures. One night he enters a darkened sound stage only to discover the dead body of ambitious, would-be actress Maggie Baumann. When the police investigate, they immediately zero in on Joe as the perp. Short on evidence they attempt to frame him and almost succeed. Who really killed Maggie? Was it the over-the-hill actress trying for a comeback? Or the talentless director with delusions of grandeur? Or maybe it was the hapless leading man whose career is headed nowhere now that the "real stars" are coming back from the war. There is no shortage of suspects as the story speeds along to its exciting and unexpected conclusion.

Book Two—1948
WE DON'T NEED NO STINKING BADGES

Joe Bernardi is the new guy in Warner Brothers' Press Department so it's no surprise when Joe is given the unenviable task of flying to Tampico, Mexico, to bail Humphrey Bogart out of jail without the world learning about it. When he arrives he discovers that Bogie isn't the problem. So-called accidents are occurring daily on the set, slowing down the filming of "The Treasure of the Sierra Madre" and putting tempers on edge. Everyone knows who's behind the sabotage. It's the local Jefe who has a finger in every illegal pie. But suddenly the intrigue widens and the murder of one of the actors throws the company into turmoil. Day by day, Joe finds himself drawn into a dangerous web of deceit, dupliciity and blackmail that nearly costs him his life.

Book Three—1949
LOVE HAS NOTHING TO DO WITH IT

Joe Bernardi's ex-wife Lydia is in big, big trouble. On a Sunday evening around midnight she is seen running from the plush offices of her one- time lover, Tyler Banks. She disappears into the night leaving Banks behind, dead on the carpet with a bullet in his head. Convinced that she is innocent, Joe enlists the help of his pal, lawyer Ray Giordano, and bail bondsman Mick Clausen, to prove Lydia's innocence, even as his assignment to publicize Jimmy Cagney's comeback movie for Warner's threatens to take up all of his time. Who really pulled the trigger that night? Was it the millionaire whose influence reached into City Hall? Or the not so grieving widow finally freed from a loveless marriage. Maybe it was the partner who wanted the business all to himself as well as the new widow. And what about the mysterious envelope, the one that disappeared and everyone claims never existed? Is it the key to the killer's identity and what is the secret that has been kept hidden for the past forty years?

Book Four—1950
EVERYBODY WANTS AN OSCAR

After six long years Joe Bernardi's novel is at last finished and has been shipped to a publisher. But even as he awaits news, fingers crossed for luck, things are heating up at the studio. Soon production will begin on Tennessee Williams' "The Glass Menagerie" and Jane Wyman has her sights set on a second consecutive Academy Award. Jack Warner has just signed Gertrude Lawrence for the pivotal role of Amanda and is positive that the Oscar will go to Gertie. And meanwhile Eleanor Parker, who has gotten rave reviews for a prison picture called "Caged" is sure that 1950 is her year to take home the trophy. Faced with three very talented ladies all vying for his best efforts, Joe is resigned to performing a monumental juggling act. Thank God he has nothing else to worry about or at least that was the case until his agent informed him that a screenplay is floating around Hollywood that is a dead ringer for his newly completed novel. Will the ladies be forced to take a back seat as Joe goes after the thief that has stolen his work, his good name and six years of his life?

Book Five—1951
THE UNKINDNESS OF STRANGERS

Warner Brothers is getting it from all sides and Joe Bernardi seems to be everybody's favorite target. "A Streetcar Named Desire" is unproducible, they say. Too violent, too seedy, too sexy, too controversial and what's worse, it's being directed by that well-known pinko, Elia Kazan. To make matters worse, the country's number one hate monger, newspaper columnist Bryce Tremayne, is coming after Kazan with a vengeance and nothing Joe can do or say will stop him. A vicious expose column is set to run in every Hearst paper in the nation on the upcoming Sunday but a funny thing happens Friday night. Tremayne is found in a compromising condition behind the wheel of his car, a bullet hole between his eyes. Come Sunday and the scurrilous attack on Kazan does not appear. Rumors fly. Kazan is suspected but he's not the only one with a motive. Consider:

Elvira Tremayne, the unloved widow. Did Tremayne slug her one time too many?

Hubbell Cox, the flunky whose homosexuality made him a target of derision.

Willie Babbitt, the muscle. He does what he's told and what he's told to do is often unpleasant.

Jenny Coughlin, Tremayne's private secretary. But how private and what was her secret agenda?

Jed Tompkins, Elvira's father, a rich Texas cattle baron who had only contempt for his son-in-law.

Boyd Larabee, the bookkeeper, hired by Tompkins to win Cox's confidence and report back anything he's learned.

Annie Petrakis, studio makeup artist. Tremayne destroyed her lover. Has she returned the favor?

Book Six–1952
NICE GUYS FINISH DEAD

Ned Sharkey is a fugitive from mob revenge. For six years he's been successfully hiding out in the Los Angeles area while a $100, 000 contract for his demise hangs over his head. But when Warner Brothers begins filming "The Winning Team", the story of Grover Cleveland Alexander, Ned can't resist showing up at the ballpark to reunite with his old pals from the Chicago Cubs of the early 40's who have cameo roles in the film. Big mistake. When Joe Bernardi, Warner Brothers publicity guy, inadvertently sends a press release and a photo of Ned to the Chicago papers, mysterious people from the Windy City suddenly appear and a day later at break of dawn, Ned's body is found sprawled atop the pitcher's mound. It appears that someone is a hundred thousand dollars richer. Or maybe not. Who is the 22 year old kid posing as a 50 year old former hockey star? And what about Gordo Gagliano, a mountain of a man, who is out to find Ned no matter who he has to hurt to succeed? And why did baggy pants comic Fats McCoy jump Ned and try to kill him in the pool parlor? It sure wasn't about money. Joe , riddled with guilt because the photo he sent to the newspapers may have led to Ned's death, finds himself embroiled in a dangerous game of who-dun-it that leads from L. A. 's Wrigley Field to an upscale sports bar in Altadena to the posh mansions of Pasadena and finally to the swank clubhouse of Santa Anita racetrack.

Book Seven—1953
PRAY FOR US SINNERS

Joe finds himself in Quebec but it's no vacation. Alfred Hitchcock is shooting a suspenseful thriller called "I Confess" and Montgomery Clift is playing a priest accused of murder. A marriage made in heaven? Hardly. They have been at loggerheads since Day One and to make matters worse their feud is spilling out into the newspapers. When vivacious Jeanne d'Arcy, the director of the Quebec Film Commisssion volunteers to help calm the troubled waters, Joe thinks his troubles are over but that was before Jeanne got into a violent spat with a former lover and suddenly found herself under arrest on a charge of first degree murder. Guilty or not guilty? Half the clues say she did it, the other half say she is being brilliantly framed. But by who? Fingers point to the crooked Gonsalvo brothers who have ties to the Buffalo mafia family and when Joe gets too close to the truth, someone tries to shut him up. . . permanently. With the Archbishop threatening to shut down the production in the wake of the scandal, Joe finds himself torn between two loyalties.

Book Eight–1954
HAS ANYBODY HERE SEEN WYCKHAM?

Everything was going smoothly on the set of "The High and the Mighty" until the cast and crew returned from lunch. With one exception. Wiley Wyckham, the bit player sitting in seat 24A on the airliner mockup, is among the missing, and without Wyckham sitting in place, director William Wellman cannot continue filming. A studio wide search is instituted. No Wyckham. A lookalike is hired that night, filming resumes the next day and still no Wyckham. Except that by this time, it's been discovered that Wyckham, a British actor, isn't really Wyckham at all but an imposter who may very well be an agent for the Russian government, The local police call in the FBI. The FBI calls in British counterintelligence. A manhunt for the missing actor ensues and Joe Bernardi, the picture's publicist, is right in the middle of the intrigue. Everyone's upset, especially John Wayne who is furious to learn that a possible Commie spy has been working in a picture he's producing and starring in. And then they find him . It's the dead of night on the Warner Brothers backlot and Wyckham is discovered hanging by his feet from a streetlamp, his body bloodied and tortured and very much dead. and pinned to his shirt is a piece of paper with the inscription "Sic Semper Proditor". (Thus to all traitors). Who was this man who had been posing as an obscure British actor? How did he smuggle himself into the country and what has he been up to? Has he been blackmailing an important higher-up in the film business and did the victim suddenly turn on him? Is the MI6 agent from London really who he says he is and what about the reporter from the London Daily Mail who seems to know all the right questions to ask as well all the right answers.

Book Nine—1955
EYEWITNESS TO MURDER

Go to New York? Not on your life. It's a lousy idea for a movie. A two year old black and white television drama? It hasn't got a prayer. This is the age of CinemaScope and VistaVision and stereophonic sound and yes, even 3-D. Burt Lancaster and Harold Hecht must be out of their minds to think they can make a hit movie out of "Marty". But then Joe Bernardi gets word that the love of his life, Bunny Lesher, is in New York and in trouble and so Joe changes his mind. He flies east to talk with the movie company and also to find Bunny and dig her out of whatever jam she's in. He finds that "Marty" is doing just fine but Bunny's jam is a lot bigger than he bargained for. She's being held by the police as an eyewitness to a brutal murder of a close friend in a lower Manhattan police station. Only a jammed pistol saved Bunny from being the killer's second victim and now she's in mortal danger because she knows what the man looks like and he's dead set on shutting her up. Permanently. Crooked lawyers, sleazy con artists and scheming businessmen cross Joe's path, determined to keep him from the truth and when the trail leads to the sports car racing circuit at Lime Rock in Connecticut, it's Joe who becomes the killer's prime target.

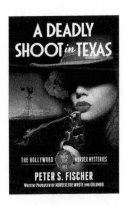

Book Ten—1956
A DEADLY SHOOT IN TEXAS

Joe Bernardi's in Marfa, Texas, and he's not happy. The tarantulas are big enough to carry off the cattle , the wind's strong enough to blow Marfa into New Mexico, and the temperature would make the Congo seem chilly. A few miles out of town Warner Brothers is shooting Edna Ferber's "Giant" with a cast that includes Rock Hudson, Elizabeth Taylor and James Dean and Jack Warner is paying through the nose for Joe's expertise as a publicist. After two days in Marfa Joe finds himself in a lonely cantina around midnight, tossing back a few cold ones, and being seduced by a gorgeous student young enough to be his daughter. The flirtation goes nowhere but the next morning little Miss Coed is found dead . And there's a problem. The coroner says she died between eight and nine o'clock. Not so fast, says Joe, who saw her alive as late as one a.m. When he points this out to the County Sheriff, all hell breaks loose and Joe becomes the target of some pretty ornery people. Like the Coroner and the Sheriff as well as the most powerful rancher in the county, his arrogant no-good son and his two flunkies, a crooked lawyer and a grieving father looking for justice or revenge, either one will do. Will Joe expose the murderer before the murderer turns Joe into Texas road kill? Tune in.

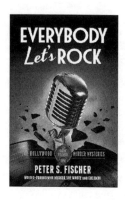

Book Eleven—1957
EVERYBODY LET'S ROCK

Big trouble is threatening the career of one of the country's hottest new teen idols and Joe Bernardi has been tapped to get to the bottom of it. Call it blackmail or call it extortion, a young woman claims that a nineteen year old Elvis Presley impregnated her and then helped arrange an abortion. There's a letter and a photo to back up her claim. Nonsense, says Colonel Tom Parker, Elvis's manager and mentor. It's a damned lie. Joe is not so sure but Parker is adamant. The accusation is a totally bogus and somebody's got to prove it. But no police can be involved and no lawyers. Just a whiff of scandal and the young man's future will be destroyed, even though he's in the midst of filming a movie that could turn him into a bona fide film star. Joe heads off to Memphis under the guise of promoting Elvis's new film and finds himself mired in a web of deceit and danger. Trusted by no one he searches in vain for the woman behind the letter, crossing paths with Sam Philips of Sun Records, a vindictive alcoholic newspaper reporter, a disgraced doctor with a seedy past, and a desperate con artist determined to keep Joe from learning the truth.

Book Twelve—1958
A TOUCH OF HOMICIDE

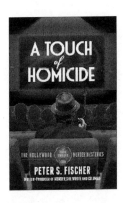

It takes a lot to impress Joe Bernardi. He likes his job and the people he deals with but nobody is really special. Nobody, that is, except for Orson Welles, and when Avery Sterling, a bottom feeding excuse for a producer, asks Joe's help in saving Welles from an industry-wide smear campaign, Joe jumps in, heedless that the pool he has just plunged into is as dry as a vermouthless martini. A couple of days later, Sterling is found dead in his office and the police immediately zero in on two suspects—Joe who has an alibi and Welles who does not. Not to worry, there are plenty of clues at the crime scene including a blood stained monogrammed handkerchief, a rejected screenplay, a pair of black-rimmed reading glasses, a distinctive gold earring and petals from a white carnation. What's more, no less than four people threatened to kill him in front of witnesses. A case so simple a two-year old could solve it but the cop on the case is a dimwit whose uncle is on the staff of the police commissioner. Will Joe and Orson solve the case before one of them gets arrested for murder? Will an out-of-town hitman kill one or both of them? Worst of all, will Orson leave town leaving Joe holding the proverbial bag?

Book Thirteen—1959
SOME LIKE 'EM DEAD

After thirteen years, the great chase is over and Joe Bernardi is marrying Bunny Lesher. After a brief weekend honeymoon, it'll be back to work for them both; Bunny at the Valley News where she has just been named Assistant Editor and Joe publicizing Billy Wilder's new movie, Some Like It Hot about two musicians hiding out from the mob in an all-girl band. It boasts a great script and a stellar cast that includes Tony Curtis, Jack Lemmon and Marilyn Monroe, so what could go wrong? Plenty and it starts with Shirley Davenport, Bunny's protege at the News, who has been assigned to the entertainment pages. To placate Bunny and against his better judgement Joe gives Shirley a press credential for the shoot and from the start, she is a destructive force, alienating cast and crew, including Billy Wilder, who does not suffer fools easily. Someone must have become really fed up with her because one misty morning a few hundred yards down the beach from the famed Hotel Del Coronado, Shirley's lifeless body, her head bashed in with a blunt instrument, is discovered by joggers. This after she'd been seen lunching with George Raft; hobnobbing with up and coming actor, Vic Steele; angrily ignoring fellow journalist Hank Kendall; exchanging jealous looks with hair stylist Evie MacPherson; and making a general nuisance of herself everywhere she turned. United Artists is aghast and so is Joe This murder has to be solved and removed from the front pages of America's newspapers as soon as possible or when it's released, this picture will be known as 'the murder movie', hardly a selling point for a rollicking comedy.

Book Fourteen–1960
DEAD MEN PAY NO DEBTS

Among the hard and fast rules in Joe
Bernardi's life is this one:
Do not, under any circumstances, travel
east during the winter months. In this way
one avoids dealing with snow, ice, sleet,
frostbite and pneumonia. Unfortunately he
has had to break this rule and having done
so, is paying the price. His novel 'A Family
of Strangers' has been optioned for a major motion picture and he
needs to fly east in January to meet with the talented director who
has taken the option. Stuart Rosenberg, in the midst of directing
"Murder Inc." an expose of the 1930's gang of killers for hire,
has insisted Joe write the screenplay and he needs several days to
guide Joe in the right direction. Reluctantly Joe agrees, a decision
which he will quickly rue when he finds himself up to his belly
button with drug dealers, loan sharks, Mafia hit men, wannabe
Broadway stars and an up and coming New York actor named
Peter Falk who may be on the verge of stardom. Someone has
beaten drug dealer Gino Finucci to death and left his body in the
basement of The Mudhole, an off-off-Broadway theater which is
home to Amythyst Breen, a one time darling of Broadway struggling to find her way back to the top and also Jonathan Harker,
slimy and ambitious, an actor caught in the grip of drug addiction
even as he struggles to get that one lucky break that will propel
him to stardom. Even as Joe fights to remain above the fray, he
can feel himself being inexorably drawn into the intrigue of under-
world vendettas culminating in a face to face confrontation with
Carlo Gambino, the boss of bosses, and the most powerful Mafia
chieftain in New York City.

FUTURE TITLES IN THE SERIES:
The Death of Her Yet
Dead and Buried

69927559R00139

Made in the USA
Middletown, DE
10 April 2018